Belle's eyes flo

All this time, she'd wondered why he'd come back. When she'd plowed into him earlier, she'd been so stunned to see him that it almost hadn't seemed real. She'd wanted to cling to him and never let go.

He lifted a hand to caress her cheek, then tenderly wiped her tears away with a gentle brush of his thumb. "I just hope I'm not too late."

This was what she'd wanted more than anything else in the world—this beautiful man, his beautiful heart. Finally, love was hers for the taking. All she had to do was grab hold of it with both hands.

"You're right on time," she whispered.

And then Cash kissed her, soft and slow, and the whiskey-soaked voice in the back of her head quieted down until it was just a low hum, drowned out by sweet nothings and promises made and the thought that this perfect bluebonnet season would stretch on forever. Like an endless dream...

Dear Reader,

Welcome back to the charming small town of Bluebonnet, Texas, home to a girl squad of fabulous heroines who recently started Comfort Paws, Bluebonnet's own therapy dog organization.

The Comfort Paws dogs have already been serving in health care settings around town, and in *Bluebonnet Season*, librarian Belle Darling is determined to expand their reach to the local elementary school. She and her Cavalier King Charles spaniel, Peaches, have been volunteering as a reading education assistance dog team, helping children who struggle with reading. With any luck, by the end of the school year, she'll get the program approved as a permanent part of the curriculum. So far, her plan is going off without a hitch...

Until Cash McAllister walks into her library. Cash's niece, Lucy, is one of the kids in the Book Buddies program, and her sessions with the dog are the only thing keeping the child going after a devastating loss. Desperate to help the little girl, Cash offers to buy Peaches.

There's no possible way Belle is just going to up and sell her dog. Not even if the library itself is named after Cash McAllister's mother...or if Belle's supervisor encourages her to make sure their wealthy benefactor stays happy...or if she might accidentally be falling in love.

Even her therapy dog, Peaches, may not be able to get her out of this mess.

If you haven't read the first two books in this series, *Dog Days of Summer* and *Fa-La-La-La Faking It*, you can still pick them up online!

Happy reading,

Teri

BLUEBONNET SEASON

TERI WILSON

Harlequin

SPECIAL EDITION

Harlequin®
SPECIAL EDITION™

Recycling programs for this product may not exist in your area.

ISBN-13: 978-1-335-40230-1

Bluebonnet Season

Copyright © 2025 by Teri Wilson

Harlequin Enterprises ULC
22 Adelaide St. West, 41st Floor
Toronto, Ontario M5H 4E3, Canada
www.Harlequin.com

Printed in Lithuania

MIX
Paper | Supporting responsible forestry
www.fsc.org   FSC® C021394

New York Times bestselling author **Teri Wilson** writes heartwarming romance for Harlequin Special Edition. Three of Teri's books have been adapted into Hallmark Channel original movies, most notably *Unleashing Mr. Darcy*. She is also a recipient of the prestigious RITA® Award for excellence in romantic fiction and a recent inductee into the San Antonio Women's Hall of Fame.

Teri has a special fondness for cute dogs and pretty dresses, and she loves following the British royal family. Visit her at teriwilson.net.

Books by Teri Wilson

Harlequin Special Edition

Comfort Paws

Dog Days of Summer
Fa-La-La-La Faking It
Bluebonnet Season

Love, Unveiled

Her Man of Honor
Faking a Fairy Tale

Lovestruck, Vermont

Baby Lessons
A Firehouse Christmas Baby
The Trouble with Picket Fences

Furever Yours

How to Rescue a Family
A Double Dose of Happiness

Visit the Author Profile page
at Harlequin.com for more titles.

For Bo. We're so happy to have you as part of our family.

XOXO

Chapter One

If there was a better smell in the entire world than the scent of old books, elementary school librarian Belle Darling had yet to find it.

Her dog Peaches obviously agreed. Belle knew this for a fact—and not just because the eleven-month-old Cavalier King Charles spaniel was her canine soulmate, even though that was also an indisputable truth. Peaches displayed her olfactory love for the written word by touching her little heart-shaped nose to each new paragraph or illustration every time one of Belle's students flipped from one page to the next. Clearly the dog was a genius who, like Belle, knew that a fragrance called Old Book Smell would've flown off the shelves of Sephora, if such a thing existed.

Or maybe the nose thing was simply a result of all the specialized work Belle had been doing with Peaches. Probably that, since Peaches was a reading education assistance dog in training. Over the past few months, Belle had taught the puppy to touch a book page on command. Peaches could also help a child turn a page with her paw. Training aside, the way her soft brown eyes seemed to light up every time she smelled a book convinced Belle that her dog was a true kindred spirit.

Take note, Sephora.

Of course, if such a perfume ever came to fruition, Belle would've been forced to place her fragrance order online since she lived in Bluebonnet, Texas. Her small hometown didn't exactly boast a fancy cosmetic conglomerate in the town square among places like Cherry on Top bakery, Sundae House ice cream shop and Smokin' Joe's, the latter of which was a barbecue establishment run out of a silver Airstream-style trailer.

But Belle made do. She'd always been more of an Ivory soap kinda girl anyway.

"Look, Miss Darling." Mason Hayes, the first grader sitting cross-legged across from Belle on the library's plush blue carpet, pointed at Peaches. The Cavalier's head rested on the open book Mason was reading out loud with her cinnamon-colored ears fanned over the pages, obscuring half the words. "Peaches fell asleep."

A snort, followed by a rumble of Peaches's muzzle followed.

"Would you look at that?" Belle winked at Mason. "You must've accidentally read her a bedtime story."

The sound of the little boy's giggles filled the quiet library, and Belle's heart soared. The reading education assistance dog program at Bluebonnet Elementary, which she'd dubbed Book Buddies, was Belle's baby. Still in its infancy, she'd yet to convince the school board to make it an official part of the curriculum. They'd given her the go-ahead for a single dog team to read with select children for one school year. At the end of May, she was scheduled to present her documentation to the board, and—fingers and paws crossed—next year, more Comfort Paws therapy dog teams would be allowed to join Book Buddies. Once the program was part of the curriculum, the number of struggling readers who could benefit from reading aloud to a dog would multiply.

Until then, Belle and Peaches were it. Period.

"Peaches is so soft," Mason said, stroking the dog as he tried to read around her sleeping form. "I wish I had a blanket made out of her."

Easy there, Cruella.

Belle's lips twitched as she bit back a laugh. Mason was a bright and curious kid. Last week, he'd asked if he could draw a mustache on Peaches with a purple crayon. Much like the blanket suggestion, the answer had been a firm no.

"You're right. Peaches is very soft. That's only one of the things that makes her so special," Belle said.

Mason nudged the dog's ear out of the way and read the last line on the page. "The End." He sighed. "Oh. I guess Peaches fell asleep because she knew the bedtime story was finished."

"It looks like our time is up for today, anyway," Belle said, scrunching her face. Each Book Buddies session lasted fifteen minutes—practically an eternity for the short attention spans of six- and seven-year-olds, not to mention a puppy who'd yet to have her first birthday. Reading time always flew by, though. The children were never ready for their sessions to end. "You'll get to read to Peaches the same time next week, though, okay?"

"Okay. Thank you, Miss Darling." Mason grinned at her, exposing a significant gap where he'd lost one of his front teeth last week—an event which he'd recounted to

Peaches in gruesome detail. He lifted one of the dog's ears and whispered, "Goodbye, Peaches."

Peaches's eyes popped open and she licked the side of Mason's cheek with a swipe of her pink tongue while her tail beat a happy rhythm against the carpet.

"Peaches kissed me!" The little boy beamed as he clutched his books to his chest and skipped back to his classroom.

Belle ruffled the fur behind her dog's ears. "Good girl, Peaches."

The Cavalier scampered to her feet and trotted alongside her as Belle made her way to her desk to document each student's progress over the past hour and a half. Six children participated in the Book Buddies pilot program every week, three from first grade and three from second. Belle kept meticulous notes documenting their progress from week to week.

All the children had made great strides since the start of the program. Since the students were still enrolled in their regular reading classes, measuring the exact level of impact that reading to the dogs had on their progress wasn't possible. But the reading and homeroom teachers all agreed that Book Buddies played a major factor in the improvement of their students' reading scores.

The only glimmer of doubt in Belle's mind was Mason's participation in the program. From day one, he'd been a great little reader. He flew through books that the other kids struggled with. But she'd left the selection process up to the reading teachers since they were the ones with firsthand knowledge of each student's abilities. Belle couldn't quite understand how Mason had ended up in a program designed for kids with limited literacy.

Guilt nagged at her consciousness. She needed to do something about that. She should at least talk to Mason's teacher and find out if there had been some sort of mistake. He was such a great kid, though. And he *adored* Peaches. Book Buddies wouldn't be the same without him.

I'll deal with it later. Belle placed that difficult situation on her list of things to do after the school's upcoming spring break. The list was getting longer by the second, but she only had so many hours in the day. Thank goodness she'd get a chance to catch up on the rest of her life when she had five blissful days in a row off work.

She thumbed through her Book Buddies binder until she reached the progress notes tab. When Maple, Adaline and Jenna—Belle's best girlfriends and the other founding board members of Comfort Paws—had gotten their first glimpse of her Book Buddies binder, they'd teased her mercilessly. Granted, it contained twice the number of progress charts than she'd originally planned, separated by whimsical dividers that were color-coded by reading difficulty and grade level. But Belle liked office supplies and organizational tools almost as much as she liked old book smell. It was basically a tie.

Not that anyone was really keeping track…

"Miss Darling, I presume?" A shadow fell over the spreadsheet she used to record which books the students read each week—alphabetized by last name, obviously.

Belle recapped her highlighter and glanced up, gaze colliding with a smooth-as-silk necktie fashioned into a crisp Windsor knot.

She sat up a little straighter and directed her attention

northward, toward steely eyes the exact hue of the sky over Bluebonnet just before one of its legendary Texas Hill Country thunderstorms. Something about the look on the man's chiseled face made her feel like she was being chastised. For what, she had no idea.

She scanned the lapels of his pinstriped suit for a visitor tag. He wasn't wearing one, which was a flagrant violation of school rules. Alarm bells started ringing in the back of Belle's head.

All campus visitors were required to check in with the school secretary. Pinstripe Guy should've had a stick-on name tag fixed to that fancy suit jacket of his. He didn't necessarily *look* dangerous, with his perfectly refined jaw and classically handsome features.

But anyone who'd seen a single episode of *Dateline* knew that looks could be deceiving.

"Yes, I'm Belle Darling and I'd love to help you, but this is my off hour." *Half* hour, technically. Belle was awarded a scant thirty minutes for lunch each day, most of which she spent working on Book Buddies and walking Peaches before downing apple slices slathered with peanut butter in the final five minutes before the library reopened. "The library is closed until one p.m."

Belle ignored the man's stony expression and pointed at him with a freshly sharpened number two pencil. "Also, you seem to be missing your visitor badge."

His gaze narrowed, and the storms in his eyes darkened to an ominous shade of charcoal. Belle half expected a clap of thunder to rattle the colorful walls of the library. She almost reached for Peaches's Thunder-Shirt—the calming compression garment the Cavalier wore during inclement weather. If there was one thing Peaches hated, it was a thunderstorm.

Brooding strangers, on the other hand, didn't seem to faze her in the slightest. Peaches hopped off the dog bed Belle kept tucked under her desk, trotted over to the man and plopped into a perfect sit position at his feet. The little Cavalier's tail thump-thumped against the carpet, and her mouth spread into wide doggy grin, seemingly oblivious to the scowl on his face. Then a single drop of slobber fell from her pink tongue onto the toe of one of his shiny wingtip shoes, and he finally deigned to meet Belle's gaze again.

"The dog isn't wearing a visitor tag," he said with an arch of a single sardonic eyebrow.

Seriously?

What. A. Jerk.

"That's because Peaches isn't a visitor. She's a volunteer who passed a rigorous background check. Hence, the working dog vest." Belle pursed her lips and cut her gaze toward the red vest stitched with the words *Therapy dog in training* directly beneath the heart-shaped Comfort Paws patch. "And she is, in fact, wearing a tag on her collar if you'd like to check."

The tag identified Peaches as a reading education assistance dog, in addition to being a therapy pet. Belle had studied long and hard for the written exam she'd taken online to get her and Peaches approved as a reading dog team. If she'd been awarded a tag like the one attached to Peaches's dog collar, she probably would've worn it stapled to her forehead.

"You can visit the school secretary in the front office, and I'm sure once you present her with proper identification, Marta will be happy to give you a name tag of your very own." Belle smiled sweetly at the stranger. A little *too* sweetly, probably. But she was trying to make a point. "Rules are rules."

This was about safety. It was about the children. Not about the expensive cut of this man's suit or the way her stomach felt like she'd done a loop-de-loop on the roller coaster at the Texas State Fair every time he looked at her with those stormy gray eyes.

That intense gaze of his flitted to the notebook on her desk that was situated immediately to the right of the Book Buddies binder. Belle's *secret* notebook—the one with the red nondescript cover. She shoved the binder to the side to cover it up.

Narrowed eyes lifted to meet hers.

"Rules are rules," he echoed with a stiff smile. "I'll be back momentarily."

He smoothed down his tie again before turning on his heel and stalking out of the library, spine ramrod straight.

Belle wondered if the tie thing was some sort of nervous tic, like the way she always wrinkled her nose when her anxiety spiked. She didn't do it on purpose. It just happened, as if all the grainy, old reruns of *Bewitched* she'd watched as a kid were lying dormant somewhere in her subconscious. Except Belle's nose wiggle was never accompanied by a cute tinkling sound effect, only the pound of her own heartbeat.

Peaches pawed at Belle's shin, pulling her out of her reverie. She gathered the pup in her arms and kissed the cute chestnut spot on top of her dog's head. "You're right.

Why am I wasting time thinking about a rude stranger when we have much more important things going on?"

Things like the contents of her secret notebook, which she hoped to finish during spring break. And things like the Bluebonnet Festival in the town square this weekend, where Comfort Paws was scheduled to have a booth about their upcoming training class for new therapy dog teams—their *inaugural* training class, which would be held in their brand-new training facility.

But even more important than the notebook, the Bluebonnet Festival or the Comfort Paws training class, the school board's final meeting of the academic year was scheduled just six weeks from now. Time was running out for Belle and her fancy color-coded binder to secure the future of Book Buddies.

"We've got this. Right, Peaches?" Belle said, and the Cavalier responded with an encouraging swipe of her tongue against Belle's cheek.

Just then, the school intercom system squawked from its speaker on the corner of Belle's desk. "Belle?"

Peaches's ear swiveled forward, and her head tilted at the sound of the school secretary's voice.

"Hi, Marta," Belle said.

"Listen…" Marta's voice dropped to a murmur. "I probably shouldn't be saying anything, but I wanted to give you a heads-up about a visitor headed your way."

Belle had to lean closer to the speaker to hear Marta, and even then, she only caught about half her words. Still, it was enough to get the gist.

"I appreciate the heads-up, but I already met him, and I can't say I'm looking forward to his return. He wasn't exactly all sunshine and rainbows," Belle said with a snort.

"Yes, but he's—" Marta started, but then the antiquated intercom system erupted into a burst of static.

Belle backed away in her wheelie chair before her eardrum burst. Peaches leapt out of her lap to run for cover under the desk.

"Marta?" Belle yelled. Well, it was more like the librarian version of yelling—so basically a raised whisper. "Are you still there? I can't hear you."

Snatches of words punctuated by white noise came from the intercom. "Family...library...important..."

Well, wasn't that just as clear as mud?

"Marta, can you repeat that, please?" Belle banged on the speaker with the heel of her hand. The charms on her silver charm bracelet tinkled.

The intercom spit out one final syllable. Marta didn't seem to be whispering anymore. Her voice came through crisp and clear. "Nice!"

Belle sat back in her chair and eyed the speaker, which was now as dead as a doornail. No static, no white noise, no red blinking light in the upper right-hand corner. Nothing.

Marta's last attempt at communication rang in Belle's ears.

Nice?

Clearly she'd no longer been talking about the visitor badge-adverse stranger. Belle could've come up with quite a few adjectives to describe the man, but *nice* wouldn't have been anywhere on the list.

Nice *looking*, maybe.

Belle's face went warm, and suddenly, he was back,

standing across the desk from her with a fresh, new, adhesive name tag stuck to his lapel. She gave a start, and her heart began beating as fast as a nervous Chihuahua's.

She really needed to move her workstation farther away from the library door. People just appeared from around the corner as if from thin air.

"My apologies for startling you," he said. A hint of a smile played around the edges of his lips.

Sure. *Now* he smiled.

"You didn't," Belle countered.

A lie if she'd ever told one. Judging by the knowing smirk on his face, she wasn't fooling anyone.

She took a deep breath, fully ready to remind him that the library was still closed. Belle usually wasn't such a stickler about her lunch (half) hour, but something about this guy screamed *entitlement*, and she really needed to finish her Book Buddies paperwork on her own time. The rest of her afternoon was scheduled with back-to-back library visits from all the first grade classes, where Belle would be reading the children a book about a sassy cow who liked to eat bluebonnets, followed by craft time for the students to write their own bluebonnet stories.

"Thank you for checking in with the front desk, Mr…." Belle glanced at his name tag "… McAllister."

Every other word she'd planned on saying withered and died on the tip of her tongue. His name was Cash McAllister? It had to be a coincidence. He couldn't be related to *that* McAllister.

But the arch of his brow said it all, as did the knowing glint in those stormy eyes of his. His gaze darted to the sign above the library door, and Belle's eyes followed, as if she hadn't seen the plaque every day of her working life for the past five years.

> *Welcome to Bluebonnet Elementary School's*
> *Evelyn McAllister Memorial Library*

Her throat went bone dry.

So *this* was what Marta had been trying to tell her over the intercom. A real, live, flesh-and-blood McAllister was in the building. Belle should be on her best possible behavior.

Marta's static-laden warning rang in her ears.
Nice!

As in, *Be nice. This man is the benefactor of your entire workplace, so you probably could've let the name tag thing slide.*

"How can I help you, Mr. McAllister?" Belle managed to squeak as Peaches emerged from beneath her desk and made a beeline straight for Cash McAllister and pranced gleefully at his feet.

At least one of them knew where their bread was buttered.

Whatever the man wanted, Belle would do it. If anyone held sway with the school board, it was him. Now that she thought about it, he might even hold a seat on the board. If memory served, the McAllister family had been granted a permanent spot on Bluebonnet's school board as a result of their generous, ongoing financial contribution to the district. None of the McAllisters had ever actually exercised the right to sit on the board, though, because it had been years since anyone in the family occupied the McAllister Mansion on Main Street.

What was he doing here, anyway?

At the moment, he was bending down to scoop Peaches into his arms. When Cash straightened, Belle's dog perched in the crook of his elbow and licked the side of his face. Peaches loved everyone, but for some reason, the sight of her lavishing affection on Cash McAllister felt like a betrayal.

"Is this the reading dog I've heard so much about?" Cash tipped his head toward Peaches.

Belle nodded, mind whirling. He'd heard about Book Buddies? Maybe whatever happened next wouldn't be so bad. Maybe he was here on behalf of the board to tell her the program had already been approved as part of the elementary school curriculum.

A girl could dream, right?

"Yes, that's Peaches, Bluebonnet Elementary School's very first reading education assistance dog." Belle squared her shoulders, beaming with pride.

"How much?" Cash said flatly.

Belle blinked. Surely she hadn't just heard him correctly. "Excuse me?"

"How much?" he asked again, enunciating each syllable with annoying precision.

Obviously, he wasn't here to give her good news about Book Buddies. A girl could dream, but in this particular instance, that might make her delusional.

Belle's fingers twitched. She had to stop herself from snatching Peaches straight out of Cash's arms as he held the Cavalier closer and gazed down at Belle as impassively as if he were inquiring about the cost of a carton of milk at Bluebonnet General.

"Name your price. I'd like to buy this dog."

Chapter Two

Belle Darling didn't say anything for a long moment—long enough that Cash began to wonder if she was about to throw out some absurdly huge sum just to see how serious he'd been when he'd told her to name her price.

He'd been too aggressive, which was a recurring theme for Cash in his business dealings. But he was a McAllister, and that's what McAllisters did. Just like they always got their way, come hell or high water.

Still, it was difficult to think of the absurdly cute bundle of fur currently nestled in his elbow as part a business transaction. Even though that's precisely what this was.

"Miss Darling," he prompted, eager to get the financial details over with so he could get the dog home to Lucy.

She snapped out of her trance with an endearing little wiggle of her nose. The gesture seemed vaguely familiar, but Cash couldn't quite place it.

She cleared her throat. "Peaches isn't for sale."

Had she not heard the part where he'd said she could name her price?

"I realize that, but this is an extenuating circumstance.

I believe you're acquainted with my niece, Lucy?" He flashed her his best attempt at a charming smile as her dog started climbing up his shoulder like he was a tree.

The librarian's eyes flashed, and Cash could tell it was taking every ounce of self-control she had not to reach for the dog and snatch it away from him. To her credit, she simply crossed her arms and sighed in resignation as Peaches curled into a warm ball in the curve of his neck.

Cute. No wonder Lucy was so enchanted with the pup. Cash held the puppy in place as she snuggled in.

Miss Darling dragged her gaze away from Peaches and glared at him. "Are you talking about Lucy Milam?"

Her tone softened as she said Lucy's name. Cash's niece had that effect on people, Cash himself included. Hence the fact that he was currently standing in a public school library in Bluebonnet, Texas, on a weekday afternoon instead of his corner office on the top floor of the tallest skyscraper in Dallas.

"Lucy Milam McAllister," Cash corrected. The adoption papers had just gone through three days ago. Clearly Miss Darling hadn't gotten the memo from the school registrar's office.

Peaches's breathing grew heavy. Apparently, the dog had decided to take a nap cuddled against Cash's neck while he and the librarian hashed out the details of her future.

"I'm sorry, Mr. McAllister. I didn't realize that you were Lucy's…"

"Guardian," Cash said, filling in the invisible blank. He didn't expect Lucy to call him Dad—not when she'd always known him as Uncle Cash.

Maybe someday, though. Not that Cash had the first idea how to be a father.

The librarian's big hazel eyes filled with sympathy, and Cash gathered this was the first she'd heard about Lucy's family situation. Then again, how would she have known that Lucy's mother had passed away six short months ago or that she'd never known her actual father? Belle Darling wasn't the child's teacher. In fact, to his knowledge, Cash had never heard the librarian's name until just this morning. If Lucy had ever mentioned it in passing, it had been drowned out by her constant chatter about Peaches.

The permission slip he signed allowing Lucy to read to a dog once a week had come from Miss Hastings, her first grade teacher, so Cash had assumed she'd been responsible for bringing the animal to school.

Who knew that signing that innocuous slip of paper would change everything?

Cash sure hadn't. But he'd seen the change in Lucy the first day she'd come home and told him about Peaches. She'd asked Cash to read a bedtime story with her that night. He caught a glimpse of a smile on her face as she drifted off to sleep. A few days later, her footsteps had slowed when they'd walked past Bluebonnet Bookshop on the way to the ice cream parlor in the town square. They'd come home that Saturday afternoon with an armful of colorful picture books. Every single one of them featured a prominent dog character.

"My niece loves this dog," Cash said, and much to his horror, his voice nearly broke.

McAllisters didn't go around wearing their hearts on their sleeves. How many times had that message been drilled into his head as a kid when he'd called home from boarding school, begging to come home to Bluebonnet?

Now, all these years later, he'd finally come back. Not for himself, though. For Lucy.

"I'm not sure you understand what kind of impact Peaches has had on my niece," he said, swallowing his emotions until they settled deep in the pit of his stomach where they belonged.

Miss Darling's nose did the wiggle thing again. "I'm glad Lucy has grown so fond of Peaches. She's made such significant progress these past few months. Without so much one-on-one attention, I'm not sure her potential dyslexia would've been caught so early."

Cash narrowed his gaze at her. "You're the one who picked up on that?"

She nodded but didn't elaborate.

Again, the note Lucy had brought home indicating Cash might want to have her checked by a dyslexia specialist had come from Lucy's teacher. Reading to the dog had clearly had an even bigger impact that he'd realized.

Which only strengthened his resolve.

"Like I said earlier." He extricated Peaches from her snuggle spot on his shoulder and gathered her into one arm. All the easier to reach the checkbook nestled in his suit jacket's inside pocket. "Name your price."

This time, the librarian didn't hesitate. She reached right out and plucked the dog from his grasp before he even registered what was happening. If possession was truly nine-tenths of the law, Cash was officially out of luck.

"Like *I* said earlier, *my* dog isn't for sale." The impenetrable Miss Darling's pageant queen–worthy smile seemed to freeze into place.

Cash was getting nowhere fast.

"I'm genuinely sorry if Lucy is having a hard time. Helping students like your niece is precisely why I started Book Buddies. But you don't seem to understand how the whole therapy dog thing works. Therapy dogs aren't the same thing as guide dogs or service animals. A person who acquires a guide or service dog needs an animal to help them perform daily tasks. These dogs are highly trained and often bred for the sole purpose of becoming working dogs."

She paused as if waiting for him to back down in the face of this new information, none of which seemed to apply to either him or Lucy.

Cash wasn't interested in some hypothetical wonder dog. He wanted *this* dog.

This was the dog Lucy had bonded with. *This* was the dog that had finally pulled her out of the fog of grief. *This* was the dog that had gotten her interested in reading, despite the challenges that came with her suspected dyslexia.

"The focus of a therapy dog team is helping others. Peaches is my dog, and we're working on her therapy dog certification, so we volunteer and help people in the community." Miss Darling's pretty, bow-shaped lips pursed in judgment. *"Together."*

Cash regarded her through narrowed eyes. "So you and the dog are a package deal, then."

"Yes." She nodded but then seemed to think better of it. "I mean, sure. But just so you know, Mr. McAllister—I'm not for sale, either."

They stood there for a moment, locked in silent warfare. If Cash hadn't looked closer, he might not have noticed that Belle Darling's eyes sparkled when she was angry. Or that her cheeks flushed a deep pink that reminded him of the dogwood trees that bloomed in the town square every spring.

Cash had missed those dogwoods. He hadn't realized quite how much he'd missed them until his first morning back in Bluebonnet when he'd gone out for coffee and found himself caught in a whirl of delicate, blush-colored petals. It was dizzying. Their sweet perfume lingered in his senses long after the March breeze had carried them away.

Cash had a feeling the memory of Miss Darling's quiet determination would do the same.

He wasn't accustomed to people telling him no. Surely once the novelty of it wore off, he'd realize how very much he disliked it.

"Duly noted." Cash's jaw clenched. He should probably leave before he tried to make her an offer she couldn't refuse.

But this wasn't over. Not by a long shot.

Belle somehow got through the rest of the afternoon with a smile plastered on her face for the first graders as she seethed through every word of the adorable story about the bluebonnet-eating cow.

She was unreasonably angry on the cow's behalf, given that the cow in question was a fictional book character. But Belle had spent weeks searching for the perfect book to read aloud for story hour during the week leading up to the Bluebonnet Festival. She'd also devoted hours of her personal time to cutting out tiny tissue paper petals in various shades of blue for the decorative bulletin boards that spanned the walls of the library. Just this morning, a stray blue petal had somehow gotten stuck to Peaches's nose.

And now Cash McAllister had gone and ruined everything. All that work, and she couldn't even enjoy the experience, because the man thought he could *buy her dog*.

Just who did that jerk think he was?

"Mr. McAllister is extremely important to this school." Ed Garza, principal of Bluebonnet Elementary, sat across from Belle looking down his nose at her like she was a naughty student.

For the first time in her entire career, she'd been called into the principal's office. Actually, not just the first time in her career, but the first time in her *life*. Belle had always been a good student. A model employee. Last year, the vice principal had even put a little foil gold star in the upper right-hand corner of the first page of her annual performance review. Belle was fairly certain it was supposed to be tongue in cheek, but she'd loved that little gold star as much as she had when she'd been a little girl in knee socks who spent her lunch hours reading in the school library instead of eating in the cafeteria with the rest of the kids.

Now here she was, sweating bullets through her cute floral A-line dress as if she'd tried to blame Peaches for eating her homework...

All because of Cash McAllister.

"I realize that, but—" Belle started, but Ed cut her off with a sharp shake of his head before she could finish.

"The McAllister family have donated vast sums to

Bluebonnet Elementary. The library is *named after his mother*." Ed's face went as red as a shiny red apple.

Belle's stomach churned. She wasn't going to get fired over this, was she? "Yes, I'm aware."

"Then would you please explain why it seems as if you've purposely gone out of your way to antagonize Mr. McAllister?" Ed folded his hands on the surface of his desk and peered at her over the top of his black-rimmed bifocals.

Belle had always liked Ed. He'd been the principal since she'd started working at Bluebonnet Elementary as the library assistant while she was enrolled in remote classes at the University of Texas to earn her master's degree in library science. Three months after she graduated, the librarian retired, and Ed Garza had offered her the job on the spot. On her first day in her new role, he'd brought in a cake from Cherry on Top bakery. *Congratulations, Belle* had been spelled out in pink frosting atop a stack of books made out of fondant.

Oh, how the mighty had fallen.

"Ed, I promise that's not what happened," Belle said, hating the way her voice went wobbly.

"So, you didn't refuse to speak to him upon his arrival this morning?"

Belle swallowed. "I did, but that was because he wasn't wearing a visitor tag."

Ed sighed. "That's a very important school rule, but from what I hear, you weren't exactly polite about it."

"I wasn't rude," she countered.

Ed's eyebrows crept farther toward his receding hairline.

"I might've been a little short after he made a crack

about Peaches not wearing a visitor tag, but that was before I knew who he was." Belle felt her nose wiggle. Ugh, would this awful day ever end? "Once he returned with proper visitor identification, I was happy to help him."

"Happy?" Ed's gaze narrowed. "Perhaps you're not aware that when the intercom system froze, the entire school office heard every word of your exchange with Mr. McAllister."

"What?" Belle's eyes darted everywhere all at once, in a blind panic. She didn't even know what she was looking for, except maybe a paper bag to breathe into.

But wait, this might be a good development. Now Ed, Marta and everyone else in the front office knew that Cash had tried to throw his weight around and get her to sell him her dog. Surely they would understand why she was so upset.

"You're right. I didn't realize our conversation had been broadcast over the intercom." She sat up a little straighter and reminded herself that whatever she'd said or done couldn't have been anywhere near as bad as trying to strong-arm a person into selling one of their beloved family members. Even if that family member had four legs and a tail. "But did you hear the part where he insisted I sell him Peaches?"

Belle sat back in her chair and waited for Ed to react with proper outrage.

He didn't. Not even close. Instead, his expression turned sheepish. "Would that really be the worst idea in the world?"

"Ed!" Belle gaped at her boss. "You can't be serious."

Thank goodness she'd left Peaches in her office. Was

Belle even going to be able to bring her on campus any-more without worrying she might get dognapped?

"I'm sorry. Forget I said that." Ed dropped his head in his hands, and when he looked back up at Belle, she finally saw the worry etched into the lines around his eyes. It had probably been there all along, but she'd been too wrapped up in her own problems to notice. "Of course I don't expect you to part with Peaches. I know how much that sweet little dog means to you—not just you, but to all of us here at school. She's a treasure."

"Thank you for saying that." Belle breathed a little easier but something still wasn't right. Ed wasn't normally this tense. "Is everything okay, though? I'm getting the feeling that there's more going on here than a benefactor trying to throw his weight around."

Ed glanced at the closed door to his office and lowered his voice. "Everything isn't okay. Please don't say anything to the rest of the staff. I don't want to cause a panic, but the county is cutting our funding."

Belle's heart sank. "Again?"

Last year, district budget cuts had forced the school to disband its elementary orchestra program. The music teacher's hours had been slashed to just two days a week.

"I'm afraid so, yes." Ed ran a hand through his thinning hair.

Belle gnawed on her bottom lip. "Are we going to lose the music program in its entirety?"

She hoped not. Kids needed to learn about more than just reading, writing and arithmetic. Social development and artistic expression at this age were just as important as academic achievement.

"More than just that, I'm afraid. I've been poring over

the new budget for weeks now. If something doesn't change, every grade level is going to lose at least one teacher next year."

"Oh no." Belle swallowed.

She didn't have the heart to ask about the library. She'd surely lose her assistant, which was fine. Tess was only there three days a week anyway. Belle could make do on her own. But she'd heard of several elementary schools in rural areas that had been forced to shutter their libraries altogether. That couldn't happen in Bluebonnet.

Kids *needed* libraries in schools. So many children developed a lifelong love of reading because of their access to library books. Libraries also exposed students to new technology. Even more important, they were a safe space for kids who sometimes felt like they didn't fit in with their peers. Belle would've been completely lost as a child if she hadn't been able to sneak away and disappear into a book during lunch and after school.

"Is the decision final?" Belle asked with her heart in her throat.

Ed nodded. "I'm afraid so, yes. Which is why I was planning on asking the McAllister Family Foundation if they might consider another endowment for our school."

No wonder he'd wanted to roll out the red carpet for Cash.

Belle cringed. "I feel terrible. I had no idea."

But he technically *had* violated school rules. And as much as she loved her job, the library and her students, she'd rather let the entire building crumble to the ground than give up her dog.

Not that now was the proper time to mention either of those things.

"It's okay, Belle. Going forward, though, I would really appreciate it if you could do your best not to alienate Mr. McAllister. We need him on our side. Understood?"

She nodded. "Understood."

Belle got the message loud and clear. From now on, she needed to play nice with Lucy Milam's—correction—Lucy Milam *McAllister's* uncle. As impossible as it seemed, she needed to pretend he'd never tried to pressure her into selling her dog. It was a tall order, but she'd do it.

Whether she liked it or not.

Chapter Three

Cash returned home at the end of the school day, dog-less, with Lucy in tow and her backpack bulging with library books. As usual, the minute the wide double doors of the McAllister Mansion shut behind them, Lucy slid the backpack off her slender shoulders. It landed on the marble floor of the foyer with a thud just as Ellis, the caretaker who'd resided at the estate for as long as Cash could remember, shuffled toward them.

"Good afternoon, Mr. McAllister," Ellis said, despite the many, *many* times that Cash had asked the older man to call him by his first name.

Ellis was old school, though. He wasn't going to drop the formalities any sooner than he'd give up his chosen uniform of a crisp, linen *guayabera*—commonly known across Texas as a Mexican wedding shirt—and black dress pants.

He bent to greet Lucy, and a smile creased his weathered face. "I have milk and cookies for you in the kitchen."

Her wan expression brightened ever so slightly.

"Oreos." Ellis waggled his eyebrows. "Your favorite."

Lucy glanced up at Cash, questions shining in her

big blue eyes. Every day he hoped she'd feel more comfortable moving about the big house. It was as much her home now as it was his. She'd taken a shine to Ellis, but even the daily after-school treat he prepared for her hadn't managed to fully lure her out of her shell. Lucy still behaved as if everything about her new life was temporary and one day she might wake up to find herself back in Dallas with her mommy.

Cash would've given everything he had to make it true. But there were certain priceless things that even McAllister money couldn't buy.

He rested a hand on her dainty shoulder. "Go ahead, Luce. I have some work to catch up on. Maybe later on, we can read one of your library books together."

She nodded.

"What do we say to Ellis?" Cash prompted.

"Thank you, Mr. Ellis," Lucy said in a small voice, made even smaller by the foyer's high ceiling, grand curved staircase and black-and-white marble floor.

"You betcha, kiddo. Come on, now. You can tell me all about your day while I get dinner started." Ellis motioned for Lucy to follow him as he headed toward the large open-concept kitchen.

When he'd decided to bring Lucy here, Cash had imagined the broad kitchen island littered with crayons, toys and school books, the way it had always been back in his early years. Cash and Mallory had spent nearly every afternoon at that kitchen island busying themselves with jigsaw puzzles or homework while their mother flitted around the kitchen and Ellis did handyman tasks around the property.

Turning back the clock was proving to be more difficult than Cash had imagined.

He tried to push that thought away as he settled into his home office and combed through the emails that had piled up while he'd been trying to abscond with Belle Darling's little dog. The McAllister Foundation's fiscal year was coming to a close, and he had countless reports to review and decisions to make before the end of the month. Ordinarily, things at the foundation ran like clockwork. But now that Cash no longer occupied his office in the Dallas headquarters, things had begun to slip through the cracks. He was behind on nearly everything. Dozens of charities were depending on him for funding decisions, and for the past few months, he hadn't managed to look at a single grant request or progress report.

Sitting at the desk that had once been his father's didn't help matters. When he'd been a boy, the home office had been strictly off-limits. Cash had always wondered what his father did all day behind the thick oak door. One day, he'd tucked himself beside the trash can underneath the big executive desk. He could still remember the lemony smell of the dark wood and the way his heart had felt like it might beat out of his chest when his father peered under the desk and found his hiding spot. Cash had been so sure he was about to be punished. Instead, his father had pulled him onto his lap and told him all about the family business. He'd shown him flowcharts and dollar signs with long numerals lined up beside them. Cash had squinted at those numbers and done his best to make sense of them, but it was all too much for him to understand. He pretended he did, especially the part where his dad told him that with great privilege came great responsibility.

Since then, Cash had heard various versions of the same sentiment, everywhere from classic literature to superhero movies. Those words always took him straight back to the day he'd hidden under his dad's desk. Cash had never felt so close to Arthur McAllister before... or since.

Less than a week later, his father told him to pack his bags for boarding school.

The mandate felt like a rejection or a delayed form of punishment, even though someplace deep down, Cash knew better. For years, he'd heard stories about prep school from his elder relatives. Boarding school was a family tradition. How else would he ultimately earn a place at an Ivy institution like Harvard or Yale?

With great privilege comes great responsibility.

Unlike the generations before him, Cash didn't thrive at sleepaway school. He struggled in every subject, especially the ones that required hours of outside reading. The words in the school's thick musty volumes sometimes seemed as difficult to decipher as the columns of long numbers his father had shown him. At Bluebonnet Elementary, his teachers had always been patient with him, offering him one-on-one help or a second chance on assignments when he missed the mark.

Boarding school was different. There was no coddling, either socially or academically. Not even the McAllister name could keep him safe. He was just one of hundreds of boys who came from equally, if not more affluent, backgrounds. For the first time in his life, school had become a sink-or-swim environment.

Cash sank like a stone in every possible respect.

He begged to come home to Bluebonnet, but his parents wouldn't consider it, especially his father. It wasn't until he failed his first term that someone at Kingsley Academy finally put a name to all the trouble he was having.

Dyslexia.

If anyone should've known what was going on with Lucy, it was Cash. The signs were all there—slow reading progress, difficulty remembering anything in sequential order, poor concentration. He'd been so ready to chalk everything up to her grief over losing her mom. Even the way she sometimes mixed up words hadn't clued him in to the fact that they shared the same learning disability. He thought it was cute when she said *flutterby* instead of *butterfly*.

Could he be any worse at this fatherhood thing?

Thank heaven for Miss Darling and Book Buddies. She'd noticed what Cash and Lucy's teacher had both failed to identify. He should've been nicer to her at the library today. Cash could add that interaction to the long list of mistakes he'd made since becoming Lucy's guardian.

The librarian had given as good as she got, though. Was it weird that Cash had almost enjoyed their sparring?

Definitely weird. Cash's temples ached. *She's an important person in Lucy's life. Get your head on straight, man.*

His gaze strayed toward the window directly across from his father's old desk. Beyond the antique restoration glass, bluebonnets swayed in the spring breeze.

The sun was already dipping below the horizon, and he could barely tell where the pink sky ended and the rolling, blue hills began. It was so beautiful his chest ached.

The feeling lingered long after he'd looked away.

"Which book would you like to read tonight?" Cash asked later that night as he tucked Lucy into bed.

She sifted through the pile of library books he'd removed from her backpack and fanned out on the bedspread. The stories all appeared to be variations on the same theme: dogs. An illustrated pup appeared on the cover of each and every book, taunting Cash from behind the clear plastic book jackets.

"This one." Lucy handed him a slender volume that boasted a cartoon golden retriever prancing up the steps of a library. A book dangled from the dog's mouth.

"*Buddy Goes to the Library*," Cash read aloud. "Sounds like a good one."

Lucy burrowed into her pillows and blankets. A quiet smile danced on her lips. "Peaches likes this story."

"I bet she does," Cash said as he stretched out beside Lucy on top of the duvet. "Maybe you can read it to me instead. I'm sure I'll like it, too."

The book opened with a crack of its spine, and the smell of soft pages with just a hint of vanilla filled his senses—a scent he would forever associate with Miss Belle Darling.

"'Buddy the dog belongs to Max,'" Lucy read, slowly enunciating each syllable.

Cash nodded. "Very good."

Lucy continued, underlining the next sentence with the tip of her finger. "'Buddy doesn't like to…'"

She stalled halfway, scrunching up her face in concentration.

...stay home alone when Max goes places.

"Buddy doesn't like to *eat*," Lucy said triumphantly, pointing at the overflowing bowl of dog food next to the dejected golden in the illustration.

She was guessing instead of trying to sound out the words, no doubt because the letters looked like a jumble of nonsense to her. Cash knew the feeling all too well. He'd done the same thing as a kid.

"Look here," Cash said gently, pointing at the *s-t* combination at the start of the word *stay*. "What do these two letters sound like together?"

She made a few attempts and finally got it right on the third try. By then, she'd slumped so far down under the covers that it looked like she was trying to disappear.

"Uncle Cash," she whispered as he slowly turned the page. "I wish Peaches was here."

Me too, sugar.

He pressed a kiss to the top her head, inhaling the childhood scents of baby powder and lavender shampoo. She was just a little girl, and her entire world had been turned upside down. She didn't deserve to struggle this much with something that came easily to other kids. Cash knew all too well that life wasn't fair, but couldn't it be just a little gentler? Just this once?

Me too.

"Wait a minute." Maple Bishop, local veterinarian and one of Belle's dearest friends held up a hand. "He seriously tried to *buy* Peaches from you?"

"He sure did." Belle eyed the generous slice of peach

pie in front of her, and her stomach clenched. It had been nearly three hours since she'd been called into the principal's office at school, and she still couldn't muster up an appetite. Not even for pie, which meant things were definitely dire. "You wouldn't have believed it. It was almost like he wouldn't take no for an answer."

Peaches gazed up at her and wagged her tail, angling for a bite of piecrust. Perhaps holding the Comfort Paws board meetings in a bakery wasn't the best idea in the world.

Tonight wasn't an official meeting, though. Belle, Adaline, Maple and Jenna had agreed to get together one last time to discuss their plans for the Comfort Paws booth at the Bluebonnet Festival, which was scheduled to kick off bright and early tomorrow morning, and they wanted to make sure everything was under control before the crowds descended on the town square. Meeting after hours at Adaline's bakery, Cherry on Top, had become something of a tradition for the four friends, because it was centrally located and came with the added benefit of baked goods. Sometimes Adaline even whipped up homemade dog treats.

Tonight, industrial-sized cookie sheets covered in neat rows of bone-shaped dog biscuits covered half the bakery's countertops. After a quick bite, the girls were going to form an assembly line to get them each bagged up in crinkly cellophane and tied with blue curly ribbon to sell at the festival tomorrow...much to the obvious disappointment of their four dogs. Lady Bird, Maple's golden retriever, had parked herself directly beneath the countertop where the dog bones were arranged. Every time Maple averted her gaze, the golden tried to rise up onto her hind legs and sneak a bite while she wasn't looking.

So far, the dog was oh for three for her efforts. Adaline kept catching her in the act and giving her a gentle swat with her cherry-print dishrag.

"I'm going to need you to elaborate." Jenna, whose Cavalier King Charles spaniel Ginger had given birth to littermates Peaches and Fuzzy, Adaline's pup, in a harrowing late-night emergency last year at Maple's veterinary clinic, pointed her fork at Belle. "What do you mean when you say he wouldn't take no for an answer?"

"'Name your price,'" Belle said, dropping her voice to a low, gravelly tone in an exaggerated imitation of Cash.

All four dogs cocked their heads.

"Please tell me he didn't say that." Jenna's fork, now loaded with pie, paused halfway to her mouth.

Adaline laughed from the opposite side of the counter. "Also, please tell us that's not an accurate impression."

"Seriously. I had a German shepherd in the clinic today with inflammatory laryngitis, and that's exactly what his bark sounded like." Maple laughed.

"Word for word, that's what he said," Belle clarified. "And pretty much what he sounded like. You know the type—all growly and masculine."

Maple snorted. "Again, are we talking about a dog or an actual human man?"

A man, unfortunately. If he'd been a dog, she might've had half a chance at getting through to him. Dogs were trainable. Men, not so much.

At least not in Belle's experience.

"His first name is Cash, the literal definition of money. I shouldn't have been so surprised that he

thought he could buy me." Belle finally picked up her
fork and stabbed at her pie with a bit too much force. "I
mean, my dog."

Why had it felt like one and the same?

Belle throat constricted as she tried to swallow. She
knew why. She just didn't want to think about it. *Ever.*

"What a jerk. I can't believe he got you in trouble
with the principal," Jenna said.

"Dogs are family members, full stop. Offering you
money for Peaches was borderline rude, but even if we
give him the benefit of the doubt and assume he was
well intentioned in the beginning, he should've let it go
after you said no." Maple pushed her empty plate across
the counter and toward Adaline. "Could I pretty please
have another slice? I'm rage-eating now."

"Of course you can." Adaline winked. "Although,
what was your excuse at our last meeting when you ate
three slices?"

Maple wadded up her pink paper napkin and tossed
it at her.

"You've been uncharacteristically quiet about Mon-
eybags McAllister, Adaline," Jenna said with a scrunch
of her forehead. "It's not like you to keep your opinions
to yourself."

Adaline slid her gaze toward Jenna, dressed in a
wraparound ballerina sweater with a perfect bun in her
hair, as usual. She and her dog Ginger had come straight
to the bakery from the dance school she owned around
the corner from the town square. "I'm going to take that
as a compliment."

"And that's exactly how I meant it," Jenna said with
a grin.

"Seriously though." Belle cast a questioning glance at Adaline. Jenna was right. It wasn't like Adaline to bottle up her emotions. Belle had expected her to be the first of her friends to come to her defense. "Tell us what you think."

"Okay." Adaline took a deep breath. "Don't shoot the messenger. I get why you're upset, but maybe you should think of this as a good thing."

Belle felt herself frown "A *good* thing?"

Was she joking? The wealthiest man in town wanted her to sell him her dog, and if she didn't make nice with him, her work friends might lose their jobs. Book Buddies probably wouldn't become part of the school curriculum, the school library might even close, and Belle might end up unemployed. What could possibly be good about any of that?

"Think about it. The reason he wants Peaches is because your dog has had an amazing impact on little Lucy. That's something to be proud of. Book Buddies is changing lives and helping struggling readers. This is the best proof of your dog's impact on the community that you could possibly get." Adaline beamed at her.

Belle didn't know what to say, so she sat quietly and turned her friend's words over in her head.

Jenna gave Belle a gentle shoulder bump. "She's right, you know."

Maple nodded with a frown. "She actually is."

"Try not to look so surprised." Adaline aimed a mock glare at each of them, in turn. "I can be the voice of reason around here every now and then."

"I'm going to credit Jace for this turnaround in your

personality. True love really does make all the difference, doesn't it?" Maple grinned.

That's it. No more pie for me. Belle wanted to barf.

She was happy for her friends. She really was. But something about all three of them falling madly in love over the course of the past year made her feel left out every now and then. That was only human, wasn't it? Even if she had zero intention of following their footsteps and walking down the aisle?

"Thank you for the reminder that Peaches and I are doing good work," she said, eager to switch the subject back to dogs. "I'll try to keep that in mind next time I run into Cash at school."

Maybe if she could switch her way of thinking, she wouldn't be tempted to throttle the man.

Jenna swiveled on her barstool to face her. "So, that's your plan? You're just going to wait to apologize until you accidentally bump into him again?"

"Apologize?" Belle's stomach churned again. "Do you really think I should?"

Ed had asked her to be nice to Cash, but was an apology really necessary when she technically hadn't done anything wrong?

Please, no. She swallowed hard. *Anything but that.*

Adaline shrugged. "Maybe it would help. You don't have to say you're sorry for not letting him walk away with your dog, but perhaps an apology for accusing him of trying to buy *you* might help smooth things over."

She was right...again.

Belle blew out a breath. "Fine. I'll do it. The next time I see him, I'll bat my eyelashes at him and go heavy on the sweet talk."

Maple snorted. "This, I've got to see."

"For now, can we get back to our plans for the festival?" Belle could think about Cash McAllister on Monday morning when school was back in session. Thank goodness she had an entire weekend to herself before she'd have to deal with him again.

"Absolutely," Adaline said.

Peaches pawed at the legs of Belle's barstool, so she gathered her puppy in her arms and held her close while the conversation turned toward the dog biscuit fundraiser and recruiting new therapy dog teams for the upcoming training class.

With any luck, she and her dog would have two blissful, billionaire-free days until they had to face reality again.

Chapter Four

Cash held tight to Lucy's hand as he guided her toward the town square bright and early Saturday morning for the Bluebonnet Festival.

Crisp white tents lined the streets, and country music blared from the gazebo that stood in the center of the park. Sunlight glinted off the silver Airstream trailer that was home to Smokin' Joe's Barbecue. The festival had been up and running for less than half an hour, and already nearly every one of the picnic tables that surrounded the food truck was occupied.

Cash hadn't been sure what to expect, seeing as he'd been about Lucy's age the last time he'd attended the Bluebonnet Festival. Looking back, the memory felt like it was bathed in golden light. Glittering, pure and steeped in a feeling of nostalgia that he now knew he couldn't quite trust.

Life had been so simple and perfect back then—or so he'd thought. Then his parents had shipped him off to boarding school, because that was the McAllister way. Seemingly overnight, everything had changed. Then, after his parents' accident, things had gone from bad to worse.

"Look, Luce." He plucked a cake of hand-milled soap from one of the vendor tables and turned it over to show her the blue flower petals mixed into the fragrant bar. "Bluebonnet soap. Doesn't it smell nice?"

She nodded. "Pretty."

Her voice was barely above a whisper, and it just about broke Cash's heart. She'd always loved flowers. Her bedroom back at the house in the upscale Dallas neighborhood where she and Cash's sister Mallory had lived had been decorated in a pink rose theme. Soft blush-colored blossoms covered the duvet, the pillows, the area rug. The walls looked like something out of fairy tale—pale gray castle stones crisscrossed with climbing vines tipped with delicate pink rosebuds.

Three short months after the diagnosis—pancreatic cancer, stage four—the doorbell rang round the clock with flower deliveries. Sympathy bouquets filled every downstairs room of the grand house. Cash had lain awake at night in the spare bedroom feeling like he might choke on their sickly sweet perfume. The scent hung in the air for weeks, even after all the blooms had dried up and been thrown away. He'd never wanted to see another floral arrangement as long as he lived.

"Would you like to take some of this nice soap home?" Cash patted the pockets of his suit jacket in search of his wallet. "Maybe some bluebonnet bubble bath too?"

"No, thank you." Lucy shook her head and wrinkled her nose as if she, too, could no longer stand the smell of fresh flowers.

Maybe bringing her to the festival hadn't been such a great idea, after all.

Cash was tapped out, though. Attempting to acquire

Peaches the dog had been his Hail Mary pass—a move born out of sheer desperation. The past six months had been rough. Cash tried, but nothing about Lucy's old life was the same without her mom. Her father was still uninterested in being a parent, which was probably for the best since Lucy had never met him face-to-face. Even so, seeing the document where he'd signed away all his parental rights to pave the way for Cash to adopt her had made Cash sick to his stomach. Who could abandon their own child like that?

He'd managed to convince himself that what he and Lucy needed most of all was a fresh start, so he'd brought her to Bluebonnet. Life in a small town was supposed to be kinder…gentler. More forgiving. And it had been, for the most part.

Until his run-in with Belle Darling yesterday.

"Look, Uncle Cash." Lucy squeezed his hand and pointed toward the booths situated closer to the gazebo. "Peaches is here."

A flicker of…something…skittered through Cash. If Peaches was here at the festival, then so was Miss Darling. She'd made things crystal clear yesterday. She and the spaniel were a package deal, full stop.

Sure enough, as he followed Lucy's gaze, he spotted the little dog dressed in a bright red working dog vest at one of the booths flanking the gazebo. And there was Belle Darling at the other end of the Cavalier's leash, with her caramel brown hair tumbling over her shoulders and dark eyes twinkling as she spoke to a man in cowboy boots who'd stopped by the table to pick up a brochure.

"Can we go see her?" Lucy asked, tugging him away from the rows of flowery bath products. "Pleeeease?"

Cash would've rather eaten a bar of bluebonnet soap, petals and all, than spend his Saturday morning in the company of the school librarian. But Lucy was already dragging him across the town square, and he didn't have the heart to tell her no—not when this was the most animated he'd seen her in months.

"Slow down, sugar. Let's make sure and wait your turn. It looks like Miss Darling is busy talking to someone." Cash couldn't help but notice the generous smile she bestowed on the cowboy, and his jaw tensed.

She sure as heck hadn't smiled at him like that yesterday. Not once.

Maybe because you tried to strong-arm her into giving up her dog.

"Hi, there. Would you like some information about Comfort Paws?" The blond woman sitting directly beside Belle waved at Cash and Lucy. Her blond hair was pulled back into a high ponytail, and the stitching on her red Comfort Paws polo shirt said *Adaline & Fuzzy*.

Cash shook his head. "No, thank you. We're actually waiting for—"

Belle Darling's gaze flitted over to him. The instant their eyes met, her mouth fell into a flat line.

An ache hit Cash square in the chest. He would've liked to chalk it up to irritation, but it felt more like interest…like *attraction*, even. Which irritated him all the more.

He redirected his gaze back to the woman sitting beside her at the booth. "We're waiting to speak to Miss Darling when she's free. My niece is a student at Bluebonnet Elementary, and she just spotted Peaches."

"Of course. But while you're waiting, I bet you might

enjoy meeting my dog, Fuzzy." Adaline winked at Lucy, then gathered a sleeping bundle of fur from her lap and placed it on the table. The puppy's eyes fluttered open, and he stretched his mouth into a wide, squeaky yawn. His tail beat happily against the tabletop as his big brown eyes landed on Lucy. "Fuzzy and Peaches are litter-mates."

So, that explained the resemblance, at least. The little dog was a dead ringer for Peaches.

Lucy's eyes went as big as saucers. "Does that mean they're twins?"

Adaline shrugged one shoulder. "Not quite. But they look a lot alike, don't they?"

Lucy's head bobbed up and down. Then she aimed a pleading expression toward Cash. "Can I pet him?"

"You should probably ask Miss Adaline first, don't you think?" Cash tipped his head toward the booth.

Lucy took a tentative step forward, and Fuzzy's tail wagged harder. "May I pet your dog?"

"Thank you for asking so nicely, and of course you can. Getting petted is Fuzzy's job." Adaline ran a hand over the pup's back. He wore a red vest similar to the one that Peaches had on. "Spreading doggy joy is what Comfort Paws is all about."

Lucy reached a hand toward the Cavalier. Fuzzy craned his neck and licked her fingertips. She let out a giggle and glanced up at Cash, eyes sparkling.

"So, is Fuzzy a reading dog like Peaches?" Cash asked.

Adaline shook her head. "No, but Fuzzy and Peaches are both therapy dogs in training. Therapy dog teams do all kinds of volunteer work in the community. We have our first official training class coming up, and hopefully once we have more dogs certified, the Book Buddies program at Bluebonnet Elementary will expand, and we can put more reading dogs to work."

Cash was doing his best to concentrate on what Adaline was saying, but with Belle sitting directly beside her, it was a tall order. She lingered in his periphery like an annoying thorn in his side. Cash was pretty sure bluebonnets didn't have thorns, but if they did, they'd probably have soft brown eyes and a penchant for rule-following.

As for Belle, she kept up her end of the conversation with the other booth visitor, but Cash could tell that his presence was distracting her. She kept stealing glances at him while the cowboy pulled out his phone and started showing her pictures of a black Labrador retriever.

Was he *hitting* on her?

Cash bristled from head to toe.

"Hellooo?" Adaline waved a hand in front of him, dragging his attention back where it belonged.

"Sorry." He cleared his throat. "You were saying?"

Adaline narrowed her gaze at him like she was trying to see inside his head. She opened her mouth to say something, then glanced at Lucy and appeared to reconsider. "No worries. I just asked if you had a pet at home that might be a good candidate for Comfort Paws. If so, we still have spots available in our upcoming training class."

"No, we don't, I'm afraid," Cash said, staring daggers at the cowboy who'd still yet to move on.

"You could always adopt one today," Adaline said with exaggerated cheer.

Cash's head snapped back toward her. "Excuse me?"

Lucy gasped. "Can we adopt Fuzzy, Peaches's twin?"

He hadn't breathed a word to Lucy about his attempt to acquire Peaches. He'd planned on bringing the dog home and surprising her. Adopting another dog wasn't an option. He wanted one like these dogs—a pet that was trained to help Lucy deal with her grief. A dog that could help her overcome her struggle with dyslexia. A miracle dog. Either Peaches or her clone, basically.

Was cloning a viable option? Cash wondered. He made a mental note to do an internet search later when he got home. Although, the likelihood of Belle giving him access to Peaches's DNA didn't seem likely.

"Fuzzy is my dog, hon. I'm afraid he's not up for adoption." Adaline offered Lucy a hopeful smile. "But see over there, in the gazebo? A local rescue group has a lot of really sweet dogs looking for forever homes. Some of them might even make perfect candidates for Comfort Paws."

"I don't think…" Cash shook his head, ready to offer up an excuse, but then Lucy interrupted.

"Do they have any puppies like Fuzzy and Peaches?" she asked, voice trailing up at the end of the question.

Cash couldn't remember the last time his niece had spoken so freely and easily with a total stranger.

"They don't have any Cavaliers, but there's a Frenchie over there with really big eyes and a smushed face. I bet you might like her." Adaline aimed a purposeful glance toward the gazebo.

A huge banner that read Pet Fair was strung from one end of the structure to the other. Cash stared at it for a beat.

This wasn't at all what he'd had in mind. Adopting a puppy on a whim and expecting it to turn into a reading dog for Lucy seemed like a long shot, at best. At worst, it seemed like a disaster in the making.

Cash had had his fill of disasters lately. He didn't have it in him to deal with another one.

But Lucy was already gazing longingly at the pet fair.

"A smushed face," she whispered, and another burst of giggles bubbled up her throat.

Cash narrowed his eyes at Adaline. "You're saying that if I adopted a puppy today, you could train it to be like these dogs."

He motioned toward Fuzzy and Peaches, who'd begun to squirm in Adaline's arms in an attempt to nudge her way toward her littermate in a bid for Lucy's attention. Adaline's peaches-and-cream complexion was growing more flushed by the second.

"That's not what I'm saying at all. I mean that *you* could train your puppy to be a therapy dog." Adaline rested her hand on Fuzzy's back. "With our help, of course."

"Thanks so much for stopping by." Belle shoved a Comfort Paws brochure at the man who'd just shown her no less than fifteen pictures of Cody, his black Lab. The dog was cute and sounded like he might be a great fit for the program, but she really needed him to move on so she could find out what in the world Adaline had just said to Cash McAllister. "Give us a shout if you'd like to sign up for our training class."

"Thank you. I'll be sure and give it some thought." The man tipped his black Stetson at her, slid the brochure into the pocket of his Wranglers and gave Peaches one last pat on the head before moving on to the next booth.

Belle whipped her head toward Adaline. "Do you know who you were just talking to?"

"First of all, calm down, hon." Adaline looked at her askance. "Your face is as red as your Comfort Paws shirt right now."

Of course it was. Belle wasn't capable of hiding her emotions. Like her dad had always said, she wore her heart on her sleeve at all times. Or, in this case, she wore it right smack on her face.

"That was *him*," she hissed under her breath. "Cash McAllister."

Adaline shrugged. "Um, yeah. I kinda figured that out already."

Belle gawked at her friend. Adaline had always been a bit on the quirky side, but this really took the cake. "And you thought it would be a good idea to *invite him to join our training class*?"

Maybe she'd heard wrong. After all, she'd been trying to pay attention to two different conversations at once. There was no way Adaline had tried to recruit Cash for Comfort Paws. No. Possible. Way.

"I did." She hitched a thumb toward the gazebo. "Have you seen the Frenchie puppy they have up for adoption over there? So freaking cute and sweet as pie."

Belle didn't even know where to start. "Why does everything always come back to pie?"

"Occupational hazard," Adaline said with a grin.

Fuzzy wiggled in Adaline's arms, and she leaned over to place the Cavalier on the ground beside Peaches, who'd scrambled to be let down the instant Cash and

Lucy had vanished in the direction of the gazebo. Belle had subsequently watched in horror as her dog strained at the end of her leash as if begging to scamper over to her potential dognapper.

Didn't Peaches realize that if Cash had gotten his way, she'd be living in a fancy mansion on Main Street?

Sure, that kind of lifestyle might sound nice, but Belle knew better. Besides, Peaches was *her* dog. She belonged in Belle's cute little shabby chic cottage situated behind the row of Sunday houses near the town square…even if the aesthetic tipped a teensy bit more toward *shabby* than *chic*.

Belle dragged her gaze away from Peaches, who was still pining for either Lucy or Cash—she was afraid to know which—and turned back toward Adaline. "You realize that you just tried to recruit the man who thought he could buy my dog?"

"I do realize that, and let me just say, 'You're welcome.'" Adaline flashed her an unashamedly self-satisfied smile. "You said you were going to be nice to him from now on, remember? I took one for the team and did it for you."

"How is that helpful when I'm the one who's supposed to be getting on his good side?"

"I'm one of your best friends. You'll look good by association." Adaline's gaze strayed over Belle's shoulder toward the gazebo. "Don't look now, but Cash is checking out the Frenchie."

"Why would I look? I couldn't care less what he does." Belle rolled her eyes, and somehow, they kept on moving until she'd completely turned her head to scope out the pet fair.

Volunteers from a local pet rescue milled about the gazebo with large dogs, all sporting Adopt Me bandanas. Two wire pens had been set up on the lawn near the foot of the gazebo's white steps. One contained a menagerie of fully grown small dogs, and the other held younger puppies. Most of the pups looked like some variety of Chihuahua or terrier, save for a lone roly-poly French bulldog.

A volunteer leaned over the railing of the pen to scoop up the Frenchie and gently place it in Cash's arms.

Belle's heart gave an inexplicable tug.

"Yes, you seem completely disinterested in the handsome billionaire and his adorable niece." Adaline snorted. "If I didn't know better, I'd think there was some sort of weird attraction going on between you two. Cash definitely didn't enjoy watching that guy flirt with you earlier."

"My only interest is in the dog he's holding. That poor Frenchie has no idea what she's getting into if he adopts her." Belle tore her attention away from Cash long enough to fully absorb what Adaline had just said. "And what are you even talking about? What guy?"

Adaline blinked. "The guy who was *just here*—the one who told you the entire life story of his black Lab."

"Because he's interested in the training class."

Adaline wagged her eyebrows. "He's interested in *something*, that's for sure. And I'm not the only one who thought so. Cash nearly turned into a green-eyed monster right before my eyes."

"I could see it—the monster part, I mean," Belle said. As far as green-eyed...no. That sounded beyond absurd.

Cash wasn't attracted to her any more than she was attracted to him.

Which, for the record, was not at all. *Anyone* would go a little weak in the knees at the sight of a nice-looking man dressed in an impeccable suit holding a squishy, baby-faced French bulldog puppy. It didn't necessarily mean anything…only that she was a dog lover. And she could appreciate a nicely cut herringbone.

But honestly, who wore a suit to an outdoor festival?

"Don't look now, but I think he's really going to adopt that dog." Adaline aimed a meaningful glance toward the gazebo.

Lucy sat on the white steps with the puppy cradled in her slender arms while a volunteer from the pet rescue chatted with Cash and tapped away at the iPad in her hands. Adaline was right. It looked an awful lot like the volunteer was helping him complete an adoption form.

Cue the Sarah McLachlan music.

The entire scene could've been a television advertisement for doggy adoption. If the Frenchie's rescuer had been anyone—literally any other person on the planet—besides Cash, Belle's heart probably would've melted.

It didn't. Instead, it froze into a furious block of ice in her chest.

No.

She simply wouldn't allow it. He was doing this on a whim. He had no idea what kind of commitment raising a puppy required, especially a pet he expected to serve the community as a therapy dog. Belle didn't know what he'd said to Adaline to make her think he'd be a great candidate for the Comfort Paws training class, but clearly he'd pulled the wool over her eyes. He wanted a reading education assistance dog for Lucy, period. He had zero intention of doing volunteer work, and that's not how the process worked. Someone really needed to put a stop to this nonsense before it was too late.

Unfortunately, it looked like that someone was going to have to be Belle.

"Can you watch Peaches for a second?" She handed the little Cavalier to Adaline as she rose to her feet.

"Um, sure," Adaline said as Peaches and Fuzzy began to wrestle on her lap. "I've got everything under control here. It only looks like total chaos."

"Thanks. I won't be gone long." Only long enough to restore the universe to its proper order, or get herself well and truly fired. Whichever came first.

"Just one question…" Adaline gave her a sidelong glance. "Where are you going?"

Belle's gaze flicked toward Cash and back again.

Adaline shook her head. "Oh, no."

"Oh, *yes*," Belle corrected.

"Oh boy."

Chapter Five

"This all seems great." The pet rescue volunteer scrolled through Cash's adoption paperwork on her iPad. "I'll just run your credit card through for the application fee, and then we can set up a time for your home visit next week."

"Home visit?" Cash laughed.

The volunteer glanced up from her screen. "Something funny?"

"Oh, you're serious." He held up his hands. "Sorry. I didn't realize. Anytime next week is fine."

The volunteer nodded. "Good. You can take the pup home today, but the adoption won't be final until someone from the rescue group signs off on the setup you've arranged for her at your place of residence."

Cash felt himself frown. This process was proving to be nearly as rigorous as legally switching from Lucy's guardian to her adoptive parent had been.

Maybe this wasn't such a great idea after all.

"Can we name her Sparkles, Uncle Cash?" Lucy grinned up at him from her perch on the gazebo steps with the newly christened Sparkles splayed belly-up across her lap.

Too late to back out now.

He flashed his niece a wink. "We can name her whatever your little heart desires."

"Any questions before I process your payment and check our home visit schedule?" the doggy adoption counselor asked.

"What happens if I fail the home visit?" Cash asked. Surely that wasn't a thing.

Was it?

"If your home isn't deemed a safe and nurturing place for the dog, we reserve the right to cancel the adoption."

Okay, so maybe it was a thing.

Cash was beginning to sweat beneath his suit jacket. "Has that ever happened before?"

"It happens more often than we'd like." The volunteer, a serious young lady with a strawberry blond pixie cut and earrings shaped like paw prints swinging from her ears, narrowed her gaze at him. "In the event we reclaim the dog, your adoption fee is not refundable. Is that going to be a problem?"

He should've just kept his mouth shut and pretended the McAllister Mansion came equipped with a theme park for puppies. Doggy Disneyland, or whatever else the rescue group deemed *safe and nurturing.*

Cash gave her a tight smile as he handed over his credit card. "No problem whatsoever."

Except now he wasn't sure what qualified as an appropriate rescue puppy setup. He'd had enough trouble figuring out how to decorate a room for a seven-year-old girl. Somehow, though, he didn't think a canopy bed and a profusion of pink bows was going to cut it where Sparkles was concerned.

"I'll be right back," the volunteer said and then disappeared with his Amex, presumably to ring up the adoption fee while also ordering a full criminal background check.

Once again, he wondered if he should've given the therapy dog plan a bit more consideration before jumping in with both feet and adopting a dog. But the Frenchie had pretty much gotten the stamp of approval from Comfort Paws already. All he had to do was show up at class a few times and, boom, Lucy could have her own version of Peaches.

It almost sounded too good to be true...

Maybe it was.

He had to act now, though. That little bulldog was as cute as a button. If he didn't adopt her on the spot, someone else would. He was doing this, period. The rescue lady had rattled him, that's all. Everything was fine.

Until all of a sudden, Belle Darling planted herself in front of him with her arms crossed and her pretty bow-shaped lips turned down into a pout, and something told Cash things weren't so fine anymore.

"Can we have a word?" she said primly.

At least the cowboy was no longer monopolizing her time. That was a plus. Although for the life of him, Cash couldn't figure out why he cared.

He arched a brow. "Hello, Miss Darling. Enjoying the festival?"

A cute little pucker formed in her forehead, as if the fact that he was making polite conversation confused her to no end.

"Yes," she said and then her lush bottom lip slipped between her teeth. He really needed to stop looking at her mouth, but he couldn't seem to help it. What was wrong with him? This woman didn't even like him. "I mean, not really. Not anymore."

"That's a shame. It's a lovely day," Cash said, knowing full well her comment had been a thinly veiled dig at him.

"What do you think you're doing?" she blurted, cutting straight to the chase. So much for pleasantries.

At least she had the decency to keep her voice low enough to prevent Lucy from overhearing their conversation. Although, Cash was fairly certain his niece only had eyes for Sparkles at the moment. She hadn't so much as noticed Belle.

"I'm adopting a dog," Cash said. Was he, though? That didn't seem like such a certainty anymore. "She's going to be a reading dog, just like Peaches."

Belle eyed him like he was a misbehaving child she was about to send to the principal's office. "You have no idea what you're getting yourself into, do you?"

She was correct. He didn't, but what business was that of hers?

He studied her until she did that cute nose-crinkle thing of hers. "You seem overly invested in my personal life, Miss Darling."

She glowered at him. "Don't flatter yourself."

Cash laughed. What was it about this woman? Was she always this confrontational, or did he, specifically, bring something out in her? "I'm being sincere. In retrospect, I can understand your rather hostile reaction yesterday when I inquired about purchasing Peaches. But Sparkles isn't yours. What objection could you possibly have to this arrangement?"

"You're naming your dog Sparkles?" Her lips twitched, which Cash only noticed because he was looking at her pretty, impertinent mouth again. Clearly, small-town life was getting to him, because she was quickly becoming the most fascinating thing about Bluebonnet.

"Go ahead and laugh," he said without cracking a smile. "You obviously want to."

She shook her head. "I can't. I'm trying my hardest to be nice to you. I kind of have to."

This was her being nice? "You seem to be finding that a bit of a challenge."

"It's a tall order." She tapped her foot against the grass. "You have no idea. Listen, I'm going to try to put this as sweetly as I can. I know Adaline told you that the Frenchie would make a great therapy dog, but the Comfort Paws training class isn't going to be easy."

"So, your friend was just trying to be nice to me, too? She doesn't think I can hack it?" Cash's gut churned. He was used to people acquiescing to him at every turn. It had been happening all his life, thanks to the McAllister name.

Perhaps that's why he found Belle so interesting. At least he could trust that she was being honest with him.

"Volunteering for Comfort Paws isn't just about training a dog to help Lucy read. It's about serving the community. Only half of the class will be about dog training. The other half of the curriculum is aimed at training the dog's handler." Belle raised her brows as if waiting for him to say something. When he didn't, she sighed. "That means you."

"Believe it or not, I read to my niece all the time. I

know my way around a bedtime story, if that's what you're worried about. If you want me to help out with your Book Buddies program at school, I'll do it." Cash hadn't anticipated doing so, but if it meant Lucy could have her own reading dog at home, he was game.

It might be nice spending more time in the library that had been named after his mother. He'd felt her presence wash over him the instant he'd entered the space yesterday. Before she'd married into the McAllister family, she'd been a librarian herself. Cash had been just a kid when she'd passed away, but he still had vivid memories of her tucked away on one of the window seats in the McAllister Mansion with a book in her lap and a cup of tea close by.

Bluebonnets had always been her favorite flower. The plush blue carpeting in the school library couldn't have been an accident.

"In order to obtain Comfort Paws certification at the end of the class, you and Sparkles will need to pass all the requirements necessary to be a therapy dog team, not just Book Buddies volunteers. That means learning how to visit people in healthcare settings," Belle said.

Cash crossed his arms.

"You'll be required to go through a mentoring process and put in hours with Sparkles someplace like Bluebonnet Senior Center or County Hospital," Belle said.

Cash was no stranger to spending time in hospitals. Toward the end of last year, he'd spent more hours at his sister's bedside than he could count.

Been there, done that. Never again.

As much as he hated to admit it, Belle Darling might

be right. There was more to this therapy dog business than he'd bargained for.

"Can you still honestly say that you're interested in joining the training class?"

He glanced at his niece cradling the puppy that no one seemed to think he was equipped to handle. Lucy was clearly besotted.

Despite his better judgment, and despite the fact that he'd rather gouge his own eyes out than be forced to re-visit the kind of suffering his sister had gone through, Cash dug in his heels. Lucy *needed* this dog. He'd made a promise to Mallory that he would take good care of her little girl, and he intended to keep it.

And if, in the process, he proved to Miss Darling that she was wrong about him, all the better.

"Are you and Peaches enrolled in the class?" he heard himself ask, as if that should have any bearing whatso-ever on his decision.

"I'm not sure how that's relevant, but yes. It's our first certification class. For now, Peaches is a therapy dog in training. Since we're part of the group that started Comfort Paws, we've had a bit of a head start. But we'll have to pass the class, just like all the other new teams."

Cash nodded. "Then Sparkles and I look forward to joining you. May the best dog team win."

He winked. He was joking, of course…mostly. He knew it wasn't a contest, but a little friendly competition might make things interesting. Especially when every-one around him seemed to think he wasn't up to the task.

Belle threw her hands in the air. "You haven't heard a single word I just said, have you?"

Oh, but he had. He'd probably be replaying this entire conversation in his head tonight while he was staring up at the ceiling, unable to sleep—particularly the little slip of her tongue where she mentioned she was supposed to be nice to him.

Someone at the school had obviously gotten wind of their tense exchange in the library. Afterward, as he'd stalked out the door and down the front steps of the school, not one person had made eye contact with him. That alone should've been a telltale sign. Cash was willing to bet that Miss Darling had found herself in the hot seat in the principal's office by the end of the day. Ed Garza had probably warned her to treat him with kid gloves from here on out.

That was the last thing Cash wanted. He didn't want to her to be nice. He wanted her to be real. He wanted to feel something again, and heaven help him, at long last he did. Cash had felt more alive during their two brief encounters than he had in months. Maybe even years.

Mallory's diagnosis had been a turning point. For the second time in his life, the McAllisters had been faced with circumstances they couldn't control. Losing his parents had been difficult enough, but he wasn't supposed to lose Mallory. Ever. She was all the family he had left. From the instant she'd broken the bad news, Cash had felt like he was drowning…slowly slipping under, moment by moment, day by day, week by week. He'd grown so accustomed to it that he hadn't even realized that the numbness had become his new way of life.

Until the fire in Belle's eyes had shaken him awake.

Cash didn't want to start sleepwalking his way through life again. Not yet…

"We'll see you at class, Miss Darling." *Assuming I*

pass the home inspection. "And don't worry—your secret is safe with me."

Heat stained her cheeks. "What secret?"

"The fact that you seem to have no idea whatsoever how to play nice."

Belle woke up Sunday morning with a weight pressing down on her chest.

At first, she chalked it up to Peaches, who liked to wake her up by settling on top of her sternum and licking her face until she opened her eyes. Her fault, really. All the puppy training manuals said that dogs were supposed to sleep in crates at night. Small enclosed spaces were supposed to make dogs feel safe and relaxed. They also helped with potty training in younger pups. But had Belle actually followed any of that advice?

No.

No, she hadn't.

Maple originally discovered Peaches and Fuzzy's dog mama, Ginger, abandoned on the front steps of her veterinary practice late one night last summer. Ginger had been in distress in the late stages of labor, and Maple had acted quickly to save her life, along with the two puppies. Afterward, she taken Ginger, Peaches and Fuzzy home with her, where she and Lady Bird had doted over the little family until they were ready to go to their new homes. Jenna had been drawn to Ginger right away, while Adaline and Belle had taken turns helping out with supplemental bottle-feeding for Fuzzy and Peaches. After all Ginger had been through, her puppies had been blessed with a perfect upbringing. Maple followed all the rules of puppy raising, down to the letter. She was a veterinarian, after all.

Then Belle had gone and ruined it all by letting Peaches sleep in her bed the night she'd brought the little Cavalier puppy home.

It was supposed to be a temporary arrangement, sort of a celebratory homecoming treat. Peaches had other ideas, though. She steadfastly refused to set paw inside the crate now. In fact, she gave it such a wide berth that Belle wondered if Peaches might be pretending it didn't exist.

Situations like this were precisely why Belle had never been a rule-breaker. She'd learned at an awfully young age that few things in life were within her control. So she gravitated to scenarios where she had as much agency as possible, and she always followed the rules to the letter. It was all she could do to ensure everything in her life turned out as perfect and predictable as possible.

Belle had a deep, dark secret, though. She actually enjoyed letting Peaches sleep in her bed. She liked falling asleep at night to the cute snuffling sounds Peaches made. She liked the way her dog's soft, warm body felt pressed against her shoulder. She even liked waking up to a face full of puppy breath in the mornings.

That wasn't the case on Sunday morning, though. As Belle squinted against the golden sunlight streaming through her bedroom window, she spotted Peaches still curled into a tight little ball beside her, which meant the Cavalier had nothing to do the weight on Belle's chest. On the contrary, that weight was the realization that despite her promise to her boss, she'd gone and doubled down on her tense relationship with Cash McAllister.

Not that they had any sort of *relationship*, per se. The very thought of it made Belle's stomach flip. Weirdly, it wasn't an altogether unpleasant sensation.

Was it just her, or had it seemed like there was a twinkle in Cash's eye when he'd said her secret was safe with him?

You seem to have no idea whatsoever how to play nice.

It had almost felt like he was *flirting* with her. Surely not, though. That would've been crazy. They didn't even like each other. The whole reason she'd been conversing with him was to try and talk him out of adopting a dog and joining Comfort Paws. Which, in the cold light of a new day, didn't seem very nice at all.

Maybe Cash had a point…maybe Belle didn't have the first idea how to play nice.

Ugh. She flipped over and groaned into her pillow. Peaches stirred at the sudden movement, and within seconds, she was nuzzling her tiny face against Belle's cheek with her tail beating wildly against the mattress.

Ordinarily, that would've been enough to make Belle forget her troubles. But Cash had a very particular way of getting under her skin.

Belle didn't have any problem whatsoever playing nice with normal people. Cash wasn't normal, though. He was a McAllister, which meant he could probably snap his fingers and get whatever he wanted, no questions asked. That's how people with McAllister money operated.

Belle had seen it before with her own two eyes.

Did any one family empire really need millions of dollars? Sure, a person could do a massive amount of good with those kind of resources, but in Belle's experience, it never failed to come at a price.

In Belle's case, that price had been her family.

"He wasn't flirting," she whispered against the cinnamon-colored fur of Peaches's ear. "And even if he had been, it definitely wasn't reciprocated."

She'd rather die than go on a date with that man. Not that he'd asked…

Then why are you even entertaining the notion?

Belle groaned again. What had gotten into her? Sure. Objectively speaking, Cash was an attractive man. And maybe the sight of him with a dog in his arms made her feel like she was looking at one of those charity calendars that pictured hot firemen posing with adorable puppies and kittens.

But Cash wasn't a heroic first responder. He probably didn't even know CPR.

Belle's phone rang just as she was chastising herself for making assumptions about a person's first aid abilities when she herself had skipped out on Bluebonnet Elementary's optional CPR in-service training last month because she'd been too immersed in the latest thriller novel from one of her favorite authors to leave her apartment.

Her father's contact information flashed on the screen of her cell, and she answered with a smile. "Hey, Dad."

"Good morning, honeybun," he said, using her old childhood nickname. No matter how old Belle got, she'd always be honeybun to Maurice Darling.

"Is everything okay? We're still on for today, right?" Belle climbed out of bed and began straightening the covers as she spoke. She and her father had a standing date for family dinner on Sunday evenings.

"Of course we are. I'm making a pot roast," Dad said. "Homemade."

Over the years, Belle had tried to get family dinner switched to her cottage instead of the double-wide trailer where she'd grown up and where her father still lived. She loved that old trailer, but she was constantly trying to get her dad to slow down a little and let her dote on him instead of the other way around.

"A pot roast?" Had she heard him correctly? A pot roast was a far cry from the burgers and macaroni and cheese they'd had last Sunday…and the Sunday before… "That sounds fancy. You know you don't have to go through all that trouble."

When had he even learned how to cook something like that?

Belle didn't think she'd eaten a Sunday roast since her mother had been the one to prepare their Sunday family dinners. That had been ages ago. Belle had been a gangly, bookish nine-year-old girl when her mother packed up and left the family without a backward glance. Afterward, she and her dad had started their new tradition— burgers with mac and cheese.

Belle and her dad had been fine without pot roast. Just like they'd been fine without her mother.

Belle had made sure of it.

In those early days, when she'd wake up in the middle of the night to the sound of her father weeping quietly in the living room, she vowed to be such a perfect daughter and take such great care of her dad that he'd forget all about her mother. All she wanted to do was make her daddy smile again.

Day by day, month by month, year by year, he did. And now, twenty years later, Maurice Darling was still Belle's best friend in the entire world—along with Peaches and the Comfort Paws girls, of course.

At the other end of the phone line, her father cleared his throat. "Actually, I wanted to make something a little special because I've invited a guest to join us for family dinner tonight."

"A guest?" This was a first. "Wow, Dad. That's awesome."

She wondered who it might be. Dad was part of a bowling league with some of his friends from work, but to her knowledge, he'd never invited any of them over before.

Sometimes she wondered if he kept to himself because of what had happened with her mom. Mostly, though, she tried not to think about it. She was proud of her father, and she was proud of her upbringing, full stop. Children of divorce weren't supposed to have to choose one parent over the other, but once Belle's mother had put the trailer park in her rearview mirror, she'd never looked back, never once invited Belle to come stay in her fancy new house with her fancy new husband. A man with more money than he knew what to do with had swooped right in and taken what hadn't belonged to him: Belle's mother.

Was it any wonder she didn't trust anyone who'd been born with a silver spoon in his mouth... Cash McAllister very much included? With his legacy seat on the school board and that big family mansion on Main Street, his spoon was no doubt the biggest and most silver one of all.

"So you don't mind, then?" Dad asked.

How sweet. He sounded nervous. "Of course not. I'm excited to meet your friend."

"Music to my ears, honeybun," Dad said, and Belle could hear the smile in his voice…

Which made it all the more surprising why she didn't see the next part coming.

"Cathy is excited to meet you, too."

Belle felt her smile freeze on her face, and she was suddenly very glad she'd never gotten her dad to learn how to use the video chat feature on his phone.

Cathy?

The friend was a woman. Was her father trying to tell her that he had a girlfriend? After all this time?

Belle didn't want to believe it. She wanted to keep her dad's heart tucked away in bubble wrap for the rest of his days so he wouldn't get hurt again. But the pot roast spoke volumes. Whoever Cathy was, she was more than a casual friend.

"Great," Belle said, and the rest of the conversation seemed like white noise. She tried to pay attention, but her head was spinning faster than Peaches on one of her late night running fits.

Zoomies, Maple called them. Belle still didn't know if that was a real term or something Maple had made up on her own.

All she knew for sure was that she had a very sudden, very intense craving for a burger with a side of mac and cheese.

Chapter Six

"Uncle Cash, did you know that your eyes changed color overnight?" Lucy studied him from across the breakfast table, cereal spoon dangling from her dainty hand. "Yesterday, they were grayish-blue, and today they're red. Like, really, *really* red."

"You don't say?" Cash snorted into his coffee cup—his third serving since giving up on sleep on and stumbling to the kitchen with Sparkles romping on his heels, chasing the trailing tie of his bathrobe.

The Frenchie hadn't slept longer than twenty minutes in a row last night. Cash felt for the poor pup. He realized the McAllister Mansion was a strange, new place. A massive one, at that. But sometime around three in the morning, he'd started feeling sorrier for himself than he did for the animal.

Ellis hadn't slept a wink either. Cash had found the caretaker sitting at the kitchen island when he flipped on the light switch in the predawn hours. He was fairly certain the huge mug of coffee in the older man's hands included a sizable dollop of whiskey, but he didn't ask. If Cash had thought a good, old-fashioned Irish coffee could lull him into sleep while a French bulldog cried at the top of his lungs, he would've tried it. As it was, unless that coffee had come with a set of noise-canceling headphones, the situation seemed hopeless.

Is this what dog ownership was supposed to be like? If so, how did Belle Darling manage to look as fresh as a daisy every time he set eyes on her?

"I'm full." Lucy nudged her cereal bowl toward the center of the table, her gaze shifting from Cash's bloodshot eyes toward Sparkles, who was now sleeping soundly in his lap. Because of course she was. "Can Sparkles get up from her nap now so we can have a tea party?"

"No!" Cash and Ellis said in unison.

They looked at each other and chuckled. At least their senses of humor were still somewhat intact. When they dropped dead from sleep deprivation, at least they'd go with smiles on their faces.

Lucy's forehead scrunched. "What's so funny?"

Cash schooled his expression. "Nothing, Luce. I'm afraid Ellis and I are just a little tired. Sparkles didn't sleep much last night, and neither did we."

Ellis ruffled Lucy's hair. "The doggy didn't keep you awake, little one?"

She shook her head.

Thank goodness Cash hadn't caved and let the puppy sleep in her crate in Lucy's bedroom. Otherwise, there would be three zombies sitting around the breakfast table this morning instead of two.

Lucy's bedroom was situated in the turret on the east side of the house. The mansion was a vast, Victorian-style building with two turrets and its own gazebo that mirrored the one in Bluebonnet's town square. A white picket fence surrounded the property. The instant Lucy set eyes on the house, she begged for a bedroom in one of the turrets. Cash had reluctantly agreed. He would've preferred her to occupy a room closer to his. Now, he was thanking his lucky stars she'd missed out on last night's doggy choral performance.

It was hard to believe that a pup that small could make such a big racket.

"I think we should let Sparkles sleep for a bit so we can all get a little rest this morning," Cash said. The Frenchie's muzzle rumbled with a soft, snuffling sound as she slept in his lap. He didn't dare budge, lest he wake her up. At the very least, he wanted to be fully caffeinated before she opened her big round eyes.

Lucy sighed. "Okay, but when she wakes up, I want to draw her picture. I'm making a book about Sparkles."

"A book?" Cash felt a glimmer of wakefulness somewhere beneath the layers upon layers of exhaustion. Or maybe it was a flicker of something else entirely.

Hope.

It had been so long since Cash knew the feeling that he almost didn't recognize it. Could it be that he'd actually done the right thing in adopting the nocturnal monster in his lap?

He'd been so sure at the pet fair. So smug, even when Belle, the self-appointed dog expert, had tried to warn him that he had no idea what he was getting into. Somewhere around two in the morning, he'd accepted that she might've been right, even though he'd never admit as much to her face. Cash was keeping this dog for the long haul, even if he never slept again.

"I want to make a book all about Sparkles so I can bring it to school and read it to Peaches," Lucy said.

"That's a wonderful idea." Cash nodded. Sparkles was clearly no replacement for Peaches. He could adopt all the dogs in the world, and that Cavalier King Charles spaniel would still have Lucy wrapped around her furry little paw.

He was never going to rid himself of Peaches and her fiery librarian mistress, was he?

Is that really what you want?

"After I draw all the pictures for the book, can you help me with the words, Uncle Cash?" Lucy's nose crinkled. Her crestfallen expression sent Cash straight back to his own elementary school days—days when he stopped trying to read aloud in class because the silence between words and syllables often stretched out so long that he could hear the kids around him beginning to squirm in their seats. It was better to let everyone suspect he couldn't read than to try and fail, proving them all right. "I'm bad at that part."

You're doing this for her, remember? Everything—the puppy, the Comfort Paws class, dealing with the maddening librarian—it's all for her.

"You're not bad at it, Luce." Cash's heart squeezed so tight he could barely breathe. "Peaches doesn't think so, does she?"

Lucy shook her head, and a hint of smile danced on her lips.

Bless that dog, and bless her saucy owner. The pain in Cash's chest morphed into something different—something that felt more like an ache.

"And Miss Darling doesn't either, right?" he asked.

"No," Lucy said in a still, small voice.

If he looked closely, Cash could see a glimmer of confidence in her eyes—just a tiny spark, but it was there. A precious gift.

Maybe he needed to make an effort to be nicer to Belle. He needed her. *Lucy* needed her. He couldn't screw up this dog thing.

"You're not bad at it. You're learning, that's all. Trust me, sugar, you'll get there. I had trouble with words when I was young, too. I promise it will get easier." Cash ought to know. He'd been there, and unfortunately he hadn't had someone like Belle rooting for him. He wondered how different his childhood would've been if he had. "But of course I'll help you with your book about Sparkles. It'll be fun."

"Thank you, Uncle Cash. I love Sparkles." She slid off her barstool and came around the island to wrap her arms around him.

Just as he feared, the sudden movement jostled the Frenchie awake in his lap. Her jaws stretched into a wide yawn that ended with a squeak that made Lucy giggle.

"Sparkles! You're awake!" Lucy gingerly gathered the puppy into her slender arms, and the bulldog's nub of a tail wagged like crazy.

Cash glanced up and found Ellis watching them with a tender expression. And just like that, Cash knew his sliver of peace and quiet had come to an end.

He didn't mind much, though.

That's what coffee was for.

Bluebonnet Acres, the mobile home park where Belle had grown up, was situated four blocks away from the town square and surrounded by rolling hills dotted with the colorful wildflowers the Texas Hill Country was so famous for. It was a small community, with six rows of trailers, and the property boasted its own white picket fence and a flower garden near the entrance.

When Belle was a little girl, she'd knelt in the dirt next her daddy while he'd tended to the blooms every spring alongside their neighbors. They planted zinnias and lantana in bright bursts of hot pink, orange and ice-box yellow, flowers that thrived in a hot Texas summer. As neat and pretty as they were, perfectly spaced out along the bold white fence posts, she'd always preferred the lavish beauty of the wildflowers. She liked the idea of the bluebonnets and pink evening primroses growing all on their own, without any help or planting from anyone. They didn't need a gardener…or a mother figure. They just appeared, strong and glorious every spring, year after year, no matter what nature threw their way.

The hills were especially lovely today as she turned her car onto the red dirt path that led toward Bluebonnet Acres. She paused to admire the endless swath of blue flowers, punctuated with fiery bursts of vermilion from the Indian paintbrushes that often grew alongside the Texas state flower. So many Hill Country artists painted the landscape as a monochromatic blur, but Belle had always loved those unexpected pops of crimson in real life.

Her father once told her that Indian paintbrushes grew best when their roots became intertwined with those of a nearby bluebonnet. They shared nutrients without harming each other and the two flowers thrived side-by-side, complementing the other.

Just like us, Belle had said. *Red and blue, like me and you.*

When Elizabeth Darling had packed up and left, she hadn't only left her husband. She'd left her daughter behind, too. Belle never heard from her mother again, but so long as she still had her father, she knew everything would be okay. He'd take care of her, and she'd take care of him. They'd be just like those two wildflowers.

What now, though? Belle thought. *What happens to the bluebonnet and the Indian paintbrush when another flower enters the picture?*

The hillside blossoms went watery as her eyes filled with tears. Seriously? She was *crying* over a silly date to a Sunday family dinner?

Belle sniffed and shifted the car back into Drive. She was being ridiculous. Her father was a grown man—a *good* man—and he deserved to be happy. Besides, she was getting way, way ahead of herself. Dad had invited a friend to family dinner, and that friend happened to be a woman. That was it. They were talking about a simple Sunday pot roast, not wedding bells.

Peaches wiggled in her sherpa-lined doggy car seat as the car crawled toward her dad's mobile home. By the time Belle parked and opened the back door to unclip the dog's harness from the safety leash attached to the car seat, Peaches was whining with excitement. Cavaliers were famous for their loving nature. They fell in love at first sight with most everyone they met. But if Peaches had a favorite person in the world other than Belle, it was Maurice Darling.

"Oh, good," her dad said as he stepped out of the double-wide trailer's front door and onto the wooden deck he'd built himself when Belle had been in kindergarten. "You brought my grand-dog."

"Do you seriously think she would've let me leave her home alone?" Belle said with a laugh.

She lifted the dog from the car. Peaches squirmed to be let down, and the instant her paws touched the ground, she scurried up the steps of the deck toward Belle's father.

The dog pawed at his shins. As a therapy animal, she should've known better, but trying to make her behave around Dad was hopeless. He hoisted her into his arms to let her cover his face with puppy kisses.

"Well, hello there, little one," he cooed. He offered Belle an easy grin. "And hello to you, too, honeybun."

"Hi, Dad." She gave him a hug and finally relaxed. Today felt like any other Sunday. She wasn't sure why she'd gotten so worked up earlier.

Then a woman with a neat silver bob stuck her head out of the trailer door.

"You must be Belle." She wiped her hands on the floral apron tied around her waist, a relic left behind by Belle's mom. "I'm Cathy. It's such a pleasure to meet you."

Belle blinked at the apron, and her throat went dry. Cathy clearly felt right at home here if she'd managed to find that old thing. Belle hadn't set eyes on it in years. "I...um...pleased to meet you, too."

She offered her hand for a shake, but Cathy pulled her into a hug instead. Her embrace was warm and soft in a way that made Belle's eyes sting. The temptation to sink into it was almost too much to bear.

Cathy pulled away but held onto Belle's shoulders so

she could study her at arm's length. "Look at you. You're every bit as lovely as your father said you were. He talks about you all the time, you know."

Funny...he hasn't said a single word about you. Belle forced a smile. Exactly how long had Dad and Cathy known each other? She definitely seemed like she was in full hostess mode.

"Supper is almost ready. I hope you're hungry," Cathy said, holding the door open wide and ushering everyone inside.

"So, you're the one who made the pot roast." Belle narrowed her eyes at her father. "Everything makes much more sense now."

Dad offered her a sheepish grin.

Belle just shook her head. "Cathy, please tell me what I can do to help."

She needed to contribute, even if it was something as simple as setting the table. She was beginning to feel like a guest in her own childhood home.

Thankfully, Cathy put her straight to work. Belle cut fresh vegetables for the salad and arranged a bundle of wildflowers in a Mason jar and placed it in the center of the kitchen table, just like she always did for Sunday dinner. Cathy chatted all the while, regaling Belle with stories about her twin sons, who'd both studied agriculture at Texas A&M and now worked on a cattle ranch in Montana. After a while, the tension left Belle's shoulders, and by the time the meal was over, her cheeks hurt from smiling so much.

Most of those grins had been aimed at her dad. It was nice to see him like this. She couldn't remember the last time he'd made a new friend, much less shown any romantic interest in anyone.

It was kind of cute how nervous he seemed. He blushed when Cathy placed her hand on top of his and squeezed his fingertips. During dinner, his leg jiggled so hard that his napkin kept sliding out of his lap. The third time it happened, Peaches pounced on it and dashed around the trailer with it, goading him into a game of chase. Cathy laughed so hard that tears streamed down her cheeks while Peaches ran circles around Dad, who finally gave up, grabbed a roll of paper towels and plunked it down in the center of the table.

The gesture immediately transported the dinner into more normal territory. For as long as Belle could remember, there'd been a roll of paper towels on the family dinner table, propped right beside a cluster of wildflowers she'd picked in the field just beyond the white picket fence surrounding the mobile home park.

It was nice to know some things never changed, especially now when Belle had the strangest sensation that the life she'd known for so long was about to slip away.

It's one *family dinner. Stop letting your thoughts run wild.*

Belle was far too old to feel anxious about her father dating again. She was a grown woman, for goodness' sake. But the day her mother left, her entire world had fallen apart. It had taken a long time for the little trailer to feel like home again. Dad had done his very best, and they'd made it through the woods…together. Cathy seemed perfectly lovely, but less than twenty-four hours ago, Belle hadn't known the woman existed. She couldn't bear the thought of her father getting hurt again.

Getting to know someone takes time. Belle sipped her sweet tea and reminded herself there was no rush. She wasn't writing the woman's biography. She'd get to know Cathy better eventually.

But the next thing she knew, Dad took Cathy's hands in his, cleared his throat and gave Belle a look filled with a tenderness she hadn't seen in his gaze in a long, long time.

"Honeybun, there's something we want to tell you," he said.

They were a *we* now? Already? When had that happened, and why hadn't her dad thought to tell her what was going on in his life before now? Dad had always been her biggest cheerleader—her best friend in the world, other than Peaches and the Comfort Paws girls. She'd never doubted for a minute that he felt the same.

But the hand he was holding now wasn't hers, and she knew what was coming even before the words left his mouth.

"Cathy and I are getting married."

Chapter Seven

"Seven months?" Adaline's mouth dropped open into a perfect O. She stared at Belle from across the counter at Cherry on Top, wordless, while Belle attacked a slice of warm peach pie with gusto.

Breakfast of champions, Belle thought. But also, *Hey, whatever gets me through this day.*

It was Monday, also known as the day after the enlightening family dinner with Dad and Cathy, plus her first day back at work since she'd all but ignored her boss's plea and further antagonized Cash McAllister at the Bluebonnet Festival. Belle needed sustenance. Specifically, sustenance in the form of sugar and piecrust, along with a hearty dose of girl talk. Fortunately, Adaline always got to Cherry on Top at an absurdly early hour to bake.

"Seven months," Belle repeated, stabbing a fork into her slice of pie. "Can you believe it? They've been dating for over *half a year*, and Dad waited to tell me until after he'd put a ring on it."

"Do people still say 'put a ring on it'?" Adaline tilted her head. She looked like one of their Cavalier puppies. "Never mind. We'll circle back to that later. I don't understand what your father was thinking. You two are so close. Why would he wait this long to tell you he'd met someone?"

Belle sighed and dropped her gaze to the flaky piecrust. She should've known Adaline would press for more details. It's what good girlfriends did. But her dad's explanation wasn't something she necessarily wanted to share, especially with someone who'd recently fallen head over heels in love and gotten engaged.

"Did he give you *any* sort of explanation for the secrecy?" Adaline prompted.

"His reasoning is the worst part of all," Belle said, finally relenting. If she couldn't share the ugly details with Adaline, who else would she tell? Peaches was a great listener, but not the best at doling out advice. And that's what Belle needed right now—someone to tell her what to do.

About *everything*.

For an introvert who loved her small little life filled with her novels, her notebook and her dog, her world had suddenly gotten exponentially more complicated. She felt like she'd been strapped into a tilt-a-whirl ride and couldn't find the way off.

"Dad said he waited to tell me about Cathy because he was afraid it would make me feel lonely." Belle swallowed hard. "Not because he's moving on and worried that I might lose him to someone new. He knows better than that. All I've ever wanted is for my father to be happy."

Adaline shook her head. "I don't get it. Why would you feel lonely, then?"

"Because, and I quote, I haven't 'found a special

someone of my own,'" Belle said and then dropped her head in her hands.

Even pie wasn't helping her feel any better. That's how far she'd fallen. Her own father thought she was so pathetically lonely that she'd have felt left out to know he'd started dating.

She lifted her head and sighed. "I don't know where this is coming from. It's not like I've never dated."

Adaline said nothing, and Belle wanted to scream. *Not helping!*

In high school, she'd been the trailer park girl. Dating back then had simply been out of the question. Belle hadn't minded much. She had her books and she had her dad, and that was all that really mattered.

In tenth grade, she'd started jotting down stories of her own. By the time she graduated, she had piles of notebooks filled with poems, fairy tales and little novellas. All she'd wanted was to become a real author someday. She'd dreamed of writing books for children like her—kids who had trouble making friends and liked to lose themselves in stories and picture books where anything seemed possible. Where a girl could grow up and be anything she wanted to be. Where it didn't matter what her family or her home looked like. Where mothers didn't leave and happily ever afters were real.

But Belle knew better than to gamble her entire future on getting published. She knew all too well that she needed a backup plan, a concrete way to take care of herself. After all, she could still do that and stay immersed in the written word. The University of Texas offered an online program in library science that included a school librarian certification. So she'd stayed put in Bluebonnet and done just that.

She'd bloomed where she'd been planted, just like all those bluebonnets that still sprang to life every spring along the Texas highways, decades after Lady Bird Johnson spearheaded the Highway Beautification Act that had led to the planting of the native blossoms along the roads that crisscrossed the vast state. And along the way, Belle had dated a handful of nice, if not terribly exciting, men. They'd all been perfectly fine. It was just that Belle couldn't seem to move past casual dating to a committed relationship. Invariably, there'd come a point where the guy she was dating wanted more, and she just couldn't do it. She'd never met anyone who made her feel safe and loved enough to allow herself to be wholly and truly vulnerable.

Honestly, that was okay. She'd made peace with being alone. Belle rarely gave dating or relationships any thought whatsoever.

And then Cash McAllister had come along, and for reasons that completely defied logic, she suddenly missed being kissed. Touched. Loved…

She sizzled when she was around him. Which was completely insane, because that man was anything but safe.

"I love my life, and I love being alone," she said, and she wasn't entirely sure if she was trying to convince Adaline or herself.

"There's nothing at all wrong with being alone if that's truly what you want." Adaline offered her a sympathetic smile. "I'm sure your dad didn't mean to make you feel bad."

Of course he didn't. Belle knew better than to believe that, but it didn't stop her from feeling the tiniest bit pathetic. Under the circumstances, who wouldn't? Her own father had been lying to her face for seven months because he thought she was a lonely singleton à la Bridget Jones.

"When I was a little girl, we used to have this card game called Old Maid. I think Dad picked it up at a charity shop for a quarter. Anyway, the entire object of the game was to avoid being the player left holding the Old Maid card at the end. She had gray hair piled in a bun and wore wire-rimmed glasses and a jaunty straw hat with flowers piled on top of it," Belle said. Now that she thought about it, the game seemed a tad sexist, even though she'd always secretly loved the old maid. Who wouldn't want to wear a hat like that? "That's how my dad sees me, isn't it? Tragic and lonely, albeit with amazing taste in hats."

Maybe she should go full Old Maid and get a bunch of cats. Peaches had never met a cat before, though. She might hate them, although it was difficult to imagine the sweet dog disliking anyone or anything.

"It's true. I'm the Old Maid card," Belle groaned.

If Adaline dared to laugh at her misery, she just might end up with a slice of pie in her face.

She didn't, though. Instead, she reached out and gave Belle's hand a tender squeeze. "First of all, that's not at all how your dad sees you. He just wants you to be happy, which is the same thing you want for him. That's a completely different concept than thinking you're an old maid. Trust me on this. My own grandmother tried to give me a matchmaking service for Christmas last year, remember? I know what I'm talking about. He messed up, but his heart was in the right place, just like Gram's was last Christmas."

Was it, though? Why did Belle have to have a significant other? She had a dog. Wasn't that enough?

"You're thinking about Peaches right now, aren't you?" Adaline asked with a twinkle her eyes.

Belle narrowed her gaze at her friend. "How did you know?"

"I told you I've been there. When Gram gave me the gift card to the matchmaker, I insisted all I needed was Fuzzy," Adaline said.

And then she'd met Jace, and now they were living happily ever after.

But that was different. Besides, what were the odds that another burly Christmas tree farmer with a heart of gold would roll into Bluebonnet anytime soon? Belle wasn't holding her breath.

"What's the second thing?" Belle asked before Adaline could try and tell her she was wrong about Peaches. Everyone knew puppies trumped men, just like paper covered rock and rock crushed scissors. "You said, 'first of all,' earlier. So you must have had a second point in mind."

"Oh, right. I almost forgot. It was about Old Maid," Adaline said.

Belle made a mental note to check and make sure the games corner in the school library didn't have an old deck of those cards collecting dust somewhere. Enough generations of women had been traumatized by that game already.

"Gram taught Ford and me how to play Old Maid

when we were kids. You don't need a special deck of cards. Gram showed us the way she learned when she was a little girl. Back in her day, she played with a regular deck and removed all the queens, except for the Queen of Diamonds." Adaline arched a brow.

Belle shook her head. "I'm not following. What does the Queen of Diamonds have to do with Old Maid?"

"She takes the place of the Old Maid card," Adaline said.

"But ending up as the Queen of Diamonds doesn't sound bad at all." On the contrary, it sounded rather fabulous.

"Exactly!" Adaline did a little dance, complete with a twirl of her apron strings.

Belle laughed. "You're ridiculous, you know that?"

"Yes, but you love it." Adaline grinned. She wasn't wrong. "I'm ridiculous, and I own it. Just like you need to own who you are and feel proud. You're one of the most amazing people I know—queen of all things sparkly and wonderful. You're basically Mary Poppins…if Mary Poppins had a puppy sidekick. I promise you that's how your dad and everyone else sees you. You just need to start looking at yourself in the same way."

Against all odds, Belle felt herself smile. "I'm the Queen of Diamonds."

"Yes, you are. And don't you forget it."

Later that morning, Belle sat cross-legged on the library floor opposite Mason Hayes while he read a picture book aloud to Peaches. As usual, he'd chosen a story with a dog as the central character. The book was part of a popular series that followed the adventures of a shaggy golden retriever named Buddy who belonged to a boy called Max. In this particular story, Buddy snuck onto the school bus to follow Max to school one day.

"Buddy, dogs aren't allowed at school," Mason read. Then he grinned and stroked one of Peaches's copper-colored ears. "But Peaches is allowed to come to school."

"That's right," Belle said.

For now.

Who knew how long that might last? She'd been so preoccupied with Dad's love life that she'd barely thought about Comfort Paws in the past twenty-four hours…or her notebook and her secret project. How was she going to find time to get anything finished properly while also outperforming Cash and his French bulldog puppy at training class?

It's not a contest, remember? Cash's face flashed in her mind, complete with that arrogant smirk of his, and a not-altogether-unpleasant shiver ran up and down her spine. The sensation was equal parts luscious and mortifying.

Fine, it's totally a contest, she vowed. *One that I intend to win.*

"Peaches is allowed at school because she's special," Mason said, drawing Belle's attention back to where it belonged.

"That's right. Peaches is a very special dog," she said.

Mason lifted one of the puppy's silky ears and leaned closer to whisper against her fur. "Can I tell you a secret, Peaches?"

Peaches's tail thumped against the library's deep blue carpet.

"I have a stuffed animal at home covered in really

soft fur, and sometimes I like to pretend that it's you," Mason whispered.

Belle's heart just about melted on the spot.

Maybe she didn't need to be in such a hurry to talk to Mason's teacher about his participation in the program. Clearly his sessions with Peaches were having some sort of positive impact.

But how was she supposed to track Mason's progress in a way that she could present to the school board when he was already reading at an advanced level?

Rules existed for a reason. Wasn't that precisely what she'd tried to explain to Cash on multiple occasions?

A throat cleared nearby, and Belle blinked, grateful for any interruption that prevented her from dwelling on the fact that a man she wholeheartedly disliked had begun to invade her thoughts with alarming regularity.

But then she turned in the direction of the noise only to discover that the throat that had just been cleared belonged to none other than Cash. In the flesh.

What was he doing here? *Again?*

She frowned at him before she could stop herself. He winked and tapped his pointer finger against the visitor badge pinned to the lapel of his suit jacket. At least he'd followed proper procedure this time.

Still, she couldn't help but grit her teeth. He was the last person she wanted to deal with today.

"The End," Mason said, and shoved the open library book closer to Peaches's smushed little face so she could see the pictures on the final two pages. "I think Peaches liked this story. Maybe I should read it again."

Belle glanced at the clock. As much as she would've loved to make Cash wait, Mason's Book Buddies session had already run a minute or two long. He needed to get back to class.

"I'm afraid that's all the time we have today, Mason. But you're right. I think Peaches really liked the story. It's time to tell her goodbye, though," Belle said.

Panic splashed across the little boy's face. "Just for today, right? Will I still get to read to her again on Wednesday, like usual?"

Belle nodded. "Of course you will."

Mason's expression brightened. "Good." He pressed his cheek against Peaches's soft head. "Goodbye, Peaches. I love you."

Peaches scrambled to her feet and kept her gaze glued to the child as he exited the library to make his way back to class. Once he was out of sight, the dog's head swiveled toward Cash waiting by the circulation desk, and she began to pant with excitement.

The corner of Cash's mouth tugged into a half-grin. Clearly he was used to prompting such displays of unfettered female adulation simply by turning up someplace unannounced (#billionaireproblems).

Belle stood, smoothed down the skirt of her A-line dress and led Peaches toward the circulation desk. The sooner she found out what Cash wanted, the sooner she'd be rid of him. But if he expected her to drool with excitement over his mere presence, he was going to be sorely disappointed. She'd promised to be nice, not humiliate herself.

Still, she couldn't help noticing how the ice-blue silk of his necktie brought out the color in his normally steel-gray eyes. His irises looked as dreamy as a field of the town's namesake flowers today. It was probably just a trick of the eye. Belle chalked it up to whatever absurdly expensive designer was responsible for the necktie.

Sadly, that necktie alone made Belle feel a little less sparkly by comparison. She was wearing one of her favorite dresses today—bright blue with a swishy skirt, a Peter Pan collar and a black satin bow at the neck. Ordinarily, she felt chic when she wore it. A little French, even. Next to a man whose last name was on half the buildings in town, she felt more like an imposter. It was probably obvious she'd never set foot in Paris in all her life. Instead of feeling chic, she felt excessively sweet to the point of being juvenile.

Belle squared her shoulders. So she liked a little whimsy in her wardrobe. Maybe she was a tad overly fond of bows and never met a polka dot she didn't like. What was wrong with that?

"I'm the Queen of Diamonds," she whispered under her breath.

Cash tilted his head. "Pardon?"

"Nothing." She hadn't meant for him to hear that. "It's nice to see you, Mr. McAllister."

"Is it really?" His blue eyes danced, as if he actually enjoyed the fact that she didn't much care for him. "Come now. I thought we were past the point of pretending."

A teacher in the hallway slowed her steps long enough to gawk at the interaction, and Belle's face flamed with the heat of a thousand Texas summers.

"Did you need something, or is the sole purpose of this visit to get me in trouble?" she whispered.

A wounded expression crossed his face. "Why would you think I wanted to get you into trouble?"

Oh, I don't know. Maybe because I'm supposed to be treating you like visiting royalty, and for the life me, I just can't do it?

Peaches wiggled her entire backside as she pranced at his feet, vying for attention. At least someone seemed to be interested in charming this very attractive, and equally annoying, man.

"What do you want, Mr. McAllister?" Belle said as he picked Peaches up and cradled the Cavalier in his arms.

The dog's tongue lolled out of the side of her mouth like she'd just found heaven on earth. It was sweet…

And it irritated Belle to no end. At least, it should have.

Instead, Belle felt herself relax. She might've accidentally smiled. Every interaction she'd had with Cash had been a disaster, but the fact that he appeared to enjoy her antagonism made talking to him almost fun.

Emphasis on *almost*.

"I'm here to humbly ask for your help with Sparkles," he said.

"Humbly?" Belle somehow suppressed an eye roll. "You seemed awfully sure of yourself on Saturday. What happened to 'may the best dog win'?"

"Oh, rest assured, Sparkles and I still intend to ace the pet therapy training class with flying colors. But I might need a little help actually getting to keep the dog." He sighed, and for the first time since he'd strolled into the library and interrupted her busy schedule, *again*, Belle noticed the lines around his eyes. In a radical departure from his usually impeccable grooming, he'd also neglected to shave.

The poor guy looked exhausted.

"Someone from the rescue group is coming by tomorrow for a home visit, and I must be doing something wrong because my puppy wants to sleep all day and party all night. I'm beginning to think I adopted an aspiring rock star instead of a French bulldog."

Belle laughed, despite herself. "You just brought Sparkles home. It's completely normal to experience an adjustment period."

"But what if it's not just an adjustment period? Maybe I got the wrong dog bed or something." He glanced down at Peaches in his arms. Her eyelids were already growing heavy.

Belle wholeheartedly doubted that whatever was going on with Sparkles was Cash's fault. As loathe as she was to admit it, he seemed to have a magic touch with dogs. "Let me guess. You bought the most expensive bed the store had in stock?"

He nodded. "It's memory foam. Is that bad?"

"Not at all. I'm sure Sparkles will enjoy chewing a hole in that memory foam as much as she would any other dog bed."

Cash's gaze narrowed. "How did you know?"

"Because she's a puppy, and that's what puppies do. They chew, they cry at night, they drive you crazy, and just when at you're at your wits' end and begin to question your sanity in bringing a needy little monster into your home, you realize you can't live without them." Belle's throat clogged. Her answer had been automatic— the truth—but the more she'd said, the more she'd unintentionally revealed about herself.

When had she started feeling comfortable around Cash McAllister? And for goodness' sake, why? *How?*

He looked at her long and hard, as if turning her words over in his head. As the seconds passed, Belle nearly forgot how to breathe.

"We're already there," he finally said. Then he cleared his throat and looked away. "Lucy's attached to the puppy. Too attached, probably."

"No such thing," Belle countered.

He fixed his gaze on her again, and a whole swarm of butterflies took flight in her belly. "I can't lose the dog."

"You won't," she promised.

"So, you'll help me?" He bowed his head and gave her a look so full of hope that her heart twisted in her chest.

"Why me?" she asked in an attempt to steer the conversation to safer ground.

The sooner he admitted he was only asking for her help because he knew she was professionally obligated to acquiesce, the sooner she could go back to disliking him. Because whatever she was feeling right now fell squarely in the *like* column, and that was far too dangerous to contemplate.

"Because you know more about dogs and dog training than anyone else I know." He arched an eyebrow and cast a meaningful glance at Peaches. Her little paws twitched like she was chasing rabbits in her sleep. "And because I know you'll say yes."

And there it was.

Belle's spine stiffened. "Right. Because I have to."

"No." His brow crinkled, and so did the lines around his eyes, making him look like a young, albeit exhausted, George Clooney. "Because you made it clear on Saturday that you care about Sparkles's well-being."

Right answer. Belle swallowed. *Dang it.*

"Fine," she said and blew her curtain bangs from her eyes with a puff. Anything to make herself see more clearly.

This was about the dog's well-being. And Lucy's. Nothing more.

"I'll do it."

Chapter Eight

"Miss Darling is here," Ellis said as he peeled back the lace curtain on one of the foyer windows and glanced outside. Before Cash could respond, he frowned and leaned closer to the beveled glass. "Never mind. It looks like she's changed her mind."

Cash abandoned his pursuit of Sparkles, who'd chosen this most inopportune time for a game of chase and was busy making frantic loops around the living room sofa. Come to think of it, maybe now wasn't such an inopportune time. Surely Belle would know how to make the Frenchie stop. Assuming she was actually going to show up at their agreed upon time, which suddenly seemed doubtful if Ellis's confusion was any indication.

"What do you mean she's changed her mind?" That wasn't possible. She'd promised to come by after school, take a look at his puppy setup and maybe give him some advice on how to tame the pudgy four-legged beast who was supposed to be helping Lucy learn how to read.

Granted, he'd had to twist her arm a little to make her agree. But Belle didn't seem at all like the type of person to go back on her word.

"She got halfway to the door and then suddenly turned

around and hightailed back toward Main Street." Ellis started to turn away from the window but stopped and did a double take. "Wait. It looks like she's coming back."

Cash sidled up next to Ellis to take a look. Belle stood at the foot of the steps leading up to the mansion's wide front porch, biting her bottom lip while Peaches strained at the end of her leash. Belle placed a foot on the bottom step, then shook her head and turned around again.

"This is a real will-she-or-won't-she situation, isn't it?" Ellis chuckled and turned his gaze toward Cash. "Son, what did you do to make this woman so skittish?"

"Why do you automatically assume it's my fault?" Cash frowned. He didn't have time for this. He'd just given up on chasing his puppy, and now he needed to go chase down a librarian. "Don't answer that."

"It seems likely. That's all I'm saying," Ellis said as Cash hoofed it for the door, laughing under his breath.

At least Ellis was beginning to drop the formality. It was a wonder how bonding in the middle of the night over a noisy puppy could change a relationship. Cash's father would've never allowed a member of the household staff to speak to him like that. Then again, Cash was no longer interested in emulating his dad. If that had been the case, he wouldn't have relocated to Bluebonnet. He would've hunkered down in his sleek Dallas office and left Lucy's emotional well-being to a nanny.

Also, like it or not, Ellis was the closest thing Cash had to family besides Lucy. The older man had known him most of his life. He might just be the last person left on God's green earth who felt comfortable enough to call Cash out when he needed it.

Not quite the only *one.* Cash's jaw tightened as he

set his sights on Belle's determined stride. She'd certainly never passed up the opportunity to criticize him, whether warranted or not.

He'd thought they'd made progress earlier today in the library, though. For a minute there, it had almost seemed like they might eventually be friends.

Cash huffed out a breath. What did he know about friendship? Not one of the guys from boarding school had contacted him after his sister passed away. Most of the mourners at the funeral had been business acquaintances, leaving Cash no doubt whatsoever about where his priorities had been for the past decade and a half.

"Where's the fire?" he asked, possibly a bit too sharply. But what did she expect? She'd never minced words with him before, and turnabout was fair play.

Peaches whipped her head around at the sound of Cash's voice and bolted toward him, dragging a reluctant Belle along for the ride.

"Oh." She gave him the fakest smile he'd ever set eyes on. "Hi."

That was it? *Oh, hi.* He'd just caught her running away from his house, and now she was going to pretend she hadn't been planning on standing him up?

She wrinkled her nose, and Cash suddenly recognized the endearing quirk for what it really was. *She's afraid.* That little nose crinkle was a dead giveaway. "Hi, yourself," he said in as gentle a tone as he could manage. "Where are you going, Scaredy Cat?"

"Scaredy Cat?" Her eyes flashed. Ah, there she was— the sassy librarian he knew and…liked. More and more every day, it seemed. She lifted her chin. "Who says I'm scared?"

He took a step closer, pausing to give her ample time to back away before he touched her. She stayed rooted to the spot even as her breath hitched. Then her lips parted, and for the life of him, Cash felt like everything was suddenly moving in slow motion. Every ounce of his attention was drawn toward her mouth, as pretty and pink as a smooth satin bow.

He swallowed and resisted the obviously inappropriate urge to kiss her. Instead, he pressed a tender fingertip to the tip of her nose.

"This," he said. "Right here."

Her bottom lip slipped between her teeth.

Busted.

Cash drew his fingers back and tucked both hands into his trouser pockets. "Did you know that you wiggle your nose when you're nervous?"

"Yes. I can't help it. It's just something I do when I'm anxious." Her fingertips fluttered to her nose, tracing the place where he'd just touched her. "I didn't realize you'd noticed."

She crossed her arms and looked away.

Oh, I've noticed. Cash pulse pounded in his ears. *I've noticed far more about you than I care to admit.*

"There's no reason to be anxious. I promise," he said quietly. He gestured toward Peaches pawing at his shins. "See? Peaches isn't nervous. Word on the street is that dogs are excellent judges of character."

"Peaches would leave me and run off with a total stranger for half a piece of bacon," Belle countered.

"I promise I'm not going to try and lure your dog away from you with salt-cured pork." Cash held up a hand. "Scout's honor."

Belle's gaze narrowed. "You were a Boy Scout?"

"No, but the vow still stands." He grinned, but she still looked like she wanted to bolt. Cash had to stop himself from reaching for her hand and weaving his fingers through hers. *Lucy needs her as much as she needs Peaches. Do* not *screw this up.* "Come inside, Belle. I promise I don't bite. I can't make any promises about Sparkles, but that's why you're here, remember?"

"Right." She nodded, then her gaze flitted to house and back at him. "Somehow when I agreed to this, I forgot where you lived. Just so you know, I grew up in a trailer park."

"Just so *you* know, I didn't grow up here." He hitched a thumb over his shoulder toward the portico, where ceiling fans whirred above a line of white rocking chairs. "Technically, I grew up several hundred miles away in a boarding school dormitory that smelled like sweaty adolescent boys and unwashed lacrosse gear. Trust me on this. I would've strongly preferred the trailer park."

He was being sincere, not patronizing. Although, he knew better to expect sympathy for being born with a silver spoon in his mouth.

Thankfully, Belle seemed to pick up on his earnestness. The corners of her mouth inched into a smile. "Sometimes you almost make it easy to forget that you're rich."

He flashed her a wink. "I'll take that as a compliment, Miss Darling."

How had she forgotten the man lived in an actual mansion?

Because he charmed you this morning at the library, just like he's charming you now, she thought as she carried Peaches over the threshold.

Belle wouldn't have stood Cash up, despite how

things looked. She would've turned around on her own. Eventually. She'd just needed a moment to prepare herself for whatever opulence lay behind the big double doors of the Southern Gothic–style home, a second or two to put on her emotional armor and forget that her mother had left her and her father to start a whole new family in a house that looked an awful lot like this one.

But Cash had chased her down before she was ready, and she'd shown him a side of herself that few people, if any, ever got to see—the soft, tender, vulnerable part of her heart that Belle preferred to pretend didn't exist.

Had she really just blurted out that she grew up in a trailer park? Cash probably thought she was unhinged.

He hadn't acted like it, though. Just when she'd least expected it, he'd treated her with a gentleness that took her breath away. When he'd touched her nose, her entire body had gone all aflutter. For a second, she'd felt like he saw a completely different person when he looked at her. Not the guarded, careful librarian who never set a foot wrong, but a brave, beautiful girl who took chances and wasn't afraid to walk out of the pages of a book and live a little...

A real, live Queen of Diamonds.

Belle's heart lodged in her throat as an older man dressed in a starched Mexican wedding shirt and black dress pants greeted her with a slight bow. "Good afternoon, Miss Darling."

"Good afternoon," Belle said, cutting her gaze toward Cash.

Did he have an actual *butler*? Were butlers even a thing in Texas?

"This is Ellis," Cash said, waving a hand at the man. "He's an old family friend."

Cash and Ellis exchanged a glance, and Belle knew the truth had to be more complicated than Cash was letting on. That was fine, though. It wasn't as if she was going to be a frequent visitor here.

Then, just as Belle was reminding herself that this visit was a one-off thing—a fluke that would never be repeated—Lucy came flying down the grand, curved staircase with several stapled sheaves of paper clutched in her hands. Sparkles scampered after, deftly navigating the spiral steps despite her roly-poly form.

"Peaches is here," Lucy cried. "At our house."

"She sure is. I thought she might like to visit with you and Sparkles while your uncle Cash and I have a chat about puppies." Belle placed the squirming Cavalier on the ground, and the Frenchie welcomed her with a play bow and a friendly yip.

"I think they like each other," Lucy said with a giggle. She'd been so shy and withdrawn when she'd first started reading to Peaches. Belle's heart gave a tug looking at her now, beaming at the dogs with a gap-toothed grin.

"Lucy, didn't you have something you wanted to show Miss Darling?" Cash prompted. He turned his smile on Belle. "Lucy's been making a book all about Sparkles so she can bring it to school and read it to Peaches."

"She's been working very hard on it the past few days," Ellis said.

Lucy glanced down at the papers in her hand and her face fell. "It's not finished yet, though."

Belle squatted so she was eye level with the child. "That's okay. I'd still love to see what you've got so far."

"Some of the letters aren't right. I'm not good at those."

"I think Peaches will like your book just the way it

is." Belle winked. "You know how much she loves stories."

Lucy's smile crept back in place. "She does. Do you really think she'll like mine?"

"Why don't you show her and we'll see?" Belle gathered Sparkles into her arms in case the puppy proved to be a distraction.

Thankfully, the move worked like a charm. As soon as Lucy lowered the makeshift book to dog-level, Peaches bounded toward it.

"It's called *Sparkles the Marvel*," Lucy told the Cavalier. "My Uncle Cash helped with the title."

Adorable. Belle's gaze flitted toward Cash.

He dragged a hand through his hair and gave her a sheepish grin. "Writing and letters aren't really my thing, either."

"I think it's precious," Belle said. Then she redirected her attention toward Sparkles before her expression gave away the fact that she suddenly had a lump in her throat. She wasn't even sure why. All she knew was that now that she'd let her guard down, she couldn't seem to get it back in place.

"Do you want to hear a secret, Lucy?" Belle asked.

The child's eyes went wide, and she nodded.

"I'm writing a story, too." There. She'd said it.

For months, Belle had been toiling away in her secret notebook, rearranging sentences and doing little sketches. She hadn't been ready to tell anyone about it, because books were so important to her...so *sacred*... that she hadn't dared to let herself think she might actually be a real author someday.

Of course, she'd been writing little stories for as long

as she could remember. No doubt there were piles of old spiral notebooks in the trailer somewhere, alongside her grade school report cards and high school yearbooks. Nothing had ever come of those early efforts, and then as she'd gotten older, she gave up on the idea of ever seeing her name on the cover of a book. She hadn't planned on letting go of her writing dreams. Somewhere along the way, it had just happened. Earning her master's degree and school librarian certification had taken years, especially since she'd had to balance her education with various full-time jobs. Belle told herself it was fine. She loved her life. She loved working at the library, and books were still a huge part of her life.

But once she'd started bringing Peaches to school and reading with the kids in Book Buddies, things changed. She started to feel inspired again. She began thinking and dreaming in verse. Rhymes suddenly came to her as easily as breathing. At first, she'd tried to resist the temptation to write anything down. She had a safe, dependable career doing something she adored. There was no reason at all to try and reach for the stars when her feet were planted so firmly and comfortably on the ground.

But in a moment of weakness, she picked up a new notebook at Bluebonnet General. Then, before she knew it, she'd crafted an entire children's book from start to finish. All she had left to do was put the finishing touches on a few illustrations during the school's upcoming spring break, and she might actually have something polished enough to submit to publishers and literary agents.

"Can I see your story sometime?" Lucy's eyes danced.

"I promise I won't tell anyone. No one will know except me and Peaches and Sparkles."

And Cash McAllister, who was standing right there, listening to their entire conversation.

Belle straightened. She was supposed to be giving Cash puppy advice, not baring her soul.

"Maybe someday. I'd like that very much." Belle couldn't bring herself to regret telling Lucy about her notebook, despite Cash's presence. She felt a kinship with the little girl, despite their vastly different upbringings. "For now, though, why don't you keep working on yours? Maybe Peaches can help you while your uncle and I talk about Sparkles. How does that sound?"

"It sounds good." Lucy clutched her pages to her chest and toyed with the frayed edges of the notebook paper. "Can Peaches come to my room?"

Belle glanced to Cash for confirmation. It was fine with her, but this was his very large, very fancy house. Not hers.

Cash nodded and ruffled Lucy's hair. "Sure thing, kiddo. Miss Darling and I will come check on you when we're finished."

"Let's show your guest to your room." Ellis gathered Peaches into his arms and she planted her head on his shoulder to gaze back at Belle while he and Lucy made their way upstairs.

Sparkles tried to follow, but Cash scooped the little bulldog up before she could climb more than the first two steps. "Oh, no you don't. You're coming with us."

Sparkles whined, but then shifted in Cash's arms to lick the side of his face, wiggling her tiny nub of a tail like mad.

Belle bit back a smile. "I'm sorry, but I'm not seeing any evidence of a problem here so far. That puppy *really* seems to like you."

"You think?" Cash tilted his head and regarded Sparkles. The dog mirrored the gesture, tilting her round head and swiveling her huge bat-like ears. They looked like two adorable peas in an even more adorable pod.

Belle really needed to get out of this mansion. Since that wasn't a viable option, she tried her to best to slip back into her imaginary armor.

"There's no accounting for taste," she said, but even she could tell that her words lacked their usual bite.

A laugh burst out of Cash's mouth and he tucked Sparkles under his arm like a football.

Belle's gaze flitted toward his before she could stop it. Those crinkles around his eyes were going to be the death of her. They made him seem warm, kind and human—all the things she'd assumed he wasn't when he'd tried to buy her dog.

"What's so funny?" she asked, heart pounding.

"Nothing." He grinned, and the lines around his eyes grew even deeper. If Belle wasn't careful, she might fall right in. "It's just nice to see that Scaredy Cat has fully left the building."

Oh, how she wished that were true.

Cash spent the next hour showing Belle all the puppy supplies he'd purchased since bringing Sparkles home from the pet fair. There were bowls, beds and puppy pads. Squeak toys, chew toys and plush toys. A play pen that Sparkles wanted absolutely no part of, and a wire crate she liked even less.

You name it, and Cash had bought it.

"You get an A for effort, that's for sure," Belle said as she took in the sight of the room he'd designated as Sparkles's play area, filled to bursting with dog equipment.

He'd half expected her to mock him for the outrageous sum he'd so obviously spent in an effort to make the bulldog feel at home, but for once, she cut him some slack. Cash would've liked to think her restraint was because they were developing a rapport, but deep down he knew it had more to do with her love for dogs. If Belle could overlook his lavish spending on anything, it was sure to be canine-related.

They'd had a moment earlier, though, hadn't they?

Cash had been certain of it. Now, he wasn't so sure. As soon as Lucy and Ellis left them alone together, Belle's countenance had changed. She'd gone back to being all business, all the time. As much as he enjoyed her occasional digs at him, he missed the fleeting tenderness they'd shared when she'd first arrived. Cash had learned more about Belle Darling in those first few minutes than he had in all their other encounters put together.

His attention had snagged on the story she'd mentioned. He would've bet money she was writing a children's book, and he knew without even reading it that it would be good. Belle had a special touch when it came to children. He'd seen her in action several times at the library and again here at his house with Lucy. There was no doubt in his mind that Peaches was a special dog, but it also took a special person to do what Belle and the Cavalier did with the Book Buddies program.

Which is precisely what she's been trying to tell you all along.

"Cash?" she prompted. "What do you think?"

Cash had no clue what she'd just asked him. He hated to blame his inattentiveness on the dog when he'd really been thinking about her writing. But seeing as the Frenchie was fully responsible for his recent sleep deprivation, it was time for Sparkles to take one for the team.

"Sorry." He held up his hands and cut his gaze toward the dog, currently disemboweling a stuffed squirrel toy. Puffs of white stuffing littered the floor between Cash and Belle's feet. "Can you repeat the question?"

Belle bent to pick up the stuffing and then deftly exchanged the squirrel for a chew bone shaped like a tree limb. Sparkles immediately acquiesced, trotting to her dog bed with the tree limb clamped in her jaws. If Cash had tried that move, he would've ended up on the losing end of a game of keep away with the flattened squirrel.

"I asked if you had any objection moving Sparkles's crate to your bedroom." Belle said. Was he imagining things, or did her cheeks go pink at the mention of his bedroom?

"No objection. Why?"

"This setup is great. Really top-notch. But you said Sparkles is keeping you up at night, and I can't help but wonder if she's lonely in here all by herself." The color in her face intensified. "I'm not saying that everyone has to have constant companionship. Being alone isn't the same thing as being lonely."

Were they still talking about Sparkles, or were they talking about Belle?

Or possibly even Cash himself?

Maybe the constant ache he'd carried around since Mallory's death was more than just grief. And maybe he wasn't merely attracted to the librarian. Maybe, just maybe, he felt a little bit less alone when she around. Less *lonely*.

Because she was right. There was a distinct difference between the two.

"Point taken," he said and made a point of averting his gaze. He wasn't ready to admit he was lonely. He lived alone for the better part of his adult life *by choice*, thank you very much. "My bedroom is next door."

He picked up the crate and carried it to his room. Belle followed, while Sparkles scurried after them.

"Any place in particular?" he asked.

"Right there, beside your nightstand. That way, she's as close to you as possible. She can see you, and she can smell you. Just your presence will be comforting, especially if she wakes up in the middle of the night."

Cash deposited the crate in the spot she indicated and rested his hands on his hips. "*If* she wakes up? You're assuming she even goes to sleep in there at all."

"I really think this arrangement will help," Belle said. Her authoritative tone alone gave Cash hope that a few hours of uninterrupted sleep might not be a pipe dream.

But he had to ask the one question that he'd been hesitant to utter out loud. "I know crate training is important. All the dog books say that it helps pups feel safe and secure."

Belle nodded. "Accurate."

"But…" Cash's gaze flitted toward his bed. It was king-sized, obviously. Massive. Certainly big enough for Cash plus one small, needy dog.

"No," Belle said before he could finish his thought.

"No?"

"No," she repeated with a firm shake of her head. "You can't let Sparkles sleep with you."

"Why not?"

"Because once you do, she'll never sleep peacefully in the crate again," she said, and Cash was tempted to ask if she was speaking from experience.

Inquiring about her bedroom habits seemed inappropriate, somehow, even as they related to dog ownership. Besides, Belle was a by-the-book kinda girl. She'd made that much clear on the day they'd met. He'd never forget Name Tag Gate. There was no possible way she'd cheated on Peaches's crate training.

"No sleeping in the bed." Cash nodded. "Got it."

"Good," Belle said, and her gaze snagged on his. For a prolonged second, it almost felt like they were in a staring contest until her eyes flitted toward Sparkles.

Belle swallowed so hard that Cash could trace the movement up and down her slender throat. Then she twirled her dark ponytail around her pointer finger.

Another nervous habit? Cash wondered.

He couldn't be sure. All Cash knew was that he'd never be able to tear his gaze away from her if she ever let her hair down.

Chapter Nine

Belle couldn't stop glancing at the clock the following day at work.

A representative from the pet rescue was supposed to arrive at Cash's house at two o'clock for his home inspection, but no matter how many times she checked the big school clock by the circulation desk, the hands never seemed to move. Time was moving at a snail's pace.

He's going to be fine, Belle told herself as she made her way through a pile of books that needed to be checked in. *He's a McAllister.*

No one in Bluebonnet would dare repossess a dog from a member of that family. She was honestly surprised the rescue group was making him go through the motions of a home visit. But good for them. That meant they were truly invested in the rescue dogs' best interests.

Still, she couldn't imagine a volunteer rolling up to the McAllister Mansion and deciding it wasn't a suitable home for one of their charges. Mainly because—somewhat to her astonishment—Cash seemed like a genuinely good pet parent. A good *person*, even.

Belle wasn't sure what to do with that information. It didn't align at all with her first impression of Cash.

It doesn't change anything. She flipped open a book, scanned the barcode on the inside front cover and placed it in the stack of books to be reshelved. *You're still you, and he's still...*

Belle breathed in and out and realized she'd stopped working altogether. She was just sitting there staring at the book in front of her with the handheld scanner dangling from her fingertips.

Who was Cash, exactly?

He was a McAllister. He was the adopted father of one of her students. He lived in a mansion, held a seat on the school board and subsequently controlled not only the future of Book Buddies, but also Bluebonnet Elementary.

But the way he interacted with Lucy turned Belle's insides to mush. That, coupled with his earnestness regarding Sparkles was almost enough to make Belle forget his last name. Or that he had a butler (of sorts, at least). Or that she was supposed to be persuading him to keep the entire school, along with its staff, afloat.

She glanced at the clock again—2:05 p.m.

Finally! Her stomach flipped as she wondered what was happening at the big house on Main Street. Was it too much to hope that Cash might text her with an update once the home visit was over?

Of course it was. The first Comfort Paws training class was scheduled for tomorrow evening. She'd be apprised of Sparkles's fate soon enough.

The intercom on the corner of Belle's desk squawked, drawing her gaze away from the clock, which—for the record—now read 2:08 p.m. Marta's voice was barely discernible amid the static emanating from the little box.

Belle frowned at the intercom. "Hello?"

The static grew louder, completely drowning out Marta.

"I can't hear you!" Belle practically shouted. So much for the hushed tone she usually used in the library.

"That thing is useless," Tess, her assistant, said as she pushed the shelving cart toward the circulation desk. At just under five feet tall and in her early twenties, Tess was nearly as tiny as some of the grade school students. When her cart was full of books, it probably outweighed her by a good twenty or thirty pounds. But as a young mom of twin toddlers, Tess was accustomed to heavy lifting. Belle had never met anyone with such impressive core strength. "Yesterday, when you were at the faculty meeting, Marta buzzed and I thought she was talking about a student who'd *flunked* an exam. Turns out, she was talking about the storage shed behind the gym getting *skunked*. There's no telling what she's trying to say right now."

"Trust me, I've had that same problem, and it wasn't without consequences." Belle no longer trusted anything she heard out of the intercom. "Also, that explains the stench yesterday when Mrs. Matthews's class came straight to library hour from the gym. Yuck."

How had Belle not heard about the skunk situation? That was prime school-day gossip. Last year, when a mama raccoon and her three babies had been found living above the ceiling tiles in the front office, word had spread like wildfire. Belle had admittedly been a little distracted lately, though.

She snuck another quick glance at the clock—2:20 p.m. Cash's home visit was fully underway at this point. Belle hoped everything was going okay.

"Do you have an appointment today or something? You've been watching the clock all day?" Tess piled a stack of books from the batch Belle had just checked in onto her cart to be reshelved.

"Have I?" Ugh, was she that obvious? "I guess I'm just excited for Reading Rumble practice after school today. It's always such a fun event."

The Lone Star Reading Rumble was an annual competition in which teams of students from all over the state competed in a daylong, game-show-style contest answering questions based on a chosen list of books. A big part of Belle's job was preparing the kids at Bluebonnet Elementary for the schoolwide contest, where the winning team of four, plus two student alternates, would be selected to move on to the district semifinals. She'd been holding after-school practice twice a week for months already in preparation for the event, which was set to take place the Wednesday after spring break.

Any and all students were welcome to come and familiarize themselves with the hand buzzers the teams used during the contest. Belle had been emceeing the Reading Rumble long enough to know that those pesky buzzers always presented a challenge. Anxious students never failed to buzz in early, before Belle had a chance to finish reading the question aloud.

A little practice went a long way. Every week, she chose a different book to focus on at the voluntary after-school drills. Today's book was a Texas-themed retelling of *The Three Little Pigs*.

"The kids are getting excited about the Reading Rumble, too," Tess said, seemingly buying Belle's excuse for keeping an eye on the time.

Just in case, Belle decided to make herself scarce. "If you don't mind keeping an eye on things for a few minutes, I'm going to go see what Marta wanted. It could be important."

"No problem," Tess said without bothering to look up from alphabetizing the books on her cart.

Belle's reason for making herself scarce wasn't totally bogus. The intercom was a legit problem. She wasn't about to let it get the best of her again.

"Hey, Marta," she said as she entered the school's central office.

The school secretary was perched just inside the door. To her left, a sliding glass window allowed her to communicate with visitors in the school's main lobby. Due to the district's ongoing budget cuts, Marta acted as support staff to the school's administrative staff as well as being in charge of attendance. Sometimes Belle wondered how she did it all, and always with a cheery attitude and a dash of school spirit. Today she was dressed in one of her many Bluebonnet Elementary T-shirts. Yellow letters spelled out the school slogan—Growing Together, Blooming Bright—over a bright blue background scattered with bluebonnet petals.

"Oh, good. You're here." Marta looked up from her computer monitor. A vase filled with silk bluebonnets sat propped beside her nameplate. "Ed is expecting you. You can go on in."

She waved a hand toward the Ed's closed office door.

Belle's red patent leather ballerina flats stopped in their tracks. "Ed wants to see me?"

Twice in the span of a week? *This can't be good.* The last time she'd been called into the principal's office, he'd wanted her to sell her dog. She was almost afraid to find out what came next.

"He needs to talk to you. I thought that's why you were here." A line etched between Marta's brows. "I just called you on the intercom."

"All I heard was static, so I thought I'd drop by and find out if it was anything important." Belle took a deep breath. "I guess it was."

"Don't be nervous. Ed adores you. You know that. I'm sure it's something boring, like asking you to be on another faculty committee." Marta's left eyebrow gave a knowing little quirk. "Or maybe he heard that you and Cash McAllister are going to be in the same dog training class together."

How on earth had Marta found out about that? The Bluebonnet rumor mill must've really been working overtime lately. Again, Belle couldn't believe the news about the school skunk had somehow escaped her.

"We *might* be in same dog training class together," Belle corrected.

First, he had to pass the home inspection. She knew he would, though. Whether or not he was serious about doing volunteer work remained to be seen, though. Didn't McAllisters simply write checks when they felt the urge to do a good deed?

That's not fair, and you know it. Belle squirmed. Her subconscious had to chime in at the least opportune moment and remind her that not only had Cash surprised her at every turn recently, but she'd actually enjoyed spending time with him yesterday. As much as she hated to admit it, there was more to Cash than his last name.

"I'm sure whatever Ed wants, it has nothing to do with Mr. McAllister," Belle said. She hoped so, at least. Their lives didn't need to become any more intertwined than they already were, even if the thought of being placed on yet another faculty committee didn't sound nearly as interesting as watching Cash with his adorable new dog.

"Belle, thanks for coming in." Ed stood and waved at one of the empty chair opposite his desk as she strode inside. "Take a seat."

"Thank you." Belle sat down and did her best to ignore the sick feeling in the pit of her stomach. Ed's expression was even more serious than the last time he'd summoned her to his office.

"I'm afraid I have some bad news," he said.

Belle's breath shook. *Please don't let this be about Book Buddies.*

"I'm just going to come out and say it." Sadness clouded Ed's features. "The district has decided to withdraw from the Lone Star Reading Rumble."

Belle blinked. The words were impossible to digest.

"What?" She shook her head, fingers digging into hard wood as she clenched the arms of her chair. "No."

"It's true." Ed's head moved up and down in a solemn nod.

Still, Belle couldn't wrap her head around what he was saying. This was far bigger than Book Buddies. The Reading Rumble was a statewide event that had been going on since Belle was a child. She'd competed as a third grade group leader back when she'd been a student at Bluebonnet Elementary. Things were obviously much more dire than she'd realized.

"The kids have been practicing for months already," she said, throat going thick.

"I realize that, and I'm sorry. But as I said, it's not just our school. It's the entire district."

"But why?" Belle had to ask, even though she already knew the answer.

Money.

Why did everything always come down to that?

"The district is over budget, as is this school. We simply can't afford to hold a districtwide event that would involve paying overtime for janitorial services, security, administrative staff, equipment upgrades and more. Funds are already being diverted to our school for a new intercom system. There's simply no money left in the coffers for extras."

"The Reading Rumble has never been classified as an extra expense. It's part of the regular school curriculum." Or it had been…until now.

"Times have changed. I'm sorry, Belle. You always do an exceptional job preparing the students for this event. Give it some thought, and maybe after spring break we can come up with a plan for a scaled back version. There's nothing stopping us from continuing to hold our own little Reading Rumble at Bluebonnet Elementary, so long as we don't incur any extra expenses or strain our existing resources."

Belle nodded. She'd make sure the students still had a fun reading competition to look forward to, but she knew they'd be crushed to learn that the glory of attending the district competition—and possibly even the state finals in Austin—was no longer on the table.

"Thank you, Ed. This is a disappointment, but I'll work hard to make the best of things for the kids." Belle offered her boss a watery smile.

"I'm confident that you will, Belle. You have my full support. And I'm here if you have any questions," Ed said, but the offer felt perfunctory. His eyes were pleading for her to go back to the library and let the matter drop.

Just one, she wanted to say. *If the curriculum is getting sliced and diced like this, is there any hope at all for the future of Book Buddies?*

She didn't dare ask, though. Because she knew she wasn't ready to hear the answer.

The following evening, Belle arrived an hour early for the Comfort Paws training class at their brand-new facility—a big red barn located just outside of Bluebonnet proper. The group had inherited the building when Adaline's sweetheart of a fiancé, Jace, lost his uncle Gus shortly after Christmas. Gus left the barn to Comfort Paws and the accompanying farmhouse with its surrounding land to Jace. Jace had immediately planted a new crop of seedlings for his Christmas tree business, Texas Tidings, and then they'd all gone to work refurbishing the barn until it was perfectly suited to support their fledging therapy dog group.

The horse stalls had been transformed into generous-sized kennels. The old tack room now held meticulously organized supplies, such as Comfort Paws logo attire, dog vests and specialized Martingale collars to assist with gentle corrections during training exercises. Bluebonnet Senior Center had donated a few old wheelchairs and walkers so the dogs could practice interacting with medical equipment. Thanks to the old wash stalls, they even had an area for dog grooming, and the indoor riding arena made the perfect space for training class.

Everything had fallen so nicely into place that the group now had long-term plans for possibly opening a doggy day care and boarding facility, but first things first. The Comfort Paws mission was all about training, certifying and placing volunteer therapy teams in the community, and tonight marked their official start.

"Adaline and Belle?" Maple glanced up from the pages attached to her clipboard, which seemed to be permanently attached to her hand. Comfort Paws had been her brainchild, after all, so she was taking lead tonight. "Can the two of you work the check-in table? There should be a printout with the names of the handlers and dogs for each team. I just need to check them off and make sure they've brought their veterinary exam forms and vaccination records."

"Absolutely," Adaline said.

Belle agreed. "Sure thing."

She'd already placed the backpack containing her training supplies—things like tiny easily chewable training treats, a water bottle and poop bags in case of accidents—at one of the folding chairs in the training arena. On a whim, she'd also saved the chair closest to hers on the right for Cash and Sparkles.

But as Adaline led Fuzzy toward the check-in table, she dropped her tote bag onto the chair that Belle had claimed for Cash. "Thanks for saving us a spot. I have a feeling things are going to get really busy in a few minutes."

"No problem at all. I think you're right. There's already a line of cars coming up the drive." Belle grinned and reprimanded herself for the stab of disappointment she felt at the thought of not getting to sit next to Cash.

He was *not* her friend...certainly not in the same way that Adaline was. There was zero reason for them to be joined at the hip during training class.

But when she'd come out of her meeting with Ed yesterday afternoon, Cash's name had popped up in her text notifications, and she'd all but sprinted to the faculty bathroom, where she'd shut herself inside a stall and nearly dropped her cell phone in the toilet in her haste to read his message. In retrospect, her behavior had been completely ridiculous.

She wasn't a book-obsessed schoolgirl anymore, and Cash certainly wasn't the popular boy she was crushing on, despite the fact that he was way, *way* out of her league...even if that's exactly how things were beginning to feel. There was no reason whatsoever to be hiding in a toilet stall. She was a grown-up. A happily single adult. And Cash was simply the parent of one of her students. Period.

Belle blamed the washroom theatrics on the bomb that Ed had just dropped on her in his office. She'd been so wrapped up in figuring out a way to save the Reading Rumble *and* Book Buddies that she'd let her emotions run away with her for a second.

No more, she vowed. The Reading Rumble was her single biggest school project of the year. If she'd been paying proper attention, she would've seen the cancellation coming. All the signs had been right in front of her face. If she hadn't been so wrapped up in Cash, she would've realized what was happening…maybe even in time to do something about it before the district decided to dash the hopes and dreams of a bunch of elementary school kids who were just learning to embrace their love of reading.

From now on, I've got to keep my head in the game, she'd told herself as she read Cash's text message.

Cash: Passed the home inspection! Endless thanks for your help.

She'd typed three different responses, ultimately deeming each one too enthusiastic, before settling on a simple thumbs-up emoji. The most impersonal emoji in the entire digital arsenal. If that didn't scream professionalism, she didn't know what would.

But then he'd responded to her thumbs up in least impersonal way possible…with a heart emoji.

And now here she was, sitting at the check-in table in the Comfort Paws barn, sort of feeling like she might need to breathe into one of her unused poop bags lest she hyperventilate at the memory of that tiny cartoon heart.

Could you be any more dramatic? It was probably a slip of his typing finger. Maybe he meant to send something else, like a paw print. Or a hamburger.

Right. Because that made total sense.

"If anyone shows up without a veterinary exam form, you can let them know that I'm offering a discount rate for annual exams for Comfort Paws dogs. I'm holding tomorrow afternoon open for back-to-back appointments."

Maple peeled a sheet of paper from her clipboard and handed it to Belle. "Just write the person's name and phone number next to the time they choose."

"Got it," Belle said.

"I can hardly believe it. We've all been working so hard in preparation for this night, and it's finally here." Maple beamed at Belle and Adaline while Lady Bird panted happily at her feet. Then Maple bent to press a kiss to the top of the golden's head and let out a happy sigh. "Pinch me if I'm dreaming, y'all."

"Nicely done." Belle nodded in appreciation. It was hard to believe it had been just under a year since Maple rolled into town, dead set on getting back to her native Manhattan as quickly as possible. "I really love how quickly and easily you've adapted to using Texas vernacular."

"So does Ford," Maple quipped. Her gaze flitted toward Adaline. "Your brother gives me a kiss every time I use *y'all* or *howdy* in a sentence."

Adaline tilted her head. "Dare I ask what happens if you combine them and say, 'Howdy, y'all'?"

"Good one. I think I'll try that when I get home tonight." Maple's eyes glittered, and Belle felt a pang that seemed a lot like envy…except that wasn't possible, because Belle didn't want what Maple and Ford had.

Liar, her thoughts screamed just as Cash strolled into the barn with Sparkles in his arms. The dog's leash was bubblegum pink, as was her collar, which was decorated with a pink leather bow. Clearly, Cash had let Lucy choose them, and somehow, that knowledge made the entire picture even more adorable.

A strange, wistful feeling coursed through Belle, almost like she was homesick for a place she'd never been before. Cash winked at her as he approached, and she shifted her gaze to the papers in front of her, staring intently at the words on the pages until they blurred before her eyes.

"Here we go! This is a huge moment for Comfort Paws." Maple took a deep breath. "Dogs and handlers are starting to arrive. Are y'all ready?"

Maybe Cash really was her friend. Would that be so terrible? And was it really so hard to imagine that someday he might be something more?

Belle couldn't think about that right now, though. Maple was right. This was a big night for Comfort Paws. That's all that mattered.

Longing wound its way through her, unspooling like a smooth satin ribbon—too potent, too exquisite to ignore.

I'm as ready as I'll ever be.

Chapter Ten

Cash had never been to a dog training class in his life. Sure, he'd talked a big game back at the Bluebonnet Festival with his "may the best dog win" proclamation. But that had been nothing but trash talk—just something to distract Belle from her righteous attempt to talk him out of getting a dog. She wasn't the gatekeeper of the entire canine population, but even Cash could admit she'd been right about a few things. He'd needed her.

And she'd come through for him, no matter how genuinely obnoxious he'd been on occasion.

That's probably why you like her so much, he thought fifteen minutes into their first class as he sat on a hard metal folding chair directly across the barn from her. *Among other reasons.*

In truth, those reasons were becoming too numerous to count. But it was becoming increasingly difficult to pretend—even to himself—that his only interest in Belle Darling was friendship, especially once he'd realized that the flirty cowboy from the Bluebonnet Festival was here tonight and that he'd somehow managed to claim a chair immediately to Belle's left.

Cash had hoped to sit beside her, but no. He'd lingered

too long at the registration desk, and the cowboy—whose real name was allegedly Stetson—had breezed right past him and plopped himself down in the seat next to the place where Cash had spotted a backpack that looked just like the sort of thing Belle would carry. It was decorated in a whimsical strawberry pattern with white eyelet trim. The chair on the other side was already taken, as well. Dejected, he'd snagged a spot opposite, which now afforded him a perfect, unobstructed view of Stetson's thinly disguised romantic overtures. His black Lab kept nudging Peaches with his big, square muzzle, his tail wagging so hard that it clanged against Belle's metal chair, despite the six feet of space between every seat.

The guy was flirting via his dog, and it infuriated Cash beyond reason.

"Good evening, everyone! Welcome to therapy dog training class." A woman in a red Comfort Paws shirt like the one he'd seen Belle wear before stood in the center of the barn, gaze flitting from one dog team to the next. "We're so glad you're here. My name is Maple Leighton Bishop, the president and founder of Comfort Paws. I'm going to introduce our trainer in just a few minutes, but first I just wanted to greet everyone and give you all an idea of how this evening will progress."

Cash forced himself to focus on Maple, but out of the corner of his eye, he saw the black Lab paw at Peaches's little head. It was clearly just an attempt to play. The Labrador's tongue was hanging out, and everything about his demeanor screamed floppy, friendly goofball, but Cash still wanted to go over there and tell the dog to keep his paws to himself.

"First off, the placement of your chairs is intentional,

and the reason for that is two-fold. We want each team to have their own space, and we also want to use this class as an opportunity to teach your dog to respect others. All the dogs here have been prescreened by our team, and they're friendly. But part of being a therapy dog is learning not to approach others unless they have permission, and that includes dogs and people alike." Maple walked straight toward Stetson. "So, if you don't mind, I'm going to show you how to keep this sweet dog in your space instead of your neighbor's."

Cash sat up straighter and tried not to look too jubilant. He must've failed, because once Belle arranged Peaches in a sit position on the opposite side of her chair from the cowboy's bull-in-a-china-shop Lab, her eyes met his. Her ordinarily bashful smile quickly changed to one of amusement.

Busted.

Fine. If she knew he was jealous, he had no reason to try and hide it. Not that he was doing such a stellar job of that, anyway.

Cash's gaze cut toward Stetson and then back toward Belle. He rolled his eyes in exaggerated fashion. She laughed, and then her plush bottom lip slipped between her teeth as she quickly regained her composure and looked away. Maybe sitting on the other side of the barn wasn't going to be the worst thing in the world.

The evening progressed with more surprises, the biggest shocker of all being that Sparkles was one of the most well-behaved dogs in the entire class. No one was more stunned by this development than Cash himself. Never once had he seriously expected Sparkles to outperform anyone, least of all Peaches. But shortly after

Maple introduced the dog trainer, the Cavalier's soft eyes landed on Cash.

She recognized him instantly and darted straight toward him, coming to abrupt halt when she reached the end of her leash. Belle's eyes went wide as her perfect little dog then proceeded to thrash about and whine. If she'd weighed more than her slight twelve pounds or so, she probably would've dragged Belle and her chair clear across the barn.

Her failure to do so certainly wasn't for lack of trying.

"Peaches, no!" Belle's entire face went as red as her Comfort Paws shirt as she dug around in her backpack for a dog treat. Once she found one, she tried to use to lure Peaches back to her side, but the cinnamon-and-white spaniel didn't even blink at it.

"Oh dear." The instructor glanced back and forth between Cash and Peaches. "It looks like someone is a little distracted."

"I am *so* sorry." Belle gave Peaches's leash a gentle tug, and the dog finally turned around long enough to see the small slice of hot dog in Belle's hand. Peaches lunged at it, but not without first pausing to shoot another glance at Cash, tail wagging so fast that it was nothing but a blur.

Belle lifted her gaze to Cash as Peaches munched on the treat, and he flashed her a wink. Beside her, the cowboy huffed.

"No worries. You handled that perfectly, Belle." The dog trainer nodded at her. "Go ahead and give Peaches another treat while you have her attention. Reward her for looking at you. Remember, class. If your dog ventures outside your immediate area, give the leash a quick, gentle tug—not enough to pull on the dog's neck, just a nudge to remind them that there's someone else at the other end of the leash, and that's who they should be paying attention to."

"Instead of the tempting stranger across the room," the handler to Belle's right stage-whispered.

Cash had already recognized her as Adaline Bishop—the woman who'd worked the Comfort Paws table alongside Belle at the Bluebonnet Festival. Before class he'd thanked her for telling him about Sparkles, and she'd told him how happy she'd been to see his name listed on the training class roster.

"That's right." The trainer laughed and pointed at Belle. "Your job is to be far more interesting than that tempting stranger." She tipped her head toward Cash.

"I'm on it," Belle said, and glowered at Adaline, who seemed to be enjoying the entire episode with unabashed interest.

The rest of class consisted of introducing the dogs and handlers to simple exercises like sit, down and settle, which was a relaxed version of the *stay* command. Sparkles excelled at that one, splaying herself between Cash's feet. It was a wonder how calm his dog could be when she wasn't throwing one of her middle-of-the-night tantrums.

The meltdowns were few and far between since he and Belle had moved Sparkles's crate to Cash's bedroom, though. Belle's advice had been spot-on, and for that, Cash owed her big-time. He'd picked up a gift for her at Bluebonnet Bookshop to show his gratitude and had been hoping to give it to her tonight at class until the Stetson-wearing Stetson had thwarted his attempts to have a single private word with her.

Peaches executed the various exercises with impressive precision. Cash knew Belle had been training her dog for months already, and it showed. But every few minutes, the Cavalier seemed to remember that Cash was in the barn, and her little head swiveled in his direction. All the hot dogs in the world couldn't drag her gaze back toward Belle. And as the end of class neared and the instructor had each handler take a turn walking their dog around the barn on a loose leash without pulling or losing focus, poor Belle didn't have a prayer. Peaches spent her entire walk veering of course with her leash stretched in a direct line toward Cash.

"What's going on here?" The cowboy glowered at him. "Do you have a steak hidden in your pocket or something?"

It was the most fun Cash had ever had in a classroom setting. For once, his dyslexia hadn't made him feel miles behind everyone else. Ticking off Stetson had simply been an added benefit.

Cash's stellar mood refused to be dampened, even when he was forced to stand around for a full fifteen minutes after class because the cowboy was once again monopolizing Belle's time. He finally seemed to get the hint when Belle politely excused herself and told him she needed to help clean up since she was a member of the Comfort Paws board of directors.

"That guy is relentless," Cash said under his breath once he'd gone.

Belle narrowed her gaze at him. "You think so?"

"One thousand percent." Cash's teeth clenched. Stetson had repeatedly let the black Lab pester Peaches, despite the instructor's repeated prompting to try and keep the dog in his own space.

Half an hour into the class, she'd finally dragged Stetson's chair three feet outside the circle, up against the back wall of the barn.

"Also, that name is ridiculous," Cash added, fully aware that he sounded like a thirteen year old kid who was angry at another boy for flirting with his middle school crush. But he couldn't seem to stop himself. "And so is his dog's."

Belle snickered. "You mean Lasso?"

Stetson and Lasso. The cringe was real. "They sound like characters in a spaghetti Western. I'm embarrassed on behalf of our entire state."

"Embarrassed, huh?" Belle's lips twisted. Why couldn't he stop looking at her mouth? "Interesting choice of words to describe what you're feeling. Adaline thinks it's something completely different."

"You've been talking about me with your friends," Cash said. That had to be a win.

Her eyes met his and held for a long, quiet beat.

"She thinks you're jealous," she finally said in a voice that was barely above whisper.

Bingo.

Cash bristled every time Stetson looked at her. When had he turned into such a caveman? It was absurd. And inappropriate. And very, *very* much real. Even now, in this dusty barn with no one around but their dogs, all he wanted to do was tuck a lock of her lush, dark hair bending her ear and utter the one word that he felt with every beat of his heart.

Mine.

"What do you think?" he asked.

A smile tugged at her lips, but before she could say anything, Peaches rose up on her hind legs and pawed at Cash's shins, begging for him to pick her up, despite the fact that he already had an armful of French bulldog.

"Peaches!" Belle gathered the dog into her arms and sighed as she pinned Cash with a mock glare. "What do I think? I think my dog has a crush on you. That's what I think."

"She's a remarkable judge of character. It must be all that training you've done with her."

"It's a problem is what it is," Belle countered.

"Regardless, Sparkles and I won tonight's class, fair and square." Cash ran a hand over the velvety fur on Sparkle's head. The bulldog released a snuffle that sounded suspiciously like a snore. Poor thing was wiped out from training class. "Just as I predicted, I might add."

"For the last time, it's not a contest." Belle groaned, but her words didn't carry the same bite they had the last time she'd told him that dog training wasn't a competition.

"Still, to the victor goes the spoils. And for my prize, I choose ice cream," he said as he scratched Sparkles behind her big bat-like ears.

Belle slid him a curious glance. "Ice cream?"

Cash nodded. "You and Peaches, me and Sparkles. Ice cream at the Sundae House."

Her face lit up, and Cash could see the gold flecks in her dark brown irises, shining like hidden treasure. "Right now? Is the Sundae House even open this late on a school night?"

"Right now. They're open until nine." Thanks to Lucy, Cash had their operating hours memorized. Ice cream was her favorite treat. Maybe he'd pick up a hand-packed carton of mint chocolate chip to take home. "I'll help you and the board with cleanup, and then we can head over there. How does that sound?"

Belle glanced toward Adaline, Maple and Jenna, who appeared to be loitering near the entrance to the barn and pretending not to look in their direction.

Her gaze flitted back to him, and she peered up at him through the thick fringe of her eyelashes. "If I say yes, you're going to keep insisting this class is a competition, aren't you?"

If it means we get to spend more time alone together... then yes.

Cash ignored the question and arched a brow at Belle's dog. "Shall we ask Peaches what she thinks?"

"Peaches would follow you to the moon and back, so I'm pretty sure I already know her opinion on the matter." Belle wound a loose tendril of her hair around one of her graceful fingers, rendering Cash spellbound for a beat. He just knew those dark lush waves would feel like silk slipping between his fingertips. He'd imagined it more times than he could count, despite every effort not to.

He was tired of fighting it, though. Tired of pretending he wasn't developing feelings for her when she'd become the calm in his storm. When Cash was with Belle, the future didn't feel as overwhelming as it had when he'd first arrived in Bluebonnet. It almost felt like something to look forward to.

Grief had stolen so much from Lucy, and in turn,

Cash. His sister's passing was the greatest loss he'd ever faced, but his heartbreak was multiplied tenfold with every tear that Lucy shed. He'd come here to give her a new beginning, and against all odds, he was beginning to think that such a thing just might be possible...for both of them. Was that asking too much? Was it okay to think of his own happiness too?

Cash knew what Mallory would say. For once, maybe he should listen, even though she was no longer around to say, "I told you so."

He smiled at Belle, and warmth curled down his spine in a delicious spiral. "Ice cream it is, then."

"I think I'm going to go with sweet strawberry cream," Belle said as she surveyed the pastel-colored ice cream varieties that filled the case at Sundae House.

Cash smirked. "Are you absolutely sure?"

"Yes." Her gaze snagged on a carton of cherry vanilla. "I mean, maybe."

She'd already changed her ice cream order three times—first from cookies-and-cream to pistachio, then to vanilla bean, and then yet again to sweet strawberry cream. The cherry vanilla looked awfully good, though.

Belle was never this indecisive. Once she set her mind on something, she stuck to it. But in her defense, it was hard to think with Cash standing so close to her—especially with his palm nestled against the small of her back as if they actually liked each other.

As if they were here on a date...

Belle's nose crinkled, entirely against her will.

Were they here on a date?

"You can relax, Belle." Cash gave the tip of her nose a playful tap. "I don't bite."

"Good, because if you did, I'd have no choice but to speak to the other members of the Comfort Paws board and get you kicked out of training class. We've got a no-tolerance policy when it comes to biting," she said, determined not to let herself get rattled. Peaches had already embarrassed them enough for one evening.

Her little spaniel was now acting like a perfect angel, sitting calmly at the end of her leash beside the toe of Belle's right sneaker. Sparkles sat beside Peaches with the majority of her bulk sagging against the Cavalier's side. The bulldog could barely keep her eyes open. Exhaustion was always such a nice little bonus after a training class. The pups were sure to sleep like babies tonight. Even Sparkles.

"Can I get you folks anything?" The teenager behind the counter adjusted his retro-style soda jerk hat.

Everything about Sundae House had a distinctly vintage vibe—from the old-fashioned ice cream parlor decor with its black-and-white checkered floor, candy-pink vinyl stools and antique Tiffany Blue cash register to the ice cream shop's name. Sundae House was a play on the words *Sunday house*, the local term for a Texas tradition dating back to the 1800s. Back then, farmers and ranchers who lived in outlying areas would keep a smaller home near town where they could stay on the weekends for attending church and social events. Quite a few Sunday houses still stood throughout the Texas Hill Country, and Bluebonnet was lucky enough to boast a whole row of them near the town square.

Most were painted in Easter egg hues with fanciful gingerbread trim, and all of them boasted historical landmark plaques. A few of the Sunday houses had been converted from residences to small businesses, like Maple's veterinary clinic. She and her husband, Ford, lived in the Sunday house directly next door to the practice that had once been occupied by her father.

"We'll have a quadruple scoop ice cream sundae, please." Cash held up two fingers. "Two spoons."

Belle stared at him. "*Four* scoops?"

"Any particular flavors?" the teen asked, reaching for the dipper well where the silver ice cream scoops were stored.

"Cookies-and-cream, pistachio, vanilla bean and sweet strawberry cream," Cash said, flashing a grin toward Belle.

"Well played." Belle laughed in spite of the fact that it was a very rich person move to order every single flavor she'd considered. She couldn't help but be impressed at the thoughtfulness behind the gesture. At least he'd been paying attention, which was more than she could say for the men she'd dated in the past.

He makes me feel special. Belle inhaled a shaky breath as she recounted all the times Cash had treated her like she was someone who mattered…like she was his equal, despite the massive difference in their social and economic standings. Other than that first awkward encounter in the library, he'd never once made her feel inferior. Quite the opposite, actually.

First impressions weren't always true. Hadn't Belle learned that very thing from numerous books she'd read—chief among them, Jane Austen's *Pride and Prejudice*? If Mr. Darcy had tried to buy Elizabeth Bennett's dog for an outrageous sum, would they have still ended up together in the end? Peaches had certainly forgiven Cash for that initial infraction. Perhaps it was time for Belle to let it go, too.

"Thank you for this," she said a few minutes later after they'd gotten settled at one of the picnic tables in the town square. Twinkle lights stretched from the gazebo to the surrounding dogwood trees, bathing the park in soft golden light. Both their dogs snoozed underfoot. "Although, I have to say, sharing an absurdly large ice cream sundae made up of all my favorite flavors kind of makes me feel like the victor in this scenario. I thought this was supposed to be your prize, not mine. You and Sparkles were the big winners tonight."

Cash shrugged as he dipped his spoon into the scoop of pistachio. "Maybe I'm finally ready to admit it's not a contest."

Belle narrowed her gaze at him and tried to figure out if he was being serious or joking, but as usual, his expression gave nothing away. "Then, why are we here, again?"

"We're here because I thought it would be nice if we got to know each other a little better. I like you, Belle." His lips tipped into a crooked smile. "Despite your best efforts to convince me otherwise."

"You think I was intentionally trying to make you dislike me?" she asked.

Well, weren't you?

Clearly the Comfort Paws girls weren't the only ones who could see right through her.

"I'm trying my hardest to be nice to you. I kind of

have to. It's a tall order," he said, parroting her own words back to her. His smile widened. "Sound familiar?"

"If it makes you feel any better, I wasn't intentionally trying to push you away. I just have a thing for rules." Belle took a deep breath. If he was willing to show her his softer side, she wanted to do the same. "Also, vulnerability doesn't come easy to me, and I'm not sure you realize this or not, but you can be rather intimidating."

He regarded her, spoon poised above the sundae between them. "And yet you've never once held your tongue around me. You always say exactly what's on your mind."

"You say that like it's a good thing." Belle swirled her spoon in the strawberries and cream so she wouldn't have to look him in the eye.

But he waited for her to lift her gaze to his before spoke, and when he finally did, the warmth in his gaze was potent enough to melt the entire dish of ice cream. "It's a very good thing."

Belle swallowed. "So, you're telling me if only I'd insulted the other men in my life, I'd be happily paired off already like the rest of the Comfort Paws girls?"

It was official. She had no filter whatsoever when she was around this man.

Belle held up her spoon. "Forget I said that."

"Too late." Cash shook his head. His smile softened, and the sudden tenderness in his eyes made it hard for her to breathe. "Is that what you want—to fall in love?"

Yes. Her answer was right there on the tip of her tongue, and she nearly let it slip out until she realized she'd sound just like a bride on her wedding day. *I do.*

"It's okay to want a family…to not want to go through

life feeling lonely. That's something I'm just now realizing about myself, too. How's that for unfiltered honesty?" Cash chuckled.

Cash McAllister…lonely? The man had the entire world at his fingertips. But money and power weren't the same things as love and companionship. As *family*. Belle's mother had made the mistake of believing that, and she'd left a trail of heartbreak and destruction in her wake.

All this time, Belle had been convinced she was the vulnerable one—the one who had everything to lose. Book Buddies, her job, her dignity. Not to mention her heart. She'd been so wrapped up in her own problems that she hadn't given any thought whatsoever to his. It was the same thing with the Reading Rumble at school.

Belle had always been so goal-oriented, forever focused on the future. So long as she kept her sights on what lay in front of her, she wouldn't have time to think about the past. Except now she was missing out on everything happening around her. She'd lost sight of the fact that this present moment was something she could never get back.

And then Cash had come along, and slowly but surely, things were beginning to look crystal clear. His parents had passed away years ago. Everyone in town had heard about the accident. The McAllister Mansion had stood empty ever since. There'd been a flurry of tributes and memorials in the months that followed. Belle had been in high school when the library at Bluebonnet Elementary had been completely renovated and named after his mother, which meant Cash must've still been at the boarding school he'd mentioned.

And now he'd lost his sister. He'd become a dad overnight, and from what Belle could tell, Lucy was the only family he had left. Nothing could prepare a person for that. There were certain things that money and a prominent name just couldn't fix.

Loneliness, heartbreak and grief were chief among them.

"You're honest with me in a way that no one else is," Cash said as the lights overhead flickered and dimmed. Sundae House was closing up shop, as were the other businesses in the town square. Without the twinkle lights, they had only the stars overhead to illuminate the small park, which all at once felt smaller and more intimate than it ever had before. "I know I can trust you, and as strange as it sounds, I can't really say that about anyone else except Lucy and Ellis."

This struck Belle as profoundly sad. Her own mother had rejected her, but she'd always had her dad. And now she had her Comfort Paws friends and Peaches, too.

"You forgot Sparkles," she whispered in the darkness. It seemed appropriate that the lights had gone out. They were feeling their way through new and unknown territory.

Cash's laugh was soft as velvet. "So, what you're saying is the sum total of my trust circle consists of a seven-year-old, a paid employee and a recently rescued French bulldog."

A paid employee? So, Ellis was indeed a butler, of sorts. Belle knew it.

"Me too. I'm in the circle. You said so yourself." She leaned forward to get a better view of Cash's face, and a gust of cool spring wind sent petals from the dogwood trees swirling all around them. Everything went pink and tender and so sweet that her heart clenched.

"Sometimes I think you *are* the circle," he said, and then his gaze dropped slowly to her mouth as he mirrored her movement, leaning closer…and closer still… until their lips were mere inches apart.

"Tell me something real," he said in a whisper. His breath, cool from the ice cream, fanned across her face.

A shiver ran up and down Belle's spine, and the truest, most authentic thing she could've said in that moment spilled right out of her.

"I can't stop thinking about you, Cash McAllister."

Chapter Eleven

I can't stop thinking about you, Cash McAllister.

If Cash had been granted one wish, he would've chosen to freeze time—to stay seated right there at the modest picnic table in Bluebonnet's town square gazing at Belle Darling with pink petals in her hair and a look on her face that made him ache in a way he'd never felt before. Dogs snored at their feet, and what was left of the ice cream sundae had long melted away, leaving the air between them rich with the scents of strawberries and chocolate.

Cash wanted to bottle it so he could revisit it time and time again—this place, this moment, this woman who'd enchanted him without even trying.

It was exquisite, this longing. The urge to close the space between them and kiss Belle was almost too much to bear. But the want itself was such delicious torture that he almost didn't want it to end.

And then it *did* end, with an abruptness that made Cash's head spin as the sudden ring of his cell phone pierced the loaded silence.

Belle gave a start. Then Cash backed up, bumping his knee on the underside of the picnic table in the process.

His grunt, paired with the sudden movement, woke the dogs, and soon Sparkles was pawing at his shins in an attempt to climb up his leg and into his lap to see what all the excitement was about.

"Don't you want to get that?" Belle's gaze flitted toward his phone ringing on the table. The light from the screen shone garishly bright in the darkness.

Cash's knee throbbed as he tore his gaze away from hers and squinted at the phone.

County General Hospital.

Someone may as well have dumped a cooler of frigid water over his head as he read the notification. His blood turned to ice, and his gut twisted in that sickening way it did so often during Mallory's illness.

Cash hated hospitals, and he couldn't think of a single reason why one would be calling him right now. Unless…

Lucy.

Panic coiled in the pit of his stomach as he grabbed the phone and jammed at the Accept Call button. "Hello?"

"Am I speaking to Cash McAllister?" The voice on the other end was calm and soothing, but that did nothing to ease Cash's worries. If anything, it made them worse.

"Yes, this is Cash," he said. Sparkles whined, and Cash was vaguely aware of Belle luring the puppy toward her and distracting the dog with a treat from her pocket in his periphery. All of his focus had narrowed to a pinprick.

Please let Lucy be okay.

Mallory had trusted him with her daughter. She *had* to be okay.

"Mr. McAllister, I'm sorry if this call has caused any alarm. My name is Pam Hudson, and I'm an RN at County Hospital." She paused, and Cash could hear the smile in her voice. "You can call me Nurse Pam. Let me start by saying I have little Lucy here with me, and she's completely, one hundred percent fine."

Cash nearly passed out from relief. Then, before he had a chance to respond, Nurse Pam continued.

"I'm calling about Ellis Graves. He gave me your number after he drove himself here this evening for treatment of an injury he sustained to his ankle at home."

There were so many alarming things about that sentence that Cash didn't know where to start. "He drove himself there?"

Ellis had been watching Lucy for the evening while Cash was at training class. Why hadn't he called Cash for help? Or at least called 911 instead of getting behind the wheel of car and driving himself to the hospital?

The answer to those questions was obvious, though. Ellis was old-fashioned—as salt of the earth and self-sufficient as they came. He'd rather drop dead in his starched uniform shirt than ask anyone for help, least of all his employer. And as much as Cash liked to think of Ellis as family, that's exactly who he was: Ellis's boss.

"Yes, he drove himself here. He insisted he was fine to drive since the injury was to his left ankle and not the right. But rest assured, I've given him a stern talking to. The injury was a result of a fall at the foot of the stairs. Luckily, he didn't suffer a concussion, but the next time something like this happens, it would really be best if he called emergency services."

No concussion. That sounded good, at least.

"How is he doing?" Cash asked, throat going thick. Employee or not, Ellis was the closest thing he had to a father. In a strange way, he always had been—even before his dad had passed away.

"He fractured his ankle in the fall and is being fitted for a special orthopedic boot. He's going to be just fine."

"I'm on my way there right now." Cash stood and began gathering his belongings with his free hand—his wallet, his keys and the messenger bag that contained the wrapped gift he'd brought for Belle. He hadn't even had a chance to give it to her yet, but that would obviously have to wait. "Please tell Lucy I'll be there as soon as I can."

He hated the thought of her spending any time at all in a hospital. She was so young, and Cash knew memories were fleeting at that age, but surely she remembered the sight of her mother, wan and pale beneath the thin sheets of her hospital bed in those final days. He couldn't imagine she'd ever forget.

"Don't you worry about Lucy. She's playing video games in the playroom with some of the kids from the children's wing. I'll tell her you're on the way."

"Thank you, Nurse Pam," he said, and his eyes nearly flooded with tears of stone-cold relief.

Cash never cried.

Even when his parents passed away and then, years later, Mallory, he hadn't shed a tear. When the headmaster at Kingsley Academy had called Cash into his office to tell him about the accident, he'd given Cash exactly ten minutes to fall apart. He'd been too stunned to cry. Shocked to his core, he'd sunk into one of the stately guest chairs in the headmaster's office and begun to shake uncontrollably. When his teeth started to rattle, the headmaster had taken Cash by his slender shoulders and told him to be strong.

It's what your father would've wanted, he'd said. *What he'd have expected of another McAllister man...*

Cash had known it was true, even though at fourteen years old, he was still more boy than man. No matter. He'd swallowed all that grief and panic and stuffed it someplace deep down inside, locked it up tight and thrown away the key.

For years, it worked. Cash moved through the rest of his life on autopilot, doing exactly what his parents would've wanted. He stayed at the boarding school until he graduated three days after his eighteenth birthday, only seeing his sister and the distant aunt who'd been appointed as their guardian on holidays. Even then, he usually stayed a perfunctory few days and returned to campus as soon as the dorms opened back up. After graduation, he attended his dad's alma mater, joined the same fraternity his father had belonged to and went on to get his MBA so he could fulfill his destiny as a McAllister and run the family foundation.

The classes had been a struggle, due to his dyslexia. Unlike the safe cocoon of Bluebonnet Elementary, the schools Cash attended had offered little to no support for his learning differences. But he'd done it, and through it all, he dated the "right" sort of women, joined the country club and hired Dallas's most expensive decorator for his corner office. Since the day he'd been born, his future had been laid out for him, and Cash never strayed from the plan, determined to make his father proud, even though he'd never hear the words from the man himself. He didn't need to. He'd known exactly what to do, and odds were, Arthur McAllister would've never said them anyway, even if he lived to see it.

But then Mallory got sick, and everything changed. Cash quickly realized that his carefully ordered life was nothing but a patchwork quilt of other peoples' expectations, self-preservation and a hearty dose of denial. His sister's illness pulled the first thread, and he'd been unraveling ever since.

He didn't want to unravel in front of Belle, though. Not here. Not now. She was his happy place, and he wanted to keep it that way.

He clamped his eyes shut, pinched the bridge of nose and concentrated on taking deep breaths until he got himself together.

"Cash? Is everything okay?"

When he opened his eyes, the worry in Belle's gaze nearly made him crack. He pasted on a smile and rearranged his belongings, anxious to get to the car, even though he had no real clue how to get to County General.

"It's fine," he said a little too sharply. "It's Ellis. He took a spill and broke his ankle. I need to get to the hospital. Lucy's there, and…" His throat tightened again. "Anyway, I've got to run. Sorry to cut things short like this."

He held his palm out and nodded toward Sparkles, a silent cue for her to hand over the dog's leash. He had no idea what kind of pet policy the hospital had, but he had a feeling Nurse Pam might cut him some slack, given the circumstances.

But Belle wasn't cooperating. Instead of giving him the leash, she wrapped it around her hand alongside Peaches's without so much as a word. Then she stood and both dogs looked up at her, awaiting instruction.

"What are you doing?" Cash asked, clenching his keys in his hand.

"What does it look like?" she countered in that adorable, argumentative way that she had. "I'm coming with you."

"Lady Bird visits patients here regularly," Belle said as she offered Cash a limp paper cup of plain black hospital coffee from the nearby vending machine. "Maple's husband, Ford, is a pediatrician on staff here, too. He usually only does rounds once a week, but we might bump into him. I'm not sure what his schedule is. He keeps regular office hours in town."

Cash nodded, and took the coffee from her as if in a trance.

They were in the hospital waiting room on the first floor of County General. Since visiting time had ended hours ago, the place was a ghost town. The silence, excruciating—and not in the tortured, intimate way the quiet had wrapped itself around them in the town square earlier. This brand of noiselessness was stifling. Belle couldn't take it. She felt compelled to fill the dead air between them with words…literally *any* words at all. They'd only been seated for fifteen minutes, but Belle had already peppered Cash with an entire evening's worth of babble.

She didn't know what else to do. Ever since Nurse Pam's call, he'd shut down. The Cash she'd gotten to know over the past week or so was gone, and the stiff, impersonal man who'd tried to buy her dog was once again standing in his place. Belle told herself he was simply in shock, which was completely understandable. They'd already spoken with Nurse Pam, who'd gone to fetch Lucy from the playroom. Once she returned with the little girl and they all got to check on Ellis in the emergency room, Cash would see that his makeshift family was a-okay. He'd drop the invisible force field around himself and everything would go back to normal.

Meanwhile, Belle chattered on as she took a seat in the vinyl-covered chair opposite him. "This hospital is one of the places where we can do our Comfort Paws mentoring later. Now that you're buddy-buddy with Nurse Pam, I'm sure she'll call dibs on you and Sparkles."

Belle glanced at the Frenchie stretched out on the carpeted waiting room floor. The dog lifted her head just long enough to twitch her nose at Cash's cup of coffee and then placed her head back on her paws with a sigh.

"What?" Cash frowned at her. At least he wasn't simply staring straight ahead anymore.

Belle would take any sign of life she could get. "Our training class includes two mentoring sessions. We have to shadow a certified Comfort Paws team on a visit to their regular facility. Then the following week, we go back with our dogs and visit under the supervision of the Comfort Paws handler who is already certified."

He looked at her like she was speaking to him in a foreign language.

"I mentioned the mentoring requirement at the pet fair during the Bluebonnet Festival when I tried to talk you out of adopting this little roly-poly bug." She nudged Sparkles with the toe of her sneaker and laughed. That incident was in the past. If tonight had proven anything, it was that they could laugh about it now.

Couldn't they?

"Remember?" she prompted while her smile wobbled off her face.

"I remember." He gave her a curt nod. Then he shook his head as a deep V formed between his eyebrows. "I just..."

Nurse Pam came bustling toward them from the corner hallway in her bubblegum-pink scrubs before Cash could finish. Lucy walked alongside her and wiggled her fingers at Belle and Cash in a dainty wave.

"Sorry about the delay," Pam said, tipping her head at Lucy. "Someone wanted to finish building her animated horse ranch in her video game before coming down here."

"No worries. I appreciate you keeping an eye on her until I could get here," Cash said, rising from his chair to wrap an arm around Lucy's slim shoulders.

She grinned up at her uncle with a mouth rimmed in a faint red stain, like she'd been eating cherry popsicles. "Uncle Cash, I played a fun game. It had horses and a pasture and bunnies in a bunny hatch."

"Stable Story." Nurse Pam winked at Lucy and then turned her smile on Cash. "The children all love that video game. Lucy made a few friends tonight on the pediatric floor, and they taught her how to play."

Cash gave her shoulders a squeeze. "Friends, huh?"

She nodded. "A girl named Amelia and a boy called Brian. Both of Brian's legs are in big casts. Amelia wears a scarf on her head like the one Mommy always wore."

Belle exchanged a glance with Cash. *A scarf like the one Mommy always wore.* Most likely, that meant cancer. So, that's what had happened to Lucy's mom. Belle couldn't imagine what the little girl had been through in her short life. No wonder Cash was so protective of his niece.

"Maybe I could come back and visit them again, Uncle Cash." Lucy cast him a questioning glance, and Belle almost found herself blinking back tears.

She'd felt a special affinity for Lucy since she'd started the Book Buddies program. Lucy didn't quite fit in with the other kids at school, much like Belle had struggled to belong when she'd been a little girl. They both liked dogs, and even though Lucy needed to take her time with reading because of her dyslexia, she adored books. Just like Belle.

But tonight Belle was seeing another side to the sweet little girl. The child had a tender heart. Her mom—Cash's sister—must've been an amazing woman. Belle just knew Lucy had also gotten a tiny bit of that compassion from her uncle, even if he seemed to be doing his best to hide that part of himself at the moment.

"I think both Brian and Amelia would like that very much." Nurse Pam beamed at Cash. "Honestly, it was no trouble looking after Lucy at all. The kids would love for her to come visit again anytime. But for now, Ellis is all patched up and ready to go if you'd like me to take you to him."

"That would be fantastic," Cash said.

Belle raised a hand. "I'll stay here with the dogs."

She didn't want to impose, and she also didn't want to drag two dogs through the emergency room without express permission.

"Don't be silly. Those two super pups are welcome here. Word on the street is that they're both part of the Comfort Paws training program. Ellis already told us all about it. He said the dogs started their certification class tonight. Come along, then." Pam turned in the direction of the ER, clearly expecting the entire entourage to fall in line behind her. Then she spun around and wagged a finger at Cash and Belle. "But I'm calling dibs on both Peaches and Sparkles when it's time to do their mentoring."

When she turned back around, Belle nudged Cash gently in the ribs. "Told you."

"You sure did," he said, then he reached for her hand, gave it a tender squeeze and held on tight.

Chapter Twelve

"Tonight was certainly an adventure." Belle yawned in Cash's kitchen as he popped a much-needed K-Cup into the coffee maker.

By the time they'd gotten Ellis home, the clock had been inching closer and closer to midnight. Of course Belle had gone with them. Sparkles needed to be walked, Lucy still had to take a bath and get ready for bed, and Cash wanted to move Ellis into one of the downstairs bedrooms so he wouldn't be in the guest cottage all by himself while he recuperated. Belle couldn't leave Cash to handle all of that responsibility on his own.

Even with her help, it was nearly two in the morning by the time Lucy and Ellis were both tucked in for the night. A row of prescription medication bottles was lined up on the kitchen counter, along with a schedule for when Ellis was supposed to take each pill and which ones were supposed to be consumed with food. Belle had packed Lucy's school backpack and placed it by the front door. Sparkles was sacked out on her huge memory foam dog bed beside the kitchen island with Peaches snuggled alongside her.

"An adventure is certainly one way of putting it."

Cash handed her a steaming mug of coffee—French vanilla, her favorite.

She'd nearly fainted with gratitude when he'd shown her the absurdly huge selection of offerings in his special coffee drawer. The coffee pods were lined up in a custom-made drawer insert, alphabetically organized by flavor. Ellis's doing, according to Cash. The man was obviously an angel sent straight from heaven—an angel who'd been ordered in no uncertain terms to stay off his ankle for the next four to six weeks.

"Thank you." She took her first sip, then another and another. Caffeine and sugar were the only things keeping her upright at this point.

"Are you kidding me right now? Thank *you* for staying and helping us out tonight. I don't know what we would've done without you." Cash dragged a hand through his hair, tugging hard at the ends as his gaze snagged on the pill bottles and dosage schedule. "Did you do all this?"

Belle shrugged. "It was no big deal—just something I threw together while you were busy getting Ellis set up in his room. I also packed Lucy's lunchbox for tomorrow, although I wasn't sure if you were planning on keeping her home since she was up later than usual tonight."

Cash's face creased into an exhausted smile. "She's got her Book Buddies session tomorrow. Wild horses couldn't drag her away from school."

"At least Peaches will be well rested." Belle motioned toward the dogs with her mug.

"They really seem to like each other," Cash said, and then the room grew quiet as his gaze met hers and held.

All night, she'd been thinking about the moment earlier in the evening when she'd been so sure he was going to kiss her. Had that really happened? It almost felt like a fever dream, too heady and potent to be real.

She'd felt it, though—the delicious pull between them. And when he'd lifted his eyes to hers in the darkness, the longing she'd seen written all over his face had taken her breath away. She hadn't imagined it. It had been real, and if the phone call from the hospital had come just a second or two later, she might've known what he tasted like…what the beat of his heart might feel like beneath her fingertips…what it would be like to just let go and let herself fall…

Everything had seemed so natural and easy in the town square when it was just the two of them. The things Cash had said to her were burned into her memory with searing clarity.

You're honest with me in a way that no one else is.

It's okay to want a family.

Is that what you want—to fall in love?

She'd been so caught up in the moment that she'd told him she couldn't stop thinking about him. Then, beneath the sterile lights of the hospital waiting room, something had shifted. Belle wanted to reel the words back in. Out here in the real world, away from the tenderness of their private moment under the stars, they felt far too dangerous. Like she was walking around with her bruised and broken heart firmly pinned to her sleeve instead of tucked away where it belonged.

She'd spent all night wishing and hoping that whatever magic spell had wrapped itself around them would come back. Every now and then, she caught a glimpse of it—only a spark, just enough to convince herself that her growing feelings for Cash hadn't somehow conjured the entire episode out of thin air. At the hospital, he'd held her hand like she was the only force capable of holding him together. Surely this was more than friendship.

Right?

"It's good that Lucy will be at school," Belle said, finally tearing her gaze away from Cash's so she could rinse her empty mug in the kitchen sink. She really needed to get going if she had any hope of being on time for work in the morning. "Tomorrow is the last Book Buddies session before spring break. I know she's going to miss reading to Peaches next week. I'll make sure she gets an extra few minutes tomorrow."

There she went, bending the rules again. Belle scarcely recognized herself anymore.

"There's no school next week?" Cash asked, brow furrowing.

"Nope. It's spring break." Belle tilted her head as she regarded him. The poor guy was so exhausted that he'd forgotten. "We're off five days in a row."

Belle had plans for every single minute of every single day. First up, finishing the proposal for her children's book. After that, she planned on living and breathing Comfort Paws. She needed to assemble the Book Buddies presentation for the school board and somehow train Peaches not to swoon every time she saw Cash. The latter was going to be a tall order.

Somewhere in there, she should also offer to help Dad and Cathy with wedding plans. They wanted a simple ceremony, with just Belle and Peaches as witnesses since Cathy's sons were busy with cattle roundup season on their ranch in Montana. Still, it was a wedding. It should feel special, regardless of Belle's complicated feelings about their surprise engagement.

"Five days in a row," Cash repeated. He was beginning to get that shocked look again. "I have an overnight trip to Dallas next week for the McAllister Foundation. It's almost the end of our fiscal year, and I have to sign off on the financials. The day after I get back, I have to attend an emergency school board meeting."

Belle swallowed and tried not to think about the fact that both of those things could possibly have a direct impact on her goals for Comfort Paws and Book Buddies. She didn't want to be the type of person who looked to Cash to solve all her problems simply because he was rich. She had a feeling he had enough people like that in his life already.

The sum total of my trust circle consists of a seven-year-old, a paid employee and a recently-rescued French bulldog. He'd said those exact words to her earlier. *And you...sometimes I think you* are *the circle.*

"Ellis was going to watch Lucy for me." Cash's jaw tightened. "He can't do that now, obviously. He'll try to say he can, but there's no way I'll let him. I'd feel better if he had someone looking after him as well as Lucy."

"I agree. If he's stubborn enough to drive himself to the hospital, he's sure to downplay any pain he might experiencing," Belle said.

"The doctor specifically said that rest is key." Cash tapped a finger on the page of discharge instructions Nurse Pam had sent home with them. "Along with ice and elevation."

Belle nodded. "He's going to need someone to fetch the ice packs and pillows."

"And that's just the tip of the iceberg. I've got Lucy and Sparkles to think about, plus preparation for my meetings." Cash cleared his throat. "I'm dyslexic, like Lucy. Sometimes I need extra time to prepare."

He stiffened, as though bracing for a dramatic reaction to his learning differences, but Belle wasn't fazed. She wasn't even surprised.

"I knew there was a good chance you had dyslexia, too. It's considered to be a neurobiological condition, passed down through genetics. Lucy's a lucky little girl. You're in a special position to support and understand her particular challenges."

Cash's brows knitted. "You think so?"

"Of course I do. And you probably know this already, but people with dyslexia often have special strengths."

"Like what?" Curiosity glittered in his eyes, and Belle wondered how much support he'd gotten for his learning disability at that fancy boarding school he'd mentioned.

"Things like thinking outside the box and creativity. Also, empathy." Belle snuck a sideways glance at him and noticed his expression had softened. "I meant it when I said Lucy is lucky to have you. You're teaching her by example how to cope with her dyslexia every single day."

He offered her a half smile. "I never thought of it that way."

"You should." She gave him a shoulder bump. It was good to see him relax a little after the night he'd had.

"I'll get right on that after I clone myself for spring break." He chuckled.

Belle took a deep breath. She was going to offer to help, despite her plans. Her plate practically seemed empty compared to Cash's, plus she adored Lucy. Ellis too...

And Sparkles, obviously.

"It sounds like you need—"

"A nanny." Cash crossed his arms and nodded.

Belle blinked. That's not at all what she was going to say. *Help* was the word she'd had in mind. *It sounds like you need help.*

"A nanny?" she echoed.

"Just for a week, while Lucy's out of school. After spring break is over, I can probably handle things on my own." His eyes slid toward hers. "You wouldn't consider doing it, would you?"

Belle hesitated.

Then guilt pricked her consciousness. Seconds before, she'd been ready to jump in with both feet and help him. She wanted to be there for him and Lucy. The word *nanny* gave her pause, though...

And the more she turned it over in her mind, the less she liked it. *A nanny.* That didn't sound like a favor or a friend helping out another friend. It certainly didn't sound like it had anything to do with love or romance or all the tempting ideas she'd finally let herself dream about during their ice cream date.

It sounded more like a job.

"I know it's asking a lot," Cash said, oblivious to the disappointment roiling through her. "You're certainly overqualified."

Overqualified, as if he was perusing her résumé. When had this date turned into a job interview?

The mood had certainly shifted after the phone call

from the hospital, but they were still on a date…or so Belle had thought.

Hot tears stung the back of her eyes all of a sudden. Belle felt like crying, either from embarrassment or anger. She wasn't sure which—probably both. She'd told him she couldn't stop thinking about him, and now he was *offering her employment*.

This was so much worse than when he'd tried to buy Peaches. How had she gotten things so completely wrong? She'd misread every single signal he'd been giving her earlier. Maybe she'd even been wrong about the almost kiss.

She had, hadn't she?

She took a deep breath and tried to tell him no. The McAllister Mansion was suddenly the last place on earth where she wanted to spend her spring break. "I—"

The words died in the back of her throat. To her horror, there was a hitch in her voice.

Could he tell how utterly crushed she was? Belle hoped not. She couldn't cry in front of him. No possible way. She was finished allowing herself to feel vulnerable in front of Cash.

"I'll pay you quite generously." He looked at her with beseeching eyes, and her heart twisted as his words from earlier came back to her.

I know I can trust you, and as strange as it sounds, I can't really say that about anyone else except Lucy and Ellis.

Belle should've been furious. He was trying to buy her…again.

This was different than last time, though. Because

they were different. Because he'd just reduced whatever delicate connection they had to a financial transaction.

And because this time, she couldn't bring herself to say no.

Chapter Thirteen

"So, Cash is your boss now?" Maple plucked one of the floral cotton day dresses that Belle had just shoved into her suitcase and refolded it into a neat square. "I'm not sure I understand what's happening."

Join the club.

"Same," Jenna said, and Adaline nodded her agreement.

Belle yanked another dress off its hanger and crammed it into the rolling bag spread open on her bed. Peaches was curled into a defiant ball in the section usually reserved for Belle's toiletries. The Cavalier always pulled this stunt when the suitcase came out, determined not to be left behind.

As if Belle would even consider moving into Cash's house without her.

"I'm taking a temporary job during spring break. It's really no big deal." Belle shrugged, but she couldn't seem to look her friends in the eye.

It was Friday night, and she'd invited the Comfort Paws girls over for a pizza-and-packing party. Cash was dropping by early Saturday morning to pick her up, and she wanted to be ready to go when he arrived at the cottage.

Intellectually, Belle knew that it didn't take four people to pack her things for a one-week stay. Plus, if she forgot something, she could always dart back home to get it. The McAllister Mansion was less than two miles from her house, easily walkable. In fact, she'd tried to tell Cash he didn't need to come fetch her in his car. He'd insisted on picking her up, either out of chivalry or professional obligation. Belle honestly didn't know which.

Her mind was all over the place lately—not to mention her heart. Hence the presence of her three best friends. She needed moral support as she prepared herself for her new nanny position.

"This is no different than that time I worked at Cherry on Top baking cupcakes during spring break. Remember that, Adaline?" Belle had been saving up for the down payment on the cottage that year, and Adaline had been looking for seasonal help at the bakery. It had been a win-win all around.

Or it would have been…if Belle hadn't had such a hard time mastering Cherry on Top's signature swirl with the frosting palette. And if she hadn't mixed up the sugar and salt once or twice. Maybe even three times.

Adaline winced. "I do, and forgive me when I say that I hope this nanny thing is indeed different than your brief but memorable tenure as a baker."

"We *all* remember," Jenna oh so helpfully chimed in.

A burst of laughter came of Maple so loud that Peaches flinched.

"Wait a minute." Belle wadded her pajama top into a ball and threw it at Maple's face. "Why are you laughing? You should know nothing at all about my foray into baking. You didn't even live here back then."

Maple swiftly folded the pajama top and tucked it into the corner of the suitcase. Her packing skills were seriously next level. Maybe it was a Manhattan girl thing. "I know, but Ford told me all about it a while back. He said he took three dozen cupcakes to the hospital staff that week, and somehow they'd ended up being both burned and underbaked at the same time."

Was nothing sacred in this town?

Of course not. This was small-town Texas. Secrets weren't a thing—not even when four full years had passed since the last time Belle had tried her hand at being a part-time cupcake queen.

"That happens when the oven temperature is set too high," Adaline said, as if anyone truly cared right then. She shrugged. "Just saying."

"Noted." Maple nodded at Adaline, then swiveled to face Belle full-on. "But back to the matter at hand. I wasn't exactly getting an employer-employee vibe between you and Cash the other night at training class. I know you two started off on the wrong foot, but I get the feeling that you two are attracted to each other. Considering that you haven't been interested in anyone else the entire time I've know you, that seems significant."

"I'm not attracted to him," Belle lied. "Maybe you're getting me confused with Peaches. She's the one who was throwing herself at him all evening."

Maple's only response was a hard stare. She knew Belle well enough to discern when she wasn't being entirely truthful.

"You're wasting your breath, Maple. I've already tried talking some sense into her, but she insists there's nothing whatsoever appealing about the man." Adaline pursed her lips. "Aside from the obvious."

"You mean the fact that he looks like he walked right out of a Ralph Lauren fragrance commercial? And he's charming? And he's got the cutest dog in the entire class?" Jenna ruffled the fur behind Peaches's ears. "Other than the Comfort Paws regulars, of course."

Belle's face went warm.

All those things were true, but none of them had anything to do with why Cash had managed to barge right through her defenses. She'd been drawn in by his softer side. By the tender way he interacted with Lucy, the affection he had for Ellis and his devotion to Sparkles and the Comfort Paws program. He made her laugh, and he never made her feel like she was too opinionated or overly ambitious. He accepted her just the way she was, and best of all, he was soulful when she least expected it. It was dizzying.

"Can we talk about something else now?" Belle asked.

She was getting confused again. Ever since the job offer, she'd vowed to keep things with Cash purely professional. That's what he wanted, right? That's also what she'd promised Ed, her *other* boss. Bluebonnet Elementary was still in financial trouble, with no end in sight. She still had to get in front of the school board, which now included Cash, to present her Book Buddies program and request that it be made a permanent part of the curriculum. And regardless of what happened while she was living under Cash's roof, they still had to attend training class together.

In a matter of weeks, their lives had become completely intertwined. Now wasn't the time to catch feelings.

"Actually, there's some Comfort Paws business we need to discuss, if you don't mind." Maple sat down on the edge of Belle's bed and folded her hands in her lap. Her expression had suddenly gone serious.

Belle's gaze flicked to Adaline and then to Jenna. Both shrugged like they, too, had no idea what was coming.

"Sure." Belle took a seat cross-legged on the floor—*like a pretzel* as they said at school. Peaches finally exited the suitcase and dove off the foot of the bed to climb into her lap.

"What's up?" Adaline asked.

Jenna gnawed on her bottom lip. "Is everything okay?"

"It's nothing too serious." Maple's forehead scrunched. "At least I don't think it is. Our puppy trainer called me yesterday afternoon while I was at the clinic. She had some concerns about Stetson. You know, the guy with black Lab?"

Adaline nodded. "Lasso."

"The trainer believes he signed up for the class for the wrong reasons." Maple's eyes shifted toward Belle.

Belle swallowed. "Cash said the same thing."

"He did seem awfully focused on you, Belle," Jenna said. "It was hard not to notice."

"The trainer thinks we should refund his tuition money and excuse him from the Comfort Paws program." Maple's eyebrows rose. "Thoughts?"

"That seems a bit harsh. Maybe we should give him another chance," Belle said, even though she knew without a doubt that Cash would've disagreed.

Adaline shook her head. "The trainer is right. In fact, I was planning on bringing this up tonight, but Maple beat me to it. Stetson didn't listen to a word the trainer said all night. He's only there to flirt with Belle."

"It's a little creepy," Jenna added.

"Does he make you uncomfortable, Belle?" Maple shot her a questioning glance.

"A little? Maybe?" She felt bad admitting it. Stetson hadn't harassed her or anything, but his behavior had disrupted class. For that reason alone, she'd been embarrassed.

"He's out, then." Maple gave a firm nod.

"Agreed," Adaline said.

Jenna raised a hand. "Me too. It's decided."

"It feels weird kicking someone out of a volunteer organization. Do we have written rules for this sort of thing?" Belle felt herself frown. "If not, we should."

Always the rule follower...what a joke. If Cash was now her boss, Belle's every waking thought was a borderline HR violation.

"We have stringent rules concerning the dogs' behavior. Why should the human handlers be held to a lesser standard?" Adaline said.

"Excellent point. I'll call Stetson tomorrow and diplomatically explain that we don't think he and Lasso are cut out to be a therapy dog team. I don't want you to worry, Belle. We'll keep this between us, and everything will be fine." Affection glowed in Maple's eyes as she offered Belle a reassuring smile.

"I'm not worried," Belle said, and she meant it.

Not about this, anyway. The doorbell rang, and she stood to go get the pizza delivery with Peaches following right on her heels. *My new temporary career as a nanny is a different story entirely.*

* * *

This was a mistake.

It didn't take long for the error of Cash's ways to fully sink in. A sense of foreboding hung over him the instant he woke up on Saturday morning. He tried to convince himself it had nothing to do with Belle, but the disquiet only seemed to grow worse the closer the time came for him to pick her up and move her things to the mansion. Then, she barely said a word to him during the short drive. Peaches's soft panting in the back seat was the only discernible sound.

"Home sweet home," he said as he set her suitcase down in the guest room closest to Lucy's. "I hope this is okay? There's an attached bathroom with a claw-foot tub, but if you prefer a shower, the guest bath down the hall has a walk-in with a steam setting."

Great. Now he sounded like a real estate agent...or the host of *Lifestyles of the Rich and Famous*. Not helpful in the slightest.

"This is lovely," Belle said with a stiff smile. "The tub is great. Who doesn't love a good bubble bath?"

He wished she sounded more enthusiastic. Instead, he got the feeling she was humoring him, and he didn't like it. Not one bit.

Where had the headstrong woman he knew so well gone? He almost wanted to start an argument with her, just to draw her out of her shell again. He didn't dare, though. He needed Belle this week. More importantly, Lucy needed her. He couldn't screw this up, even though a part of him wondered if he already had, given that Belle's expression closed like a book every time she looked at him.

At least Peaches seemed to approve of her surroundings. While Cash shifted from one foot to the other as he tried to read Belle's mind, the Cavalier took a flying leap onto the king-sized bed and proceeded to writhe around on her back in doggy ecstasy.

"Yeah, this room should work," Belle said, finally cracking a smile.

Cash took his first full inhale of the day. He'd been imagining things, that's all. The near kiss on their ice cream date was messing with his head. He'd shut down afterward at the hospital, but now that Ellis was home and everyone was safe and sound, he could breathe again. They'd get back to where they'd been that night at the picnic table.

His gaze met hers…and held. He loved those luminous eyes of hers as much as he loved her quick wit and her kind heart. But then she swallowed and shifted her attention back toward Peaches, leaving Cash aching for more. The flash of connection between them had been a welcome balm, but it proved to be as fleeting as it was precious.

Cash cleared his throat as Lucy tiptoed into the room, eager to bask in the glow of her new nanny's attention. And boy, did Belle deliver. She had a magic touch with his niece—an easy camaraderie that filled the big house with giggles and laughter. The child was even more taken with Belle than she was with Sparkles.

He tried to give them space. After all, Lucy was the entire reason Belle was here now. So he shut himself in his father's—scratch that—*his* office for the rest of the afternoon to pore over documents in preparation for his meetings this week. He had a pile of status reports to read before his trip to Dallas, as well as a multipage spreadsheet to review before the school board meeting.

The words and numbers swam before his eyes until he finally packed it in. When he ventured downstairs, he found Belle alone in the kitchen with her head bent over a spiral notebook and her dark hair spilling over the pages like a glossy, glorious curtain.

Cash's hands flexed at his sides.

The thank-you present. In the mad dash to get to the hospital last Thursday night, he'd never gotten a chance to give Belle the gift he'd gotten for her. Since then, he'd forgotten all about it. He wasn't even sure where it was now. Somewhere amid all the dog and child paraphernalia in his house—not to mention Ellis's prescription bottles, various ankle wraps and the pillows he carried from room to room to elevate his foot—he'd lost track of it.

Too bad, because now would've been the perfect time to give it to her.

He cleared his throat so she wouldn't think he was trying to spy on her, and she promptly slammed her notebook closed.

"Hey," she said.

"Hey, yourself." He tucked his hands in his pockets and strolled toward the island. The pang in his chest felt strangely wistful as he thought about all the time he'd spent sitting there as a small child. It seemed right to see Belle there now…like she'd fit into his life all along, not just these past few weeks. "I thought it might be time to think about dinner. I can run and grab us all something from Smokin' Joes if that sounds good to you."

"Actually, I've got a casserole in the oven already— King Ranch chicken. I threw it together with some ingredients you already had on hand. I hope that's okay," Belle said, pulling the notebook closer toward her as he approached.

It sounded delicious, but Cash hoped she didn't think he expected her to wait on him hand and foot or anything. They probably should've discussed the parameters of the nanny arrangement at least a little bit. "Thank you. That's a really nice surprise."

"Lucy went up a few minutes ago to change clothes. We're going to take the dogs on a walk while the casserole finishes cooking." Peaches and Sparkles both popped their heads up the instant they heard the word *walk*.

Maybe if Cash had been a dog, he would've picked up on the signs earlier. Sparkles never ceased to amaze him with her ability to read Lucy's moods. When she had a bad day or particularly missed her mom, the Frenchie never left her side. On good days, she followed Lucy around with a stuffed toy hanging from her mouth, ready for whatever adventure the child had in mind.

But Cash wasn't a dog. He was a man—a deeply flawed man who was finally beginning to understand that he'd made a mistake.

"Speaking of dinner, I need to ask you something." Belle clasped her hands together. "I need tomorrow evening off. I always have dinner with my dad on Sundays. It's kind of a family tradition. I know we didn't discuss my work hours, and—"

"Belle, stop. Please." Cash held up a hand.

She was talking to him like he was her employer, not someone who she'd almost kissed a few days ago. And as much as it hurt to admit it, it was all Cash's fault.

She'd warned him on the very first day they'd met, and he still hadn't listened.

Peaches isn't for sale....and just so you know, Mr. McAllister—I'm not for sale, either.

How many times had he replayed that conversation in his head? Too many to count. And yet, mere moments after he'd finally told her how he felt about her—or at least hinted at what an important force she'd become to him—he'd turned around and offered her money.

He should've known better. He'd seen his father throw the McAllister money around enough times to know how it made people feel. Cash had simply wanted her to know he valued her time, but there were better ways to make her feel appreciated than reaching for his wallet. And now she was looking at him like he was her boss...asking permission to have dinner with her family.

"I'm sorry," he said quietly. His hand slid across the island toward hers, stopping short of her fingertips. The space between them felt infinite, even though her hand was right there, mere centimeters away.

"For what?"

He waved a hand between them. "For this. You don't need to ask me for a 'night off.' We're in this together. I promise."

She nodded, but the wary glint in her eyes told him she wasn't entirely convinced.

This was all his fault. Cash had created this mess, and now he didn't know how to undo it. "Of course you'll have dinner with your dad tomorrow night."

She nodded. "Thanks."

"Is your mom still in the picture, or...?" He let his voice drift off so she could fill in the blank.

"She left when I was little." Belle's nose wiggled ever so slightly—just enough for Cash to know that this was a difficult subject. "I haven't really seen her since. But Dad and I are very close. He just got engaged, actually."

"I'd like to meet your dad sometime." Cash inched his hand closer, and when she didn't pull hers away, he wove his fingers through hers.

"Are you angling for an invitation?" Belle tilted her head and laughed.

"Yes, and I'm dead serious."

Her smiled dimmed. "Cash…"

"Just think about it." He winked. If he pressed, she'd never say yes. So he switched gears and nodded at her notebook. "Is that it? It is, isn't it?"

"What?" She blinked, but he knew good and well she knew what he was talking about.

"The children's book you've been writing—the one you mentioned to Lucy a while back."

"Maybe." She bit back a smile. "Lucy and I have been working on our stories together this afternoon. *Sparkles the Marvel* is all finished, and it's very sweet. She's got big plans to show it to you and Ellis tonight at dinner. I also have it on good authority that there will be a reading tonight at bedtime. Sparkles and Peaches are already on notice."

"And what about your story?" He cast a meaningful glance at the spiral.

She sighed and toyed with the edge of the notebook, ruffling its pages with the pad of her thumb. "I'm not sure it will ever be finished. Every time I think it might be ready to submit to agents and publishers, I talk myself out of it."

"Maybe you need a completely unbiased opinion from an objective reader," Cash said. He knew that whatever she'd written would be good. Belle lived and breathed books, especially children's literature.

A quiet smile played on her lips. "Let me guess—you think that reader is you?"

He shrugged one shoulder. "Why not?"

"Because sometimes I think you're not so subjective." Her smiled blossomed, and so did Cash's heart.

Maybe it wasn't too late. Maybe he could still right this ship...or at least get them back to where they'd been before. At the very least, he wanted to be Belle's friend.

It had been a long time since Cash had a true friend. The last person who'd come even close to knowing the real him had been Mallory, and now she was gone.

The grief came back to him, aching and raw. It hollowed him out like it always did, carving away at him until he had nothing left inside. Nothing to feel. Nothing to give. Just the cold emptiness he'd trained himself to embrace after losing his parents.

This was exactly why Cash always kept things on a surface level in his relationships...why he'd never dated more than casually. Opening up to someone made room for all the bad feelings to come rushing in, as well as the good. That's why he'd had such a hard time at the hospital the other night.

But Belle had stayed. And she was still here, in spite of everything, including his demons.

"What if I wasn't subjective at all when it came to you?" he asked as his throat clenched tight. "Would that really be such a bad thing?"

Cash wasn't altogether sure of the answer himself, because he cared about her enough to not want to hurt her. She deserved better, so it was a relief when Belle didn't speculate and instead simply slid the notebook toward him and let him flip through her story.

One sacred page at a time.

Chapter Fourteen

"Take a left at the next stop sign." Belle sat up a little straighter in the passenger seat of Cash's luxury SUV, even though every cell in her body wanted to sink into the buttery leather and disappear.

How on earth had she let Cash talk her into taking him along to family dinner? She still wasn't sure how it happened. One minute, she'd been putting together a King Ranch chicken casserole and contemplating tripling the amount of pepper in Cash's portion (joking... she would never, but it was funny to think about), and the next, he'd worn her down to such an extent that she'd completely caved and shown him her manuscript.

Belle still wasn't sure how it happened. Except he'd done it again—he'd dropped the impenetrable billionaire act, and she'd become putty in his hands. She'd even shown him her notebook, while her very best friends in the world still didn't know it existed.

He'd loved her story, though. And she could tell he wasn't merely giving her work lip service. He'd been specific about why he thought it would resonate with kids, even going so far as to reference several popular children's books that just happened to be some of Belle's favorites. She'd been thoroughly charmed by his knowledge of children's literature. She shouldn't have been so surprised since Lucy had told her weeks ago that her uncle read to her on a regular basis. Hearing about it was one thing, though. Seeing the way he cared for that child was another matter entirely.

Besides, books were Belle's biggest passion. A well-read man—particularly one who could wax poetic about *Skippyjon Jones*, the adorable book series about a Siamese kitten who believes he is a Chihuahua—was clearly her downfall. Hence, his presence beside her as Bluebonnet Acres mobile home park came into view.

"This is where you grew up, Miss Darling?" Lucy asked from the back seat. Her little face was pressed against the window, taking it all in.

"Yes, it is," Belle said, bracing herself for questions about why the houses had wheels.

She wasn't ashamed of where she came from, and her father was the best man she'd ever known. But her feelings about wealth were undeniably complicated, and she knew good and well that Lucy had probably never even seen a trailer in her life.

Kids had zero filter, as Belle knew all too well. Once, at school, her assistant had forgone her usual morning beauty routine because she was experimenting with the natural look—which Belle doubted was even an authentic thing, because she'd recently watched one of her favorite Instagram influencers pile on a dozen makeup products in a tutorial for the "no makeup look"—and the first child to stroll into the library that morning had taken one look at Tess, gasped and blurted, "What happened to your face, Miss Tess?"

Belle hadn't set eyes on Tess's bare complexion since.

"It's so pretty. Look at all the flowers!" Lucy said. She gasped as the hill came into view, covered in a sea of blue petals. "Can we plant bluebonnets at our house, Uncle Cash?"

"I think that's a great idea, pumpkin." Cash gave Belle a sideways glance and whispered. "Any clue how we do that?"

"You spread seeds in the fall—anytime between early September and late November. Given the right conditions, flowers should bloom the following spring," Belle said.

Cash's gaze flicked to the rearview mirror. "It's settled, then. Come autumn, we'll have a bluebonnet seed party. How does that sound, kiddo?"

"Can Miss Darling and Peaches come?" Lucy asked in her singsong voice.

"They're our friends. Of course they're invited." Cash tapped his fingers against the steering wheel, and Belle knew they were just words. They likely didn't mean a thing, but joy welled up inside her at the thought of future plans with him and Lucy.

But first she had to survive this meal with her dad, Cathy and her billionaire friend/boss/possibly-something-more. She wasn't sure what Cash was to her anymore, and she didn't want to think about it. Especially not now as he pulled his fancy SUV into the spot she indicated beside the white picket fence and her father's trailer, with its neat flower boxes filled to overflowing with colorful ranunculus.

"Your dad has quite the green thumb," Cash said as his gaze swept over the property.

Belle relaxed a little, happy to sing Dad's praises. "He does. When I was a little girl, we worked in the garden together all the time. We still do every spring. He's the one who first planted the beds near the entrance to the trailer park."

"I would've given anything at that age to do things like that with my father." Cash's expression turned bittersweet.

"I guess you guys weren't close?"

"No." He blew out a breath. "I'm glad that you and your dad are, though. Family is important."

"It is," Belle said.

He was going to be a great father figure for Lucy. She hoped he knew that. It had been obvious from the start that Cash would do anything for that little girl, but she'd really had no idea how deep that devotion ran or how earnest he was about wanting to give her a happy, well-adjusted childhood.

She felt a little silly now for worrying about bringing them here. Neither Cash nor Lucy seemed fixated on the size of her childhood home. Still, they'd yet to go inside. She couldn't quite imagine Cash sitting on the plaid sofa with the window-unit air conditioner blasting nearby.

But then her dad exited the screen door and waved to her like it was any other Sunday evening, and gratitude filled her soul anew. It was easy to look at Cash's life from the outside and think he'd always had everything. The best things in life were the ones that money couldn't buy, though. The more Belle got to know Cash, the more she realized he might not be rich in the ways that mattered most.

"Hi, Dad." She hugged her father extra tight while she tried to figure out how to introduce Cash and Lucy.

She'd called ahead this morning to make sure he and Cathy didn't mind if she brought guests. Of course they hadn't. She'd been intentionally vague about Cash and Lucy's identity, though. How was she supposed to explain that she'd brought both heirs to the McAllister family fortune to dinner on a whim?

"Hello, sir. It's a pleasure to meet you," Cash said as he shook Dad's hand. "Belle speaks so highly of you."

Dad chuckled. "That's mighty fine to hear, but I'm afraid my daughter's been keeping you a secret, son."

Cathy swatted him with her dish towel as Belle's cheeks went hot.

"Dad, Cathy, this is Cash." There was really no need to mention his last name, so she kept that little nugget to herself. "And this is his niece, Lucy."

"Come on over here, Cash. I hope you don't mind, but I'm a hugger," Cathy said as she pulled Cash into a welcoming embrace.

"I don't mind at all, ma'am," he said, all warmth and charm.

"We're awfully happy to have you. Maurice tells me that Belle has never brought one of her boyfriends to family dinner before." Cathy grinned at Belle. "Is that right?"

She wanted to die on the spot.

Someone, please bury me under the bluebonnets and call it a day.

"It's not like that," she countered. "Cash isn't my boyfriend. He's my b—"

Cash jumped in before she could utter the word *boss*. "We're friends."

"Of course." Cathy's eyes danced. "Friends."

Belle aimed a pleading look at her dad.

He quirked a brow and gave a little shrug. Great. He probably thought she'd taken his speech about loneliness to heart and immediately gone out and found herself a significant other.

As if it was that easy.

"It looks like you're not the only one who's found a special friend," Dad said as he watched Sparkles run circles around Peaches in a nearby patch of bluebonnets. Belle bit her tongue. *Not "special friend"...just "friend." Period.* This dinner was already a fiasco, and the food wasn't even on the table yet. "Who's this little monster?"

"Her name is Sparkles," Lucy said, brow crinkling. "She's not a monster, though. She's a puppy."

"By George, you're right," Dad said as he crouched down to greet Lucy. "And aren't you just as cute as a bug in a rug?"

"A bug?" She scrunched her face and giggled.

"The cute kind," Dad grinned at her. "Like a ladybug. Do you like ladybugs?"

Lucy nodded. "They're pretty."

"They sure are, and they're good for plants, too. They keep the bad kind of bugs away so the flowers stay nice and healthy. I just released a bunch of them in the yard yesterday. I bet if we look really hard, we could still find some hanging around." He held out his hand. "What do you say?"

Lucy plopped her dainty hand into his big, weathered palm. "Yes. Let's find them."

"Keep your eyes out for bunnies, too," Dad said, and Belle was instantly transported back to her own childhood.

"Bunnies!" Lucy's eyes widened, two pools of endless blue, and Belle felt such an affinity for the little girl that her chest felt like it might burst wide open.

Dad felt the same. Belle just knew it, and when he glanced at her over the top of Lucy's head with his mouth curved into a watery smile, it was all the confirmation she needed. There was a certain poetry to bringing Lucy here—like a stanza from the rhyming verse in Belle's notebooks. Even now, a story was spinning its way through her mind, and her fingers itched to jot it down.

Dad cupped his hand around his mouth and whispered into Lucy's ear. "The hills are full of wild rabbits, but they like to hide in the bluebonnets. So you have to look really hard to spot their fluffy white cottontails."

"I bet I can find one!" Lucy cried.

Dad flashed Belle a waggle of his eyebrows as he let the child lead him toward the field that backed up to the white picket fence, and nostalgia tugged hard at her heartstrings. She'd gone bunny hunting plenty of times when she'd been a child, just like she'd checked out books at the library instead of buying them and bought back-to-school clothes at the charity shop instead of the nice children's boutique in the town square. And never once had she realized her childhood was in any way lacking until she'd gotten her first look at her mother's new house.

This is what she left us for, she remembered thinking after she'd finally gotten her driver's license and driven two towns over to see for herself where her mother had gone.

She never breathed a word to her father about what she'd seen that day—the stately manor, the uniformed maid, the young towheaded children she'd spied playing in the backyard. Her mother's upgraded, replacement family in her resplendent new home. Belle had immediately locked the images away in the farthest corner of her mind, cranked the engine and driven back to Bluebonnet in a blazing trail of dust and indignation on the winding country roads.

"And to think you were nervous about inviting me here." Cash prodded her with a playful jab of his elbow, dragging her out of her reverie and back to the present. "I can't imagine anyplace more idyllic to grow up. Lucy will be talking about this for days."

The screen door slammed behind Cathy as she disappeared back inside the trailer, leaving them alone on the wooden deck.

But it all felt too personal now, too intimate, like she couldn't get enough air, even out here under the sweeping Texas sky. She'd flung open a door to Cash, and now there was no slamming it closed. They may as well have been locked in a tiny closet together, feeling their way in the dark.

Her first instinct was to shrink into the corner, as far out of reach as she could get.

"As I recall, you invited yourself." Belle lifted her chin to meet Cash's gaze, but the fight went out of her when her eyes met his. The crinkles in his eyes never failed to knock the chip right off of her shoulder. "And who said I was nervous?"

He gave her nose a gentle tap. "You couldn't hide your feelings if you tried."

This was not boss-employee behavior. Ed Garza had never once looked at her in a way that sent a shiver up her spine.

"I'll have to work on that, then," she said, and for the life of her, she didn't know why it came out all breathy and flirty-sounding.

"Don't. Your brutal honesty is one of the things I like best about you, remember?"

"I'm not sure if that makes you appealing or crazy." She made a show of rolling her eyes, but her pulse was suddenly pounding so hard that he could probably hear it. "Possibly both."

His eyes narrowed. "Did you send out your book proposal like we discussed last night?"

The change of subject was quick enough to make her head spin, but she was glad to be back on somewhat neutral territory, even if it felt weird talking about her literary ambitions out loud like this when she'd been keeping them secret for as long as she could remember.

"I emailed both of the editors I told you about," she said.

She'd shown him her list of dream publishers last night—all small artsy presses attached to Texas universities. Some of Belle's favorite books to win the prestigious Texas Library Association's Bluebonnet Award for excellence in children's literature had been published by the same two editors, both of whom accepted unsolicited submissions from in-state authors.

She wagged a finger at him. "But I'm not holding my breath."

Belle already had a job—one that she loved. Dreaming and hoping for more seemed a bit…dangerous. A few weeks ago, her life had been perfectly content. She'd had the library, her cottage and her dog. Her biggest dream had been building Book Buddies into something bigger, and even that had seemed like a reach. It still did.

Then Cash had turned up, and now she was living in a mansion, sending her children's book out to publishers and spinning more stories in her head. Even worse, she was letting her feelings run away from her, more and more with each passing day.

You've taken the whole Queen of Diamonds thing too far. All of this is a fantasy. She bit the inside of her cheek to really drive the point home. *And don't you forget it.*

Cash crossed his arms. "You're not holding your breath, huh?"

"Nope," she said flatly.

"Then I guess I'll just have to hold mine on your behalf." Cash grinned as he took in a big gulp of air and held it with his cheeks ballooned out in a ridiculous fashion.

Then he strode right past her and walked inside the trailer, barreling into yet another slice of her life…

Almost like he'd belonged there all along.

Chapter Fifteen

Never in his life had Cash imagined he might one day occupy a seat on a board of education. His feelings about his own experience in the school system was complicated, at best, and he'd never been a stellar student. But the McAllister family had been granted a permanent seat on the Bluebonnet School Board years ago, after the McAllister Foundation's memorial endowment that had funded the overhaul of the library at the elementary school.

Cash's mother had volunteered at the library most of her life. Not just writing checks, but doing actual hands-on work, like shelving books, organizing bake sales and book fair fundraisers, and helping tutor students after school for the annual districtwide Reading Rumble. When Cash had been a student at Bluebonnet Elementary in the early years before he'd been enrolled at Kingsley Academy, his mother had been a daily presence at the school. It wasn't until after her death that he'd learned she kept volunteering long after he'd left for boarding school.

When Ellis had sent him clippings from the *Bluebonnet Beacon*, documenting the library's renovation, along with photos of the plaque bearing his mother's name, Cash had sat on the twin bed in his dorm at Kingsley and wondered what it all meant. Had his mother wanted him to stay in Bluebonnet all along? Did she only go along with her father's plan to send him to Kingsley because it was a McAllister family tradition? Had she missed seeing him walk those public school hallways, with their cinderblock walls and pale yellow paint, after he'd gone?

If so, she'd never mentioned it. Not once. Thus, if he'd had any real choice in the matter, Cash would have gladly left the McAllister board seat vacant. What did he know about running a school district, anyway?

But now Lucy was a student at Bluebonnet Elementary. He had a vested stake in what went on there, especially following her dyslexia diagnosis. Cash would've moved heaven and earth if it meant she loved going to school, despite the fact that reading didn't come easy. He was her parent now, he had a seat at the table, and he intended to occupy it.

Even if he felt slightly out of place walking into the Bluebonnet High School auditorium for Monday night's emergency meeting.

"Welcome, Mr. McAllister. We're so pleased to have you join us tonight." The principal of Lucy's school pumped Cash's hand in a double-fisted shake. "Ed Garza, from Bluebonnet Elementary."

Cash recognized him immediately. The principal usually popped out of his office the instant Cash crossed the school's threshold. "Yes, of course. I'm happy to be here."

"Since this meeting was called under the school board's emergency provisions, tonight will be a closed session. Ordinarily the public is welcome to attend." He waved a hand toward the chairs at the front of the auditorium. "I'd be happy to show you to your seat."

Cash nodded. "Thank you."

Ed peppered him with chitchat and introduced Cash to various people as they made their way down the sloped aisle of the auditorium. The walls were lined with trophy cases showing off various awards for sports, academics and extracurricular activities spanning several decades. A tribute to Cam Colden, the current star quarterback of Texas's most beloved NFL team, the Houston Rattlers, occupied a place of honor. Cash paused at the display. If he'd stayed in Bluebonnet instead of leaving when he did, he and Cam would've been in the same graduating class.

He wondered what else about his life would've been different. Would he have developed a closer bond with his mom and dad if he'd grown up in their family home instead of a dormitory? Would losing them have hurt even more?

He knew this: Bluebonnet would've rallied around him and Mallory after the accident. This town took care of its own. The house would've been packed with flowers and casseroles. Teachers at school would've handled him with kid gloves. Cash would have had time and space to grieve.

To heal.

Cash's chest filled with a bittersweet ache at the thought of what could have been, and he couldn't help wondering if Belle might have had a place in that imaginary life. He liked to think so. He liked to imagine sharing dinners with her father back when they were teenagers, scraping plates and washing dishes side by side in the trailer's galley-style kitchen. Then sneaking off to the rolling hills beyond the white picket fence at sunset, bluebonnets swallowing their feet while the light turned liquid gold around them and they shared their very first kiss.

He couldn't seem to get the image out of his head. It had burrowed its way in his consciousness until he it felt more like a memory than a daydream.

But now he was trapped in this present reality, where a lifetime of losses had chipped away him, turning him into the last thing he'd ever wanted to be—his father. Cash was trying to change. He really was, but every time he took two tentative steps forward, he immediately followed it up with a giant backward step. Like throwing money at Belle at the hospital and asking her to be Lucy's nanny instead of just talking to her and asking for help.

It was a move straight out of Arthur McAllister's playbook—take control of the situation by any means necessary. Much to Cash's shame, it had worked.

He wished he could believe in a world where he could loosen his grip on the people around him, to embrace his feelings instead of shutting down every time the block of ice he called a heart began to melt.

But that world was a fantasy in every sense of the word. Growing up right here in Bluebonnet wouldn't have changed anything. Fate would've caught up with Cash eventually—it always did. His sister still would've gotten sick. No alternate reality could eradicate cancer. Mallory wouldn't have lived to see her little girl grow up, no matter what. Cash would've still ended up in this same moment, in this same room. So what did it really matter?

His body felt leaded as he took his seat and the meeting was called to order.

"Good evening, everyone." A woman with white-blond hair that flipped up at the ends in a stiff, shellacked helmet took her place behind the podium on stage. "For those who are new here—" her gaze flicked in Cash's direction, and her smile broadened "—I'm Donna Bradley, the president of the Bluebonnet School Board."

Cash gave a little head bow of acknowledgment.

"Thank you all for coming to this emergency meeting. We're here tonight to approve various changes to the district budget, as well as set the agenda for the final school board meeting of the academic year, which will take place in two weeks' time. I trust everyone received the spreadsheet our board secretary sent out via email last week outlining recent maintenance issues resulting in a deficit to the operating budget?"

The people around Cash nodded, as if by rote. He had a feeling he was the only person in the room who'd pored over the columns of numbers until they'd finally made sense...

Or partial sense, if he was being nitpicky. He understood the specific needs of the school, but the paperwork had been vague about where the extra funds were coming from. The new intercom at the school was being purchased with money from the "extracurriculars" fund, but didn't specify which, if any, extracurriculars were being cut.

Also, the email hadn't mentioned a thing about approving an agenda for the final meeting of the school year.

"The funds have already been distributed, and the intercom system is being installed while the school is closed for spring break. In accordance with the district bylaws, the secretary and I—who make up the executive board—approved the expenditure. A full board vote is now required to officially transfer the line item from the extracurriculars column to the column representing the operating budget, which traditionally covers school building maintenance." Donna Bradley pushed her glassed farther up on the bridge of her nose and scanned the crowd. "Can I get a motion to approve?"

Cash stood, least a raised hand get misinterpreted. "Excuse me."

The board president's brow furrowed. "Mr. McAllister? Did you wish to make a motion?"

"No, actually. I have questions, and I'm guessing the rest of the board might as well." He glanced around, and none of the others met his gaze.

Or not, he thought as doubt crept in.

He was new here, and for all intents and purposes, this group had clearly come together to rubber-stamp something that had already been done. The easiest course of action would be to just fall in line and vote accordingly.

But Cash had never been a rubber-stamp kind of guy, and he had no intention of changing that anytime soon.

"Ask away, Mr. McAllister." Donna Bradley's smile went tense around the edges.

Around him, the other board members settled into their chairs with reluctant resignation.

Get comfortable. Cash unfolded his printed copy of the aforementioned spreadsheet. His carefully written notes filled the margins on either side of the ledger. *We're going to be here a while.*

"I'm not sure you should trust me with this." Belle eyed the pastry bag that Adaline had just handed her and turned it over in her hands, her past spring break baking experience coming back to her in a wave of fresh humiliation.

"Don't be silly. We're not at Cherry on Top." Adaline waved a hand at their surroundings, pausing to cast a longing glance at Cash's fancy high-end oven. "We're just baking for fun. Right, Lucy?"

"Right." Lucy gave a nod, and the paper chef's hat that Adaline had brought over—along with all the baking supplies for homemade Oreos—slid so far down her forehead that it covered her eyes. Unfazed, she pushed it back in place and resumed lining up dark chocolate cookies in a neat row, ready for Belle to pipe the cream filling.

Belle had decided that a girls' night was in order since Cash was busy with the school board meeting. As soon as she'd told Adaline how much Lucy loved Oreos, Adaline volunteered to invent a recipe and come over to Cash's house to teach the little girl how to make a homemade version of the classic cookie. Belle wasn't sure who was more excited—Lucy or Ellis. Ellis had volunteered to be the official taste-tester and was sitting with his ankle propped up on a kitchen chair, supervising their efforts.

"Also, Lucy and I mixed up the filling, so there's no possible way you can mess this up. All you have to do is position the pastry bag over the cookie and squeeze." Adaline took the pastry bag and demonstrated on the first dark chocolate cookie in Lucy's lineup. "See? Squeeze and swirl."

"Squeeze and swirl," Lucy echoed from her place between Belle and Adaline, where she knelt on a chair pulled up to the kitchen island, which was dusted in a generous layer of flour and cocoa.

The last time the dogs had ambled into the room, they'd promptly sneezed in unison and walked back out. Since then, they'd positioned themselves in the hallway, where they had a clear view of the humans. Peaches and Fuzzy flanked Sparkles on either side like fluffy cinnamon-and-white bookends.

"You make it look far easier than it is," Belle said, examining the perfect coil of filling Adaline had just made with a quick flick of her wrist. She was pretty sure she still had bad memories from her last experience with a pastry bag.

Adaline placed a plain dark chocolate cookie on top of the filling, and voilà! The end result looked just like the real deal. Only better, because it was made from scratch.

"You can do it, Miss Darling. Maybe Peaches could help you, like she helps me at Book Buddies?" Lucy gazed up at her with wide, innocent eyes.

"That's a very sweet suggestion, but chocolate isn't good for dogs, remember?" Belle scrunched her face.

"I remember. No Oreos for Sparkles." Lucy gave her head an exaggerated shake. "Ever."

"That's right, pumpkin. That also means more cookies for Uncle Ellis." Ellis winked, and the child collapsed into giggles.

Belle's heart clenched. This nanny thing was becoming harder by the day, and not just because she was living in such close proximity to Cash. The more time she spent with Lucy, the more she dreaded the end of the week and her return to reality.

I could get used to this. She squeezed the pastry bag, and a blob of sugary frosting missed the cookie by a mile. *Not the baking part, but the togetherness. The* family *part.*

She reminded herself that this wasn't real. It was a paycheck. Cash wasn't hers and neither was Lucy.

"I want you to do the filling part, because that means we all made the cookies together. It's okay that you didn't get it right the first time, Miss Darling," the little girl said, and to Belle's horror, her eyes grew misty. "You can just try again."

Adaline's eyes narrowed as her gaze slid over to Belle.

"You're right, and you know what? I think you should call me Belle instead of Miss Darling." Belle reached over and tapped the tip of Lucy's nose, leaving a dab of frosting behind.

Lucy brightened. "Really?"

"Really. We might have to go back to Miss Darling at school, but we'll worry about that then, okay?"

"Okay." Lucy beamed at her. "Belle."

Belle could feel Adaline's curious gaze on her as she redirected her attention to the Oreos. She made a passable swirl, and Lucy lifted her little arms in victory as Ellis let loose with an earsplitting whoop.

"See? It's really not so bad when you let yourself loosen up a little, is it?" Adaline gave her a meaningful look, and Belle wasn't altogether sure if they were still talking about baking anymore.

Later that night, after Adaline had packed up her dog, her pastry bags and her ultra-Dutch processed cocoa—whatever that was—and gone home, Belle made sure Ellis took his meds and helped Lucy get cleaned up and ready for bed. Then they arranged some of the cookies on a platter to surprise Cash and took turns reading storybooks to Peaches and Sparkles while they waited for him to get home.

But soon, the minutes turned to hours, and Lucy's eyelids got heavier and heavier. Sparkles's big round head bobbed as the Frenchie fought sleep.

"I think it's time to turn out the light," Belle whispered. She pressed a gentle kiss to Lucy's temple, and when she didn't beg for "just five more minutes" of story time, Belle knew she'd made the right call.

She tucked the covers up to Lucy's chin, and by the time Belle had crossed the room and reached for the knob to pull the door closed, the child's chest was already rising and falling in a sleepy rhythm.

Belle tiptoed down the hall and made her way downstairs to the sitting room. Peaches and Sparkles followed close on her heels. A quick glance at the antique tabletop clock that sat on one of the dark wood-paneled bookshelves lining all four walls of the cozy room confirmed what Belle had suspected.

It was after nine o'clock already. Where was Cash?

Belle had only been to a handful of school board meetings, but none of them had ever run this late. Then again, those had been run-of-the-mill public meetings. This one was an emergency meeting to discuss the districtwide budget problem.

Ed had made it sound as if everything had been figured out ahead of time, though. Now that girls' night was over and Belle was alone with her thoughts in the quiet mansion, she couldn't help but wonder if something had gone wrong.

She grabbed a blanket from the back of the sofa and wrapped it around her shoulders. Good grief, it was soft—soft and lush. Cashmere, probably. Not everything about this house was terrible. In fact, staying here was growing on her.

Stop. She patted the sofa cushion and the dogs hopped up and settled in beside her. *It's only temporary.*

Right. Next week, she'd be back in her beloved library at school. After work, she and Peaches would go home to her quiet cottage near the town square. Everything would go back to normal, just as it should.

She picked up the remote control and aimed it at the television. Why on earth did anyone need this many channels? There was simply no end to the scrolling. She finally settled on an old black-and-white *Bewitched* rerun—comfort television at its finest—as her cell phone pinged with an incoming text message.

Belle reached for it, fully expecting it to be from Cash. Instead, Ed Garza's name lit up the screen.

She sat up straighter and scanned the words in the text bubble.

Ed: Just ended the longest school board meeting on record and wanted to be the first to let you know that the Lone Star Reading Rumble will go forth as originally planned.

Belle gasped. Finally, some good news for the library and Bluebonnet Elementary. It felt too good to be true.

Before she could tap out a response, another text from Ed arrived.

Ed: Next time you see Cash McAllister, you might want to thank him.

Belle pressed a hand to her chest. So Cash had pulled out his checkbook again, and this time, he'd found someone who was more than happy to take his money. He'd saved the day in true McAllister fashion.

Belle would definitely thank him. Ed hadn't needed to prompt her to express her gratitude, but she appreciated the heads-up. Who knew if Cash would even mention his financial contribution, considering how uncomfortable she felt every time he reached for that wallet of his?

She was happy for her students, though. The Reading Rumble was safe...for now, at least. And she was truly grateful, even though this surprise development was yet another reminder that she and Cash were from two completely different worlds. Different *stratospheres*. She didn't fit into his any more than he belonged in her dad's double-wide at Bluebonnet Acres.

Cash hadn't batted an eye when they'd pulled up to the trailer park on Sunday, though. He'd been nothing but gracious. He'd treated her dad and Cathy like they were his equals. Since Belle had specifically not mentioned the last name McAllister, her father hadn't even realized who Cash was. They'd done things like pick flowers and oohed and aahed over Cathy's Dr. Pepper cake. The only one who seemed hung up on things like money and class differences had been...

Belle.

"Hey, there."

She jumped at the sound at Cash's tired voice. How long had he been standing there in the entrance to the family room while she'd been staring at the text messages from Ed?

"Oh." She met his gaze, and despite the fresh wave of shame coursing through her, Belle's heart did a somersault. "Hi."

Peaches and Sparkles blinked sleepy eyes open. Then both pups leapt off the sofa to greet Cash in a flurry of wags and squeaky dog yawns.

He bent down to lavish them with attention, and Belle bit her lip. The three of them painted an awfully adorable picture. Surrounded by dogs, with the knot of his tie loosened and his shirt sleeves folded up to the elbows, Cash looked remarkably unguarded. She loved seeing him here, at home, where he could be himself instead of whatever everyone expected a McAllister to be.

Even Belle had pasted her expectations onto him without getting to know him first. It must happen all the time.

Cash looked up at her and the corners of his mouth turned up. "Sorry about the late hour. The meeting ran long. Was Lucy terribly upset that I didn't get home in time to tell her goodnight?"

"Don't worry. We read to the dogs, and she fell asleep with a smile on her face. I promise." Belle motioned toward the platter of cookies on the coffee table. "Adaline came over, and we had a girls' night. She taught us how to bake homemade Oreos."

Surprise splashed across Cash's face as he eyed the cookies. "Homemade? Wow, I bet Lucy loved that."

Belle lifted a single eyebrow. "For the record, so did Ellis."

"No doubt." Cash chuckled, reached for a cookie and came to sit down beside her.

He was a chaste foot or two away, but it was still too close for Belle, who was clearly experiencing some sort of gratitude-induced delusion, because before she could stop herself, she was thinking about how nice it felt to be his safe place…his home.

Sometimes I think you are *the circle.*

She wished he'd never said those words, because now she couldn't get them out of her head.

"There's a tall glass of milk in the fridge with your name on it." Belle stood. "I'll go get it for you."

He caught her wrist, wrapping one of his big hands around it like a bracelet before she could move. "You don't need to wait on me, Belle. Stay and chat for a bit? Please?"

"Sure." She tucked her hair behind her ears and sat back down, doing her best to ignore the tingle along her skin where he'd touched her.

Cash bit into his cookie and moaned. "These are incredible. What are they made with? Unicorn tears?"

"I'm afraid you'll have to ask Adaline and Lucy." Belle held up her hands. "All I did was pipe the filling. Baking isn't my strong suit."

"But it was your idea, wasn't it?" He popped the rest of the cookie into his mouth and nodded without waiting for her to answer. "I hope you know that you've officially ruined store-bought cookies for this household. RIP aisle three of Bluebonnet General."

Belle laughed. "You've committed the floor plan of the grocery store to memory?"

"What can I say?" Cash shrugged. "We go through a lot of Oreos."

"Lucy really enjoyed making them. You might have a future baker on your hands. She was so sweet and encouraging, too. You should've heard the pep talk she gave me when I balked at participating."

Cash's gaze slid sideways toward her, and his eyes went soft. "She learned that from you, you know. Her sessions with you and Peaches at school have had more of an impact than you realize."

It was possibly the nicest thing he could've said to her. "You think?"

"One hundred percent." He reached toward the platter and paused as his attention snagged on the television. Then he pointed at the screen with one of the sandwich cookies. "This is it. This is the show."

Belle glanced at the screen as Elizabeth Montgomery magically cleaned her messy kitchen with a twitch of her nose. Now that was a skill that could come in handy. "*Bewitched*? It's a classic."

"Your nose wiggle is just like hers," Cash said, and his smile went tender enough to turn her knees to water.

"My dad and I used to watch this all the time when I was a kid. The classic channel was one of the only things we could pick up without a satellite dish, but I didn't care. I loved this show."

"That sounds like a nice memory." His eyes shimmered with a sadness that Belle could only interpret as homesickness. Or maybe even envy.

This wasn't supposed to be happening. She was supposed to be helping him out for a week and then moving on with her life…not feeling more and more like they could actually have something real.

"Ed texted me the good news earlier. Sounds like you were the big hero tonight." She beamed at him.

Confusion clouded his features for a beat. "Hero?"

"I don't even know how to thank you for what you did. You saved the Reading Rumble."

He shook his head. "I'm not sure if I'd put it that way, exactly."

"Your donation is lifesaver. Honestly."

"Is that what Ed said?" Cash asked as his gaze dropped to the cookie in his hand.

"Not in so many words, but it's the truth." Belle's stomach squirmed. This conversation was beginning to feel awkward, and she wasn't sure why.

She chalked it up to the fact that they were talking about money again. Every time they did, it was like throwing a sopping wet blanket into the mix.

"Really, Cash. I mean it. Thank you for your generous financial contribution." She rested a tentative hand on his knee.

He covered her hand with his, and Belle forgot to breathe for a beat when he looked at her like he wanted to tell her something…something she desperately wished might restore the intimacy that had been percolating between them just moments before.

But then Sparkles nudged her way between them, and she crawled into Cash's lap. He let go of Belle's hand.

"I'm happy I could help," he said in a tone that was low, soft and oddly melancholy in contrast to the sentiment.

Then he gathered Sparkles into his arms and bid Belle goodnight while the television flickered in the darkness, casting shadows of its magical, make-believe world until she fell asleep right there under the cashmere throw and dreamed of a life she was too afraid to admit she really wanted.

Chapter Sixteen

Belle tried her best to give Cash a wide berth for the next few days, which was surprisingly difficult considering the space they shared was roughly equivalent to the square footage of Versailles. Late Tuesday night, she bumped into him in the kitchen while she'd been filling a kettle for the elderflower and chamomile tea she always made when she couldn't sleep. He'd been dressed in blue flannel pajamas that brought out the color of his eyes, and her toes had curled in her fuzzy slippers while the kettle whistled away. The sound hadn't even registered in her consciousness.

Since then, he'd shown up every night for her tea ritual, and they'd spent long sleepy hours with their hands wrapped around steaming mugs, whispering in the darkness. It was easier to share things with him when the rest of the world was asleep, almost like she was sleepwalking and the late-night conversations were nothing but sweet, rose-tinted dreams. Then, come morning, they'd share a secret smile or Cash would reference something she'd told him while they ate pancakes at the kitchen island with Lucy and Ellis, and it would all come rushing back.

She was falling deeper and deeper into this fantasy life, and it *really* needed to stop…starting today.

"Where's Cash?" Adaline looked past Belle, toward the open barn doors, as she and Peaches arrived at training class Thursday evening. "I expected you guys to arrive together since you're roomies and all now."

"That's not what we are," Belle said as she plunked her backpack full of training supplies down on the welcome table. Tonight, she and Adaline were charged with recording the preferred sizes for the therapy dog teams' Comfort Paws gear—shirts for the humans and harnesses for the dogs—as the students filed in for class. "I'm the hired help, and he's the lord of the manor."

Adaline rolled her eyes. "I see someone's been bingeing *Downton Abbey* again."

Belle shook her head. "Nope. *Bridgerton.*"

Queen Charlotte's over-the-top wigs were the only thing that could distract her from thoughts of Cash as she tried to fall asleep after their late-night tea parties. She'd breezed through two full seasons already.

Adaline's brow creased in concentration. "I don't remember any of the wealthy characters in *Bridgerton* having a secret love affair with a member of the household staff."

"That's exactly my point," Belle said.

Everyone knew their place. Period. Nannies didn't bring earls or dukes home to meet their fathers, and male aristocrats didn't hang out in the kitchen late at night with the servants.

Belle was fully aware that Cash would willingly poke his eyes out before he ever referred to her as a servant, but that was beside the point.

Adaline swatted at her a sample Comfort Paws shirt. "Oh my gosh, would you stop? Cash seems like a great guy. I really don't understand the problem here."

"It's complicated." At least that's what Belle continually told herself as spring break marched on.

Just a few more days. You can do it. Then you'll never have to see Cash in those inexplicably attractive pj's again.

What was it about those pajamas, anyway? She'd never realized she had a thing for blue plaid flannel.

It's not the pj's themselves. It's what they represent. They're dad *pajamas, and when he wears them, all you see is a man who's nurturing and kind...a man whose constancy you can depend on.*

"It's really not. You care about him, and he thinks you hung the moon. Sounds simple enough to me," Adaline said with all the blissful naivety of a woman fully in love with her partner.

"I adore you, but you're entirely wrong." Belle forced a smile as she wrestled Peaches into her Comfort Paws harness. "And can we please stop talking about Cash? He's going to be here any minute. We took separate cars because he's heading straight to the airport in Austin after class. He has a red-eye flight to Dallas later. He's got meetings there tomorrow for the McAllister Family Foundation."

Then he'd be back on Saturday, they'd share one more night under the same roof, and *poof*, spring break would be over at last.

Belle couldn't wait. Next Monday would be the first day back at school, plus the final school board meeting of the year was scheduled for that evening. She'd finally have an opportunity to present her Book Buddies program and get it approved as part of the curriculum.

All she wanted to do was concentrate on her future, even though somewhere in the back of her head, she felt a little bit like Cinderella as the hands on the clock crept closer and closer to midnight. At least when her dreamy existence turned into a pumpkin as the clock struck twelve, she could depend on Adaline to make pumpkin pie.

Figuratively speaking, of course.

"Since you, Lucy and Ellis will be on your own, do you want me to come over tomorrow night? We can bake again. I promised Lucy we'd do unicorn blondies next," Adaline said as she arranged the red sample shirts in ascending order according to size.

Belle straightened the collar of the extra large. "What's a unicorn blondie?"

"It's a regular blondie but topped with rainbow sprinkles." Adaline grinned. "Loads of them."

"I'm sure she will. It's a date," Belle said. Another girls' night was the only sort of date she was interested in.

That's what she thought, anyway, until Cash strode inside the barn with Sparkles walking in perfect heel position alongside him at the end of her leash.

She went all swoony at the sight of him, as if she hadn't just seen him thirty minutes prior. Also, how had he managed to get Sparkles leash-trained so quickly? Had he and his French bulldog been practicing for class when she wasn't looking?

"Hi, Cash. Welcome back to class," Adaline said

brightly. "Wow, you and Sprinkles are really looking good tonight. Right, Belle?"

Belle cut her friend a look.

"What? I meant good in the dog-training sense." Adaline's lip twitched. "Obviously."

"Obviously," Cash echoed. A grin tugged at his lips.

"We're asking everyone to choose their shirt size before class starts, along with the proper harness size for your dog." Belle waved at the display on the welcome table, doing her best to steer the conversation toward dogs. Or piqué knit cotton. Or basically anything other than his handsome face—which, for the record, was the first thing she'd zeroed in on when she'd spied him walking toward her. Not his admirable leash skills.

"Okay, let's take a look," he said as he inspected one of the harnesses.

"We can measure Sparkles if that helps." Belle reached for the measuring tape and patted the table in front of her. "Just put her up here and I'll check her neck, length and girth."

Cash hoisted the Frenchie onto the table. She wiggled her back end with excitement and her paws tap-danced on the smooth laminate surface.

"Look at that cutie-pie," Maple said as she approached with Lady Bird glued to her side like a furry golden shadow. She cupped Sparkles's sweet face in her hands and smiled up at Cash. "How does it feel to be our star pupil, Cash? You and Sparkles are going to make a great therapy dog team and do so much good in the community when all this is over. We're all so happy to have you in our group."

"Thanks. We wouldn't be here if it wasn't for Belle,

though. She and Peaches are quite an inspiration." His eyes glowed with affection, and once again, Belle's legs went wobbly.

Back when he'd first announced his intention to adopt a dog and join the Comfort Paws program, Belle never would've imagined anything close to this scenario taking place. Sometimes she wondered what else she'd been wrong about.

"They are, aren't they?" Maple wrapped an arm around Belle's shoulder and lowered her voice. "And speaking of you, Belle, I don't want you to worry about class tonight. I took care of that matter that we discussed last Friday night. It's done. Jenna invited Cam to come keep an eye on things, just in case."

At first, Belle didn't understand what Maple meant. So much had happened during the past six days that she'd forgotten all about Stetson. Although, now that she knew he wouldn't be at class this evening, relief skittered through her. It was as if her body had been on high alert without her even realizing it.

"Great. Thanks so much." She glanced at the entrance to the barn just in time to see Cam settling by big double doors with his hands clasped in front of him. She'd never imagined that a dog training class might need a bouncer, but there was a first time for everything. "Having Cam here might be overkill, don't you think?"

"Better safe than sorry." Maple gave Sparkles one last pat. "Gotta run and finish getting set up for class. We're getting the dogs acclimated to medical equipment tonight. Ford and Jace have both volunteered to role-play as patients. I need to grab a walker and wheelchair.

Good to see you again, Cash. I can't wait to see you and Sparkles in action tonight."

"Back at you," Cash said, but his eyes never left Belle, and there was a sudden seriousness to his tone that even Sparkles seemed to notice. The bulldog's forehead creased, and her ears pricked forward.

"Oh, shoot. I forgot to get the fanny packs and crossbody sling bags out. Each team gets to pick one to receive at graduation from training class, and we're supposed to mark down the choices. I think it's probably a good idea for them see the bags in person." Adaline pushed her chair back and handed Fuzzy's leash to Belle. "Can you watch Fuzzy for a second? I'll be right back."

"Sure thing." Belle took the leash. Fuzzy made a beeline straight for Peaches and the two Cavaliers sniffed each other, tails wagging furiously.

"Belle." Cash cleared his throat.

She glanced up and found him frowning down at her, that chiseled jaw of his as hard as granite. "Yes?"

"What's going on?" He arched a stern eyebrow.

"What do you mean?" she asked, although she was pretty sure she knew where this line of questioning was going. She just didn't want to make a big deal out of it, because Maple had already taken care of things.

"You know what I mean. Why is the star quarterback of the Houston Rattlers guarding the door?"

Belle glanced at Cam, smiling and greeting dog teams as they started to file inside the barn for class. She needed to cut this discussion short before more people checked in at the welcome desk. "Because he's Jenna's fiancé."

"Belle." Cash let out a measured breath. "I know I've

told you how fond I am of your headstrong streak, but I need you to be honest with me right now. There's something going on. What is it?"

"Fine, I'll tell you, but don't go bananas or anything." Belle held up a hand. He was already getting that control freak look on his face—the one he'd had when he'd first stalked into the school library like he owned the place. "The girls thought Stetson might have signed up for training class for the wrong reasons. Maple called him and explained that the instructor felt like he and his dog weren't a good fit for the Comfort Paws program."

"I *knew* that guy was trouble," Cash said through gritted teeth. He looked like he wanted to lasso Stetson with his bare hands, pun very much intended.

"There's nothing to worry about. He won't be back. End of story." Talking about it was making Belle nervous again, and she'd hardly given the matter any thought whatsoever since last Friday.

Cash's gaze darted to the barn door and back. The look he gave her was so searing that she felt it down to her toes. "End of story? Then why is there a pro NFL player here to protect you?"

"You heard Maple. It's out of an abundance of caution." She ran the measuring tape around Sparkles's midsection in an effort to get things back on track. Class was scheduled to start in less than twenty minutes. "You'll need to get a medium-size harness for Sparkles. I'm writing that down."

Cash gathered his dog into his arms, but still made no move to go take a seat in the training arena. "I don't like this."

I don't either, Belle thought. He didn't get to go into

overprotective mode and act like he was her boyfriend when he wasn't. Belle wasn't sure what they were, exactly. And she hadn't realized until just this second that the uncertainty was tearing her apart. Not just the uncertainty, but the vulnerability—the aching knowledge that when whatever they had ended, she'd get hurt. It was inevitable at this point, especially when he looked at her the way he was doing right now. Like she meant something to him. Like she was someone rare and precious. Like he couldn't bear that thought of anything bad happening to her. That single sharp look was all it took for everything to become crystal clear.

Belle had spent her entire life doing everything she could to ensure that no one could make her feel as unwanted and unworthy as her mother had. The easiest way to avoid that kind of pain was to keep her emotions—her deepest, darkest wants and needs, every fleeting hope and dream—in check. Be strong. Be brave. Be perfectly content with her own company.

For years, it had worked.

And then she'd adopted Peaches. Maybe that was the first step in her undoing. For the first time in her life, she'd loved another living soul with unabashed adoration. And Peaches had loved her right back with the kind of unconditional love she'd never known she needed.

Then she'd met Cash. And Lucy. And somehow, she'd let them work their way into the crack in her composure that Peaches had opened up. Now her heart felt full to bursting, even though her time as part of their little family had an expiration date. As much as she'd tried to deny it, that's what the past six days had felt like: a family. Belle had forgotten how nice that feeling was, because she hadn't experienced it in such a long while. Only this time, she'd gotten to see it from the other side. She wasn't a child anymore. She was a grown woman. The swell of affection she had for Cash and Lucy had given her a tiny taste of what her mother had left behind all those years ago, and now she understood it even less.

What was wrong with her that made her so profoundly unlovable? And when would Cash see it?

That's why she couldn't wait to move out of his house and get back to her normal life. She wanted to go ahead and get the pain over with before the thought of it became unbearable.

She wanted him…desperately.

And the only thing she wanted more was to not want him at all.

Training class was a disaster.

Twice the instructor had to repeat herself because Cash had been too busy watching the door to hear what was going on. He couldn't focus and neither could Sparkles, and Cash was all too aware that lackluster performance was one hundred percent his fault.

When Belle had come over to help him get the house set up for the Frenchie, she'd recommended a few books about puppy-raising, and Cash had subsequently ordered them and read each one cover to cover. The paperbacks were still in a stack on his nightstand with dog-eared pages and cracked spines. There was no way he'd adsorbed everything he'd read, but he knew enough now to understand that dogs possessed exceptional emotional intelligence—especially dogs that were well suited for work as service animals or therapy dogs. Any stress that he was carrying undoubtedly traveled straight down the leash to his canine partner.

And it showed.

The role-play exercises were especially awkward and uncomfortable, because Cash could feel himself bristling against the rising panic in his gut, just like he had at the hospital the night that Ellis broke his ankle. Only this time, it was worse. That night, all the facts had been accessible to him. He'd known exactly what he was dealing with, and while he didn't like to think about what would've happened if Ellis's injury had been worse, the logical side of his brain knew that everyone he loved was safe and sound. For a moment, he'd let his intuitive side take over—the side that made him react as if he were about to lose his sister or his parents all over again. But even in that anxious state, he'd never had to grapple with the unknown.

Tonight was different. He'd suspected all along that Stetson had ulterior motives for joining the Comfort Paws class, and now that he knew others had picked up on the same bad vibes, Cash was a mess. He wanted to protect Belle and hold her at arm's length, all at the same time. Anything to quell the sickening feeling in the pit of his stomach at the thought of that idiot making her feel uncomfortable...or even threatened.

He appreciated Maple being proactive and inviting Cam to watch over class, even though there'd been no outward sign of Stetson retaliating against Belle or the group for being excused from the Comfort Paws program. But Cash's thoughts—and worse, his *feelings*—were running wild. All he wanted to do was make it stop.

"Rough night, huh?" Maple approached him after

class with a sympathetic smile. Lady Bird dipped her head to sniff Sparkles, and her bushy gold tail swished back and forth. "Don't let it get you down. We all have them. That's how dog training goes. It's not a linear process. Some days will be incredibly encouraging and others not so much."

"Thanks for saying that," Cash said, even though it was hard to imagine Lady Bird being anything but perfect.

"I'm not just saying it. It's true. You and Sparkles have a close bond. Anyone can see it. You two are something special." She tapped a fingertip against her right temple. "You just need to stop overthinking. Your relationship with your dog doesn't come from your head, it comes from your heart."

And there it was in nutshell—the entire reason why Belle had been right when she'd tried to discourage him from joining Comfort Paws. Last week had been a fluke. He was going to be terrible at this.

"Easier said than done," he muttered under his breath.

"Don't worry. I have faith in you." Maple's eyes shifted toward Belle, who'd barely looked him after their tense exchange before class started. "We all do."

Cash wasn't so sure about that. He'd handled the situation badly and gone all caveman on Belle again. It was no wonder she was avoiding him.

"See you next week," Maple said with a wave. Then she and Lady Bird moved on to chat with another one of the trainees—a petite woman with a corgi named Queen Elizabeth.

Cash tried to take Maple's words to heart as he packed up his training supplies. The whole reason he'd joined this class was to give Lucy a reading education assistance dog of her very own. He'd had no interest whatsoever in doing real volunteer work, beyond what was required to graduate from class and get Sparkles certified. The McAllisters had a long history of supporting the community through financial contributions. Money was an important resource.

But all the money in the world couldn't have inspired Lucy to love books the way that Peaches had. Cash would've done anything to get his hands on that dog in the beginning. But adopting a dog of his own and seeing all the work and preparation that went into training a therapy animal had given him a new appreciation for the way the dogs and the handlers served others. This kind of work was a labor of love. A blessing—not just to the people on the receiving end of the visits, but to the pups and handlers, too.

Cash couldn't help but think he needed that kind of fulfillment in his life…that kind of connection to others. For a while there, he'd started to think it was possible. Now, he wasn't so sure. He hadn't realized quite how much he wanted it until tonight, when it seemed too out of reach. He'd let his dog down, and he had the unsettling feeling that he'd let Belle down, too.

The stiff smile on her face when she came to get Sparkles so he could leave straight for the airport in Austin all but confirmed it.

"I'm sure you're in a rush. Sparkles can hang out with Peaches and me while we help Maple, Adaline and Jenna straighten up," she said. Her face remained perfectly expressionless.

Cash was indeed in a hurry. His flight left at 10:00 p.m., and Austin was a good ninety-minute drive from Bluebonnet.

He couldn't seem to hand over Sparkles's leash, though. "I think it might be a good idea if I stayed."

He hadn't planned on speaking those words out loud. They just slipped right out before he could stop them.

"What?" Her eyes bore into him. "Why?"

Because there are things I need to say to you...things we need to say to each other...

She huffed out a breath. "This is because of Stetson, isn't it?"

And yes, that too.

"I'd feel better if you weren't alone," he said tersely.

"News flash—I won't be. Ellis and Lucy will be there." She waved a hand at Peaches and Sparkles wrestling at their feet. Their leashes were on the verge of becoming hopelessly tangled.

Kind of like every facet of Cash's life was becoming intertwined with his nanny's.

He crossed his arms. "Lucy is a seven-year-old child, and Ellis is can barely get around."

Belle's eyes blazed. "Ellis is doing great, and you know it."

True, otherwise Cash wouldn't have agreed to let him babysit while he and Belle went to training class. But watching a Disney movie and eating popcorn in the den with his foot propped up and Lucy snug a blanket fort for a couple hours wasn't exactly the equivalent to being able to help Belle if Stetson showed up.

"I'd like to stay," Cash repeated.

He'd deal with the other officers of the foundation later. His name was on the letterhead, not theirs. This dashing back and forth to Dallas wasn't going to work. If his and Lucy's home base was going to be here in Blue-bonnet, he needed to shut the door on the past. All of it.

"Tell me why, then." This time, when she squared her shoulders and glared at him, there was a challenge in her gaze...just like the day at the library when she'd called him out for breaking the rules and not taking the time to check in at the school's front office for a name tag. Except this time, there was more at stake. "The real reason."

Because I'm falling in love with you.

Now was the time to say it.

But they were standing in a barn filled with people and dogs. They needed privacy for this. That had to be the reason why the words just wouldn't come.

"Have a nice trip," she said as she bent to untangle the dog leashes, grabbing hold of the one that belonged to Sparkles in the process. "Goodbye, Cash."

Then she walked away with the Cavalier and the Frenchie trotting alongside her, and Cash had the awful feeling that this was more than a simple parting for a quick forty-eight-hour business trip. This was the last page of their story.

The end.

Chapter Seventeen

The barn cleared out less than twenty minutes after Cash left as the other dog teams drifted toward their vehicles. Once the guests were gone, Cam closed and locked the barn doors behind them so the Comfort Paws girls could let their dogs play off-leash while everyone helped put away folding chairs and straighten the training area after class.

Peaches, Fuzzy and Sparkles immediately took off in a game of chase, while the more dignified Lady Bird and Ginger stretched out on their bellies in the center of the arena and woofed at the smaller dogs every time they darted past them. On any other day, Belle wouldn't have been in a hurry to leave. She would've laughed with the rest of her friends when Cam pulled a few mini footballs out of his Rattlers duffle bag and tossed them around, ratcheting up the canine excitement. Her answer would've been an enthusiastic yes when Jace suggested that they order some pizzas and hang around to try and get a glimpse of the meteor shower that was expected to be visible over the Hill Country later tonight.

Not tonight, though. She just didn't have it in her to stick around and be the only single member of their friend group. Usually when the Comfort Paws girls got together and invited the guys, she really didn't mind. Ford wasn't just Maple's husband, but also Adaline's brother. Belle's entire social circle had always felt more like family than friends.

But she'd just practically begged Cash to tell her he had feelings for her, and his answer had been nothing but resounding silence.

She was furious and devastated, all at once. Granted, she hadn't exactly been forthcoming with her feelings, either, but Cash had been the one who'd tried to force the issue. He wanted to stay home with her instead of flying to Dallas...

But for how long? And just...how? With her as the family nanny, or the therapy dog handler who helps his little girl read? Because that wasn't going to be enough anymore. Belle wanted more. She'd wanted more for a while now. She'd just been too bruised by her past to think it could ever be a real possibility.

Because it's not.

Her throat clogged as she watched Sparkles and Peaches scramble after the same mini football. Then she took a deep breath, hiked her backpack onto her shoulder and gave Peaches the *come* command. The Cavalier did an abrupt about-face and scampered toward her with Sparkles following close behind.

Belle clipped the dogs' leashes onto their collars and pasted on a smile before turning to face her friends. "Pizza sounds great, y'all. I wish I could stay, but I need to get back and check on Lucy and Ellis since Cash is on his way to Austin."

"Bummer." Adaline pouted. "I understand, but I love it when we're all together like this."

"Me too," Belle said and hoped it sounded genuine. She really did mean it. Right now, she just needed some space.

Everyone gathered round to say their goodbyes, dogs included. Peaches and Sparkles were going to sleep like babies tonight after all the stimulation. Belle wouldn't be surprised if they both conked out on the way home and she had to carry them into the house.

"Babe." Jenna rested a hand on Cam's touchdown-throwing bicep. "Can you please walk Belle to her car?"

"Of course. Come on, Bells," he said.

Before she could object, he took hold of her backpack and slung it over one of his shoulders. She had no choice but to let him escort her out of the building like he was her bodyguard.

Outside the barn, stars glittered overhead like diamonds on dark velvet. Say what you will about Texas, but the stars really were bigger and brighter in the Lone Star State. The meteor shower was going to be gorgeous out here. What could possibly be prettier than stardust falling on Jace's rows and rows of budding Christmas trees?

If Lucy wasn't too sleepy, maybe Belle would spread a quilt on the mansion's back lawn so they could watch for shooting stars. She could make s'mores to take outside and make an occasion out of it. Wouldn't it have been cozy to have Cash there too?

She needed to stop thinking like this. They weren't a family, and they never would be.

"Thanks, Cam. It was really sweet of you to come tonight." Belle's steps slowed as they approached her vehicle. "Clearly, all the worry was for nothing."

"Always better to be safe than sorry." Cam tipped his head toward the barn. "Everyone here cares about you, Bells. I'm happy to help."

Belle's throat tightened. Why was she getting choked up? There'd been more than enough drama for one night. She just wanted to get home.

"Call us if you need anything, okay?" Cam said after they'd loaded up the dogs and Belle's seat belt was bucked.

She nodded. "Will do."

He pushed her door closed with an easy grin, and she began the slow crawl down the tree-lined drive that led back to the main road, until the warm glow shining from the barn windows vanished from her rearview mirror.

The drive back to Cash's house was uneventful, save for a brief moment when Belle almost thought someone was following her. The streets were unusually quiet and dark—even for a sleepy town like Bluebonnet—probably because everyone in town was hunkered down someplace waiting for the meteor shower. The only other headlights on the road belonged to a truck not far behind her that seemed to be following the same route. But once the McAllister Mansion came into view, the truck turned off of Main Street and she breathed easier.

Paranoid much? She loosened her grip on the steering wheel and shifted the car into Park.

As she'd expected, Peaches and Sparkles had fallen asleep during the brief drive. The dogs were curled against each other in the back seat like two snug spoons, the Cavalier playing the part of the big spoon with the Frenchie as the smaller one. They barely lifted their heads as she gathered a dog in each arm and carried them inside the house.

Ellis and Lucy weren't any more alert than the pups. From the look of things, Ellis had gone to bed in his room after letting Lucy fall asleep in her blanket fort with the television turned down low. *Cinderella* was nearing its end, and Belle glanced up from tucking the covers snug around Lucy's sleepy form just in time to see the coach's wheels go off-kilter and then roll away as the carriage turned into a fat orange pumpkin.

Oh, the irony.

She nestled Sparkles in the blanket fort next to Lucy and then clicked the door closed behind her.

"I guess it's just you and me for the meteor shower, huh?" she whispered, and Peaches's tail wagged.

Belle grabbed a blanket and made her way out the French doors that led to the back terrace. A falling star streaked across the horizon in a dazzling trail just as she stepped outside.

She gasped. "Make a wish, Peaches."

And for a split second, Belle was so transfixed by the glittering show that she didn't notice the low growl coming from her sweet-as-pie dog.

"Peaches?" She glanced down and found her dog standing stock-still, tail drooping straight toward the ground.

The Cavalier released another rumbling growl, and Belle couldn't believe what she was hearing. She'd only heard Peaches growl a couple of times, *ever*, and both those instances had been when she'd unexpectedly caught a glimpse of her own reflection in the full-length mirror on the back of Belle's closet door.

"Maybe *I* should make a wish."

The voice was eerily calm, but it made the blood instantly freeze in Belle's veins. Her head whipped up, and she squinted into the darkness with her heart in her throat. Then more stars began to fall, illuminating the sky just enough for her to make out Stetson's form a dozen or so feet in front of her.

"Stetson," she said, trying her best to fake a pleasant smile. The last thing she wanted was for him to know she felt threatened, but the tremble in her voice gave her away.

"Is this why you kicked me out of dog class?" He took a step closer, eyes fixed on the grand house behind her.

Belle tightened the slack on Peaches's leash and stood her ground. She wondered how loud she would have to scream to wake Ellis. What did it matter, though? Even if he heard her, he still had a broken ankle. It wasn't as if he could come running outside to help her.

Just breathe. He hasn't outright threatened you... Yet.

But what was he doing here in Cash's backyard? The property immediately behind the house was surrounded by an eight-foot, whitewashed privacy fence. Beyond that, rolling hills stretched into the horizon—the very hills where she'd hoped to help Cash plant wildflowers, come fall. There wasn't a bluebonnet in sight right now, though. Just…nothing. Every time a star tore across the sky, it lit up the surrounding landscape and reminded Belle just how isolated she was, here at the end of Main Street. The closest neighbor wasn't anywhere near. Unlike the quaint Sunday houses a few blocks away, which were situated right up next to each other.

"I don't know what you're talking about. I didn't kick you out," Belle said. Peaches's growl had transitioned into a whine, likely because the dog had picked up on the fear skittering up Belle's spine.

She wanted to scoop the Cavalier into her arms to reassure her and let her know everything was fine, but she didn't dare take her eyes off Stetson.

His gaze shifted away from the house and back at her, and his face screwed. "Don't pretend you don't know what happened. I know you do."

Belle took a deep breath, prepared to repeat the reason Maple had given him for his dismissal from class. "The board felt that you and Lasso weren't—"

"A good fit for the program," he parroted with a heavy dose of disdain. "Save it. I know that's a lie. Labs are great dogs."

"They are. Where's your dog right now, Stetson?" She was trying to buy some time while she figured out how to get out of this mess. If she turned around and ran for the back door, she wasn't sure could get it shut and locked behind her before he caught up, especially with Peaches on lead.

And Belle wasn't going to leave her best friend behind. Period.

"I was just trying to be nice to you," Stetson said, ignoring her question. His hands curled into fists at his sides. "I never did anything wrong."

Other than ignoring the instructor's repeated requests to give me and my dog space...along with trying

*to monopolize my time and lashing out at Cash when
Peaches lavished him with affection.*

The signs had truly been there, hadn't there? She
simply hadn't wanted to see them. Bluebonnet was a
safe place. Belle had grown up with unlocked doors
and windows tossed open wide to let it in the fresh Hill
Country air.

The only person she'd been instantly wary of lately
was Cash.

Cash. Tears pricked her eyes at the thought of him.
She would have given anything to turn back time and
take him up on his offer to stay. If only he were here…

She wouldn't hold back this time. She'd wouldn't keep
her soul locked up so tight that he'd have to be the one
to put his heart on the line first. That's not what love
was, anyway, was it? True love didn't need a safety net.

"No, you didn't. You were a perfect gentleman," Belle
said, humoring Stetson as best she could. She hitched a
thumb over her shoulder toward the house. "Why don't I
go inside and give Maple a call? Once I explain everything,
I'm sure everyone will agree to let you back in class."

Stetson's lips curled.

Dang it. She'd just let on that she'd left her cell phone
behind.

He took another step closer, and this time, she took
a giant backward step. Trying to talk him down didn't
seem to be working.

Stetson's eyes were wild as the meteors blazing behind him. He was getting more agitated with each passing second. "It's because I'm not him, isn't it? I never
stood a chance because I'm not a McAllister. You're *living here in his house.*"

Belle's skin crawled. How long had he been watching her?

"It's not what you think," she insisted. But wasn't it?

Deep down, the situation was precisely what Stetson thought it was. She had feelings for Cash, and everyone seemed to know it but him.

"Anyway," she said, voice wobbling as a sob lodged at the back of her throat. "Cash is right inside. He'll probably be out here any minute, so you should go."

It was a last-ditch effort to talk her way out of this increasingly uncomfortable encounter, and Stetson wasn't buying it. Not for a second.

"You women are all the same. All that matters to you is money," Stetson spat, lips twisted. The smell of whiskey on his breath turned Belle's stomach. "You won't give a regular working guy a shot, but you never hesitate to throw yourself at a rich guy. Money is everything to you. Money, money, money."

His words were the ultimate slap in the face. They dredged up something bitter and dark inside Belle until her mouth filled with bile...no doubt because he could've been saying them straight to her mother's face. And they might've been true.

But he wasn't speaking to her mother. He was saying those words to her, and they were so cruelly reminiscent of her childhood and every dark thought that she'd ever had about her mom that she could barely process them. If she could've planted her hands over her ears and prevented herself from hearing them, she would've.

"No." Belle shook her head as she reeled backward and nearly tripped on the edge of the veranda where the tile met the grass.

She hadn't realized how far she'd backed away from him already. If she let Stetson steer her any closer to the house, she'd never be able to get to the door without him being right on top of her before she took a step. He hadn't pulled out a weapon or expressly threatened to harm her, but he'd scaled a fence to corner her. She wasn't going to wait around and see what he might do next.

She had to take a chance and run. Now…

Belle spun around and took off as fast as she could, screaming at the top of her lungs, "Peaches, come!"

Bless the little Cavalier's heart, she obeyed and ran toward Belle as fast as her little legs could carry her. Stetson stumbled forward after them, and when Belle glanced over her shoulder to make sure Peaches was right on her heels, she saw him grab at the dog. The whiskey must've slowed him down, and when he realized he didn't have much of a chance of catching Belle, he went after Peaches instead.

But her training was rock-solid, and she dashed for Belle without looking back. Stetson's hands swiped at the air, and he fell to his knees just as Belle slammed the back door shut, closing herself and her dog inside the house. She paused for a beat, squeezing the doorknob tight, afraid to let it go as she rested her forehead against the smooth wood and tried to catch her breath.

Call someone. You promised Cam. Call somebody right now.

She grabbed Peaches first, because the poor dog was pawing at her shins and whining, eager to be praised for following instructions. Her little body trembled when Belle picked her up.

Thank goodness she'd growled when she'd spotted

Stetson. If she hadn't, Belle might not have even noticed him watching her in the dark. She'd had her face tipped up to the sky, swept away by the sight of the meteor shower. Anything could've happened.

She couldn't think about that now, though. She needed to dial 911. Stetson hadn't hurt her, but he'd trespassed on Cash's private property, and Belle needed to get the police here before he had a chance to get away. She could see him through the windows of the French doors struggling to regain his footing.

"I've got you," Belle whispered into Peaches's fur. "Everything is okay."

She held her dog tight to her chest as she turned to make a mad dash for her phone, but before she could take a step, she ran into a brick wall of a man. He took hold of her shoulders and said her name, and at first, Belle was so disoriented that she thought she'd gotten confused and Stetson had somehow caught up with her, right here, inside the house. But then he cupped her face and said her name again, voice tense with alarm.

"Belle!" He smoothed back her hair and forced her to meet his gaze. "Belle, you're safe. I'm here. Tell me where he is."

"Cash?" Her teeth chattered, and Peaches licked her cheek. Ever the comfort dog, eager to soothe.

"It's me, sweetheart." His voice cracked. "I'm here."

Cash hadn't made it more than thirty miles past the Bluebonnet town line before he'd turned around and barreled back home.

The farther away he'd gotten from the Comfort Paws barn, the louder the voice in the back of his head be-

came—the one that told him if he didn't stay and tell
Belle how he felt, he might never get another chance.
Not because Stetson might do something stupid, but because when Belle had given him the chance to be honest with her about how he felt, Cash had done what he
always did. He'd shut down.

He'd tried to pretend it wasn't the right time or place
for raw, aching honesty. But deep down, he knew that
wasn't the truth. He'd been paralyzed again—unable
to crack his chest open and serve his heart up on a silver platter.

People died. Sometimes it happened without warning,
and sometimes it happened slowly…painfully. Sometimes people left in other ways—not physically, but emo-
tionally. The losses piled up. It happened every day, and
in Cash's family, it seemed to happen with frightening
regularity. He'd thought he could stop it by refusing to
care, but that was the surest way to end up alone.

And Cash didn't want to be alone anymore.

He wanted Belle.

So he made a U-turn and didn't stop driving until
he neared the end of Main Street. The funniest thing
had happened as he approached the house, though. He'd
thought he spotted a familiar-looking truck parked under
a tree on one of the nearby side streets. It was a Ford
F-150, hardly out of place in small-town Texas, but it was
the same coloring as the Ford that had been parked at dog
training class last week, and it had the same dented back
fender. Cash hadn't seen the truck in the barn parking
lot when he'd left dog training class earlier, which meant
it was entirely possible the Ford belonged to Stetson.

Even if it did, its presence on a side street in close

proximity to Cash's house didn't necessarily mean anything. Stetson could've lived on this street. But as Cash sat studying the vehicle, a dog poked its head out of the unrolled passenger side window. Not just any dog, but a glossy black Labrador retriever.

Lasso.

Cash gritted his teeth. The dog's presence in the front seat of that vehicle could only mean one thing: Stetson was close by, and Cash had known exactly where.

"The police are on their way," he said to Belle as calmly as he could manage. He'd wasted no time at all calling 911 as he'd floored it the rest of the way down the street. "Where's Stetson? Is he out there?" Cash tipped his head toward the backyard, and Belle nodded.

"I went outside to see the meteor shower, and he was just…there. I tried to talk some sense into him, and when that didn't work, I ran inside and locked the door."

"You did the right thing." He pulled her into his arms with Peaches sandwiched between them as the wail of a police car pierced the air. "Thank God you're okay. I don't know what I would do if something happened to you."

"Ellis and Lucy are okay, too. They're both asleep." Belle let out a shaky breath. "Stetson's been drinking. He said some really awful things…"

Cash didn't like the sound of that, although he wasn't surprised. "What kind of things?"

Belle hesitated as the police siren grew louder. Within seconds, flashing red and blue lights swept over the darkened yard. "It's not important right now. Is that the police? Are they here?"

"Yes, we need to get out there and talk to them. I

know where Stetson's truck is parked. If he's managed to get around the privacy fence already, they'll know where to find him." He wrapped an arm around her shoulders and anchored her and Peaches to his side. There was still so much he needed to say, and until he got the chance, Cash wasn't about to let either of them out of his sight.

Never, ever again.

Belle wrapped her hands around the hot mug of chamomile and lavender tea Cash prepared for her after the police left. They'd located Stetson within minutes, and she knew she should feel relieved, but she couldn't shake the sense that something still wasn't right.

"You must be exhausted." Cash wrapped her favorite blanket—the lush cashmere one from the den—around her shoulders and pressed a gentle kiss to the top of her head.

She was perched on one of the barstools at the kitchen island with Peaches snuggled in her lap. Despite the late hour, the warm, rich scent of coffee hung in the air. Cash had forgone the single-serve machine in favor of the fancy industrial-looking drip coffee maker and made a full pot for the officers who'd come to update them after Stetson had been taken into custody.

"I am, but I'm also weirdly wired. I still can't believe Stetson had an outstanding warrant." Belle sipped her tea, hoping the warm floral blend would do its magic and make her head stop spinning so she could sleep.

Aggravated stalking.

She couldn't get those two ugly words out of her head. Apparently, Stetson's fascination with her had been part of a pattern. Eighteen months ago, he'd harassed an ex-girlfriend in Austin and was ultimately arrested for repeated unwanted contract and threatening her with a knife. After he'd failed to appear for the subsequent court hearing, the warrant had been issued. He'd been on the run ever since and only recently settled in Bluebonnet.

"In a strange way, I'm glad that he did. Like the officers said, this means he'll serve real time in state prison. He won't be back here, and that's the most important thing." Cash sat down beside her and scooted his barstool closer to hers. "But we're still getting that protective order, just in case."

Belle nodded, silently registering his use of the word *we*. He'd been like this all night. Attentive. Affectionate. Doting, even. Treating her like she was made of glass, while at the same time marveling at her composure and the way she'd handed herself with Stetson. He'd even called Maple to tell her what had happened while Belle had taken a quick bath and changed into her pajamas. Being treated with such care and tenderness was nice. It was already going a long way in taking the edge off one of the most stressful nights she'd ever experienced, but nothing could erase the things Stetson said to her.

You women are all the same. All that matters to you is money.

It wasn't true, obviously. But Belle didn't like the way that whiskey-soaked voice kept coming back to her as she sat in the grandest home in Bluebonnet, with a cashmere blanket wrapped around her shoulders and Cash McAllister waiting on her hand and foot.

"I just thought of something." Belle sat her tea down on the island and rested a hand on Peaches's tiny rib cage. It rose and fell in a slow, sleepy cadence. "What's going to happen to Lasso?"

Cash's gaze slid over to her, and the corner of his mouth lifted. "You're worried about the stalker's dog now?"

When he put it that like, it did sound a little ridiculous. But Lasso was a sweet dog, and it wasn't his fault that he'd been adopted by a bad person. Maybe the Lab could be re-homed by someone here in Bluebonnet. He deserved a fresh start.

We all do.

"Yes, I suppose I am." Belle chuckled under her breath. It felt good to laugh. "Is that silly?"

"No, it's not silly at all. It's—" Cash's smile dimmed as he struggled for words, but his eyes shone with warmth "—maybe the most Belle thing I've ever heard. And it's also one of the many reasons I've fallen in love with you."

It took a second for his words to register, and when they did, Belle's eyes flooded with tears. All this time, she'd wondered why he'd come back. When she'd plowed into him earlier, she'd been so stunned to see him that it almost hadn't seemed real. She'd wanted to cling to him and never let go. But so much had happened in the moments immediately following that she hadn't gotten the chance to ask him what he was doing here. Why he'd changed his mind and stayed...

"What did you just say?" She sniffed and tried her best to not to cry. She'd somehow managed not to shed a single tear all night. Her determination to stay strong had been resolute.

She hadn't been prepared for this, though. If there

was one thing that could break her, it was hearing Cash say those three little words.

"I said I'm in love with you." He lifted a hand to caress her cheek, then tenderly wiped her tears away with a gentle brush of his thumb. "You asked me earlier why I wanted to stay, and that's the reason. I couldn't say it then, but I'm telling you now. I love you, Belle. I just hope I'm not too late."

"You're not too late." She shook her head and bit her lip to try and keep more tears from falling.

But it was no use. Cash *loved* her, and hearing him say it, bold and out loud, had unlocked a part of her that she thought had been lost forever. She wished it didn't feel so scary…and she wished Stetson's ugly words would go away once and for all.

But surely it would. This was what she'd wanted more than anything else in the world—this beautiful man, his beautiful heart. Finally, love was hers for the taking. All she had to do was grab hold of it with both hands.

"You're right on time," she whispered.

And then Cash kissed her, soft and slow, and the whiskey-soaked voice in the back of her head quieted down until it was just a low hum, drowned out by sweet nothings and promises made and the thought that this perfect bluebonnet season would stretch on forever. Like an endless dream…

Or a wish she'd made upon a star.

Chapter Eighteen

"Belle?" Cash's breath was warm on the back of Belle's neck the next morning as the first rays of sunlight filtered through the bedroom window.

She wasn't ready to open her eyes quite yet. Everything just felt so delicious right now, snug in a warm bed with Cash's arms wrapped around her from behind and the steady beat of his heart reverberating through her... grounding her in this special time and place.

She'd asked him to sleep with her last night—just sleep. She'd been so spent from the roller coaster of emotions that she'd barely been able to keep her eyes open, but she hadn't wanted to let him go. So he'd come to her room and held her while she finally succumbed to her exhaustion, and now morning had come far too soon.

"Hmm?" she murmured without dragging her eyes open quite yet. It came out more like the purr of a contented kitten.

"There's a dog in the bed." Sleep clung to his voice, but underneath it Belle heard a smile. "And I distinctly remember someone telling me that letting my dog sleep with me was strictly forbidden."

Belle's eyes snapped open. "Oh, that."

Cash pushed up on his elbows to give her a look of mock consternation. He was still wearing his T-shirt and sweatpants from the night before and, for once, wasn't perfectly groomed in a suit and tie as soon as the sun came up. She loved seeing him this way in the fresh light of day.

"You've been holding out on me." He arched a brow and cut his gaze toward Peaches, curled into a snug little ball near Belle's hip. "I've never seen a dog look so content before. I bet she's never spent a single night in a crate."

"She totally has," Belle protested. "She slept in one every night at Maple's house until she was old enough to leave the litter and come home with me."

He left eyebrow crept even higher. "And since then?"

She had to go ahead and fess up. Also, this might be a good time to tell him that she'd let Sparkles sleep in the blanket fort with Lucy last night. "Fine. You caught me. She's been sleeping with me the entire time."

In one swift move, Cash plucked the pillow from behind him and tossed it at her face.

Belle squealed as the pillow made contact. Then she grabbed hold of it and lobbed it back at him. It landed on the side of his head with a thud just as her cell phone vibrated, skittering across the nightstand.

"You might want to get that. Your phone's been blowing up for a while now. I didn't want to wake you." He shoved the pillow out from between them and kissed her cheek. "It's probably your friends checking up on you. I'm sure they're worried. I'll go make us some coffee while you chat."

"Thank you." Belle sat up, straightened her pajama top and reached for her phone. "I'm sure you're right.

Adaline has probably been up stress-baking anxiety pies for hours already."

"Anxiety pies?"

Belle shrugged. "It's kind of her thing."

"I look forward to tasting one sometime. Tell her I said good morning." Cash winked and then shut the door behind him.

Belle couldn't wipe the smile off her face as she accepted the call without bothering to check the name on her notifications. She should've asked Cash to make her coffee an extra large. This was going to take a while.

"Hey, there. Before you say anything, I promise I'm okay." Belle took a giant inhale. "More than okay, actually."

"Er…" The person on the other end of the call—*not* Adaline, apparently, or any of the other Comfort Paws girls—stammered and then cleared her throat. "I'm calling for Belle Darling. Is this the right number?"

"Sorry. Yes, this is she," Belle said. She should've checked before pressing the Accept Call button, but she'd only been awake for a hot second. Plus, she'd been anxious to talk to her friends. She knew they had to be concerned about what had happened last night.

"Hello, this is Miranda Percell from Southern Dallas University Press. I'm calling about your recent children's book proposal. Is now a good time to chat?"

Belle tossed the covers aside and flew to her feet. Miranda Percell was calling her? Less than a week after Belle had submitted her manuscript?

She couldn't have this conversation while lounging in bed in her pj's. Southern Dallas University Press was one of her dream publishers—not the tiptop one, but a close second—and Miranda Percell was legendary in the world of children's literature. Maybe if Belle was vertical, she'd have half a chance at sounding professional.

"Yes," she blurted. "Yes, of course."

"Wonderful. I have to say, your manuscript really charmed me, Miss Darling."

"It did?" She could hardly believe she was having this conversation. The cumulative effect of everything that had happened in the past twenty-four hours was making her dizzy. She might need to sit back down again.

The editor went on to explain what she liked best about the story, speaking in glowing terms about Belle's literary voice and the unique hook she'd chosen for her story.

"Where did you get the idea for a children's book told from the point of view of a therapy dog who helps kids learn to read?" Miranda asked.

"From my own dog, actually." Belle's gaze flitted to Peaches, whose eyes were cracked open just a smidge. Her tail beat softly against the duvet cover. "We're a certified therapy dog team, and I work as an elementary school librarian. I bring Peaches to work with me twice and week. We're trying to get canine-assisted reading education approved as a permanent part of the school curriculum."

"I love to hear it. That would give us a really unique way to market your book."

Her book.

Was this really happening?

"I'm glad you think so," Belle said.

"There are a few changes I'd like to suggest. Nothing major, though. I can send an editorial letter with my overall thoughts after this call, but at this point, I'd like to extend an official offer for publication," Miranda said.

Belle clamped her hand over her mouth to keep from screaming out loud. After a second or two, when she trusted herself to speak in a normal tone that wouldn't pierce her new editor's eardrums, she swallowed and said, "I'd like that very much. This is a dream come true. I don't really know how to thank you."

"No need to thank me. I've already got a few ideas for which illustrators might be a good fit. We'll get to that later, after the contract is all signed." Miranda took a breather, and Belle could hear her tapping away at her computer keyboard. "I'm sending you the terms of the offer right now."

"Thank you," Belle said again.

"Thank *you* for submitting your enchanting story." Miranda laughed under breath. "And I suppose I also owe a thank-you to Cash McAllister."

Belle stilled. What could Cash possibly have to do with this? And how did Miranda Percell even know who he was? Granted, everyone in the state had probably heard of him—especially in Dallas, where the McAllister Foundation and Southern Dallas University Press were both located. But why would she mention him now…in this context?

"Cash McAllister?" Belle repeated, her tone wooden.

She didn't have to ask, though. Somehow, she just knew.

"Yes, his late mother was a friend of mine. She was quite active in the children's book community. I was surprised to hear from Cash when he reached out a few days ago to tell me to be on the lookout for your submission, but once I read your story, I understood right away why he spoke so highly of you."

There wasn't an ounce of judgment in her tone. On the contrary, the editor was crisp, professional and complimentary. But humiliation burned inside Belle, all the same. She'd been so proud just moments before. So ecstatic. Her lifelong dream of becoming an author was on the verge of coming true, and before she'd had a chance to celebrate, she'd found out she hadn't made it happen all on her own.

Cash had done this.

He just couldn't help himself, could he? He couldn't resist the temptation to pull out his big, fat wallet and buy whatever he wanted. She was as furious as she'd been when he'd tried to buy Peaches.

Calling an editor on her behalf wasn't technically the same thing, but it hurt just as much. Maybe even more. He hadn't even told her about the phone call. Had he been planning on keeping it secret forever? Was he planning on sitting by while she had a book launch party someday at Bluebonnet Bookshop and pretended he'd never had a thing to do with her success?

Belle ended the call as politely and swiftly as she could. Within seconds, her phone chimed with an incoming email. The subject line read, Southern Dallas University Press would love to publish your book!

It should've been one of the happiest moments of her life, but instead, shame curled in the pit of her stomach.

She pressed a hand to her breastbone and reminded herself to breathe. Cash loved her, and she loved him, and this was just a small thing that shouldn't really matter in the long run. Her book wouldn't be getting published if it wasn't good.

But the seeds of doubt had already begun to blossom into something wild and dark, fueled in no small part by Stetson's cruel assessment of her. The sickening things he'd said to her were rising back to the surface, and this time, Belle was powerless to quiet them. He didn't even really know her, and in her head, she knew his opinion was meaningless. But her heart felt differently, because the only thing worse than being abandoned by her own mother as a child would be realizing that she'd grown up to become just like her.

"Belle, what's wrong, sweetheart?" Cash loomed over her with a cup of coffee in each hand and a wrapped gift tucked under one his arms. A look of intense alarm splashed across his face. "That call wasn't about Stetson, was it?"

Belle had been so shocked into immobility that she hadn't registered his return. "No, it wasn't. Sorry. Everything's fine."

Everything was *not* fine, but she didn't even know where to start.

"Good. You looked so upset. It frightened me there for a second." He set the coffees down on the nightstand. The sweet, caramelized scent of French vanilla wafted up toward her.

"What's this?" she asked as he handed her the flat gift-wrapped package. Instead of a bow, it was decorated with the familiar embossed gold seal that Belle recognized from Bluebonnet Bookshop.

The sight of it broke her heart a little.

"This is the thank-you gift I got for you after you

helped me prepare for pet rescue's home visit a couple weeks ago. I brought it to the first night of dog training class, and things kind of went haywire after that." His mouth curved into a sheepish grin.

Things were still going haywire. Belle felt like she was on the world's most disorienting roller coaster, and at the moment, she wanted nothing more than to get off.

"Go ahead." Cash dragged a hand through his hair. She'd never seen a man look so good with bed head. It should be illegal. "Open it."

She slid a finger under the seal and peeled the paper away to reveal a fine leather notebook with gold-trimmed pages. The lined sheets inside were smoother than any paper she'd ever felt before. When she turned the notebook over, she spotted her name in the bottom right-hand corner of the front corner—Belle Darling, spelled out in gilt lettering.

"It's for your writing," Cash said. "You told Lucy about your story that day, and I could tell by the way you talked about it that your writing was important to you."

It was the most beautiful gift she'd ever received and, undoubtedly, the most meaningful.

Belle didn't want to ruin the moment, but she couldn't keep what she knew inside any longer. She'd always hated secrets, and this was the very worst sort.

She held the notebook to her chest and met his gaze. "Cash, that wasn't Adaline on the phone just now. It was Miranda Percell from Southern Dallas University Press. She said they want to publish my book."

His face lit up in an instant, and she blurted out the rest as fast as she could because she didn't want to wait and see if he'd keep pretending he hadn't pulled a string or two on her behalf. Her heart was already in pieces.

"She also said that you called her the other day and told her they should give me an offer."

Cash's expression abruptly changed—first to one of confusion and then denial. He shook his head. "It wasn't like that. Not exactly. She and my mom were friends…"

"I know. Miranda mentioned that," Belle said. He wasn't getting it, was he? He truly had no idea why she was upset.

"Sweetheart, this is good news. If anyone deserves to be a children's book author, it's you." He opened his arms as if waiting for her to step into them for a celebratory embrace, but she couldn't bring herself to take a single step.

"So, you decided to buy it for me?"

It wasn't quite fair, and she knew it. But it was how she felt in the moment, even though she desperately didn't want to.

Cash's jaw visibly tensed. "Belle, that's not true. All I did was make a phone call to an old family friend to tell her how talented you are and that they would be lucky to publish you."

"If it was so innocent, then why didn't you mention it to me?" Belle asked, and she hadn't realized that the question was a test, of sorts, until the words were already out of her mouth.

He could've answered any number of ways. All he had to say was that he hadn't told her about the call because he didn't want to get her hopes up. That would've been a perfectly acceptable explanation in Belle's eyes. Or she hoped it would be…

But that's not what Cash said. Instead, he let out a long, tortured sigh and gave the worst answer possible.

"I didn't tell you because I thought you might not like it." He held up his hands. "But, Belle, please hear me out, okay? I'm trying to change. I *have* changed. I—"

She held up a hand. "Don't. Please. Not now."

He clamped his mouth shut, and she could tell it was killing him not to take control of the narrative. At least he was respecting her need for silence. Maybe he really had changed.

But maybe Belle had changed, too, and not in a way she'd ever wanted.

"I think Peaches and I need to go home," she said quietly.

Cash's eyes went shiny. "For how long?"

"I don't know."

Chapter Nineteen

Cash knew that the only way he and Belle might have a shot at a real future was if he didn't try and force it. The best thing he could do was wait.

So he did.

He waited all day, until Friday turned into Saturday, and then he waited some more, until Saturday turned into Sunday. By late afternoon, he was fully going out of his mind. He'd spent so much time pacing around the kitchen that he was fairly certain he was going to wear a path around the island.

"Can I ask you something, Mr. McAllister?" Ellis entered the room on his crutches and lowered himself onto one of the kitchen chairs.

"Ask me anything," Cash said. *Literally anything.* Whatever Ellis wanted would be a welcome distraction from missing the woman he loved and kicking himself for making the call to Miranda Percell without talking to her about it first.

Ellis raised his brows. "How long is this going to go on?"

"I'm not sure what you mean." Cash pulled an extra chair closer to Ellis so the older man could elevate his foot. His ankle was apparently healing nicely, because it was getting harder and harder to convince him to slow down and rest.

"I'll say it bluntly then. When are you going to make up with Miss Darling so she'll come back?" Ellis's gaze cut toward the flattened pillow beneath his ankle boot. "She fluffs a mean pillow."

Cash had no doubt that Belle did indeed fluff a mean pillow, but he also knew when Ellis was putting on a show. Ellis had a soft spot for Belle. He'd been visibly shaken on Friday when Cash filled him in on the Stetson situation. He'd felt partially responsible since he'd been asleep when she got home from dog training class and still grew pensive whenever the subject came up.

Now Cash narrowed his gaze at him. "First of all, I've asked you a thousand times now to call me by my first name. I know for a fact that you call Belle by hers when I'm not around."

Ellis's forehead furrowed. At least he had the decency to look contrite. "She prefers to forgo the formalities."

"So do I." Cash sighed. "I mean it Ellis. You're like family to me."

"As you wish, Cash." He nodded, then his dark eyes fixed with Cash's. "Now, will you answer the question?"

Cash's chest tightened. "There's nothing to say. Spring break is over. Belle only signed on to be Lucy's nanny for a week. As I explained to Lucy, she had to leave a couple days early because she had a family emergency."

It was the oldest excuse in the book, but he'd been at a loss when Lucy had stumbled out of her blanket fort Friday morning and the first words out of her mouth had been, "Where's Belle?" He wanted to leave space for Belle to come back whenever she chose, and a family emergency seemed vague enough to account for any length of time. Cash had never imagined her absence would stretch on this long, though.

Ellis looked at him for a long moment until sadness clouded his features. "You might have Lucy fooled, but I wasn't born yesterday. Surely you don't expect me to buy that load of hogwash."

If Cash hadn't been so preoccupied with his current predicament, he might've laughed. The formalities had finally been well and truly quashed.

"You love her. I'd have to be blind not to have noticed." Ellis folded his hands in his lap. The concern in his eyes bordered on fatherly, but in no way reminiscent of the sort of father figure that Cash's real dad had been. Ellis was looking at him as if his unhappiness grieved him…as if he felt Cash's distress deep in his bones. "I've known you a long time, Cash. I remember when your mother brought you here for the first time swaddled in a little blue blanket. Your face was all screwed up, and you cried nonstop, like you were angry at the world. Maybe you were. Maybe on some soul-deep level you knew what the world had in store for you, so you came out kicking and screaming."

Brutal, but very possibly true.

"I care about you," Ellis continued. "Why do you think I'm still here after all these years? You're like a son to me, and it might not be my place to say it, but I'm proud of you. Your daddy isn't around to tell you, and I feel like it's something you need to hear. I've watched you grow up a lot over the past three decades, and you're a good man, son."

Cash's throat clogged with emotion. Ellis was right. He did need to hear it, and oddly, it almost meant more coming from Ellis than if he'd heard those words uttered from his own father.

"Thank you," he said quietly. Cash's body felt leaden. Why had they never talked like this before?

Because you weren't ready.

It had taken losing a sister, becoming a father and falling in love to prepare Cash's heart for healing. He'd had to know what it felt like to be utterly lost before he could build himself back up into the kind of person he wanted to be.

"I mean it. Let me say it again: You're a good man." Ellis paused, and his smile turned gentle and full of hope. "But Belle makes you a better one."

Cash wasn't about to argue. Truer words had never been spoken.

"I messed it up, Ellis. That's why she's not here."

"So fix it. McAllisters never give up, remember?" Ellis winked. Now he really did sound like Cash's dad.

If only things were that simple.

Cash scrubbed his face. "Trust me, acting like a McAllister isn't going to win her back. That's how I ruined things in the first place—by embracing the McAllister way."

"You seem to be forgetting that you're the patriarch now. You don't have to do things a certain way just because it's tradition. That was your father's choice, but it doesn't have to be yours. You don't want to fly back and forth to Dallas all the time? Move the foundation's office to Bluebonnet. You want to prove to Belle how much you care about her? Don't just tell her. *Show* her." Ellis pointed a finger directly at Cash's chest. "*You* get to decide what the McAllister way is now, no one else."

Cash sat with those words for a moment, and the longer he did, the more he realized that Ellis was right. He'd given the McAllister family name and the McAllister way so much weight that the shadow of his dad loomed over everything. Even as he'd tried to change, his motivation had been singular—to avoid turning into his father.

But Cash's destiny was his alone. The only way to embrace the future was to let go of the past, once and for all, and concentrate on building something entirely new.

"Ellis, that might've been the wisest thing anyone has ever said to me," Cash said, and for the first time since Belle packed up her dog and left, hope stirred. She herself had given him the answer when she'd told him how lucky Lucy was to have him as a parent.

People with dyslexia often have special strengths... things like thinking outside the box and creativity.

Also empathy.

"Good. Now tell me you have a plan." Ellis patted his stomach. "It's been days since I had a homemade Oreo."

"I'm getting there." Cash felt himself smile. It was time to think way outside the box and show Belle how much he cared about her and the things that were important to her.

He'd done it before, quite recently. Belle just hadn't realized it yet. But if he did it once, surely he could do it again...

"Uncle Cash." Lucy shuffled into the kitchen with

her feet clad in bunny slippers and a pile of books balanced in her arms. Sparkles scurried to catch up. "Can you watch me read to Sparkles? We need to practice."

And just like that, Cash knew exactly where to start.

Belle spent the rest of her spring break hiding away in her cottage, dodging her friends and bingeing *Friends*, her favorite comfort show. She used to think there wasn't anything in the world that Ross, Rachel, Monica, Chandler and Phoebe couldn't fix, but alas, she'd been wrong. Even the Central Perk gang was powerless when it came to a broken heart.

And make no mistake, Belle's heart was positively shattered.

The Comfort Paws girls had given her a day of peace and quiet before barging in and demanding a debrief. Belle caved and spilled her guts, and not just because Adaline had come bearing pie. She knew they were worried sick about her after the horrible incident with Stetson. Belle needed them to know she was okay…mostly. She'd accidentally gone and fallen in love, that's all.

Annoyingly, Adaline, Maple and Jenna all seemed to be #teamcash. They also thought she was completely crazy for refusing to accept the publishing deal from Southern Dallas University Press. She probably was, although Belle hadn't completely burned that bridge. She'd simply asked for a few days to consider the offer before signing on the dotted line. In turn, Miranda Percell had given her until first thing Monday morning to make up her mind.

Fifteen hours and counting. Belle forced down a sick feeling as she climbed out of her car at her dad's trailer

Sunday evening for family dinner. She still had no idea
what to do about the book deal, and time was running
out. Tomorrow would be her first day back at work, and
for once, the thought of returning to the library held little
appeal. If there'd been any way to avoid family dinner,
she'd have stayed home and clung to every last second
of solitude before her life went back to normal.

Belle couldn't do that to Dad, though. As much as she
would've preferred not to tell him about Stetson, she'd
had no choice in the matter. There were no secrets in a
place like Bluebonnet, Texas. If Belle hadn't called him
on Friday morning as soon as she'd gone home from
Cash's house, he would've heard the news from somebody else. Odds were, the story would get more salacious
with each retelling. She wanted her dad to hear the honest truth, straight from her own mouth, even if she still
wished he'd never had to hear about the incident at all.

Canceling on dinner wasn't an option. He needed to
see that she was completely fine. Once he had—and once
Belle had consumed her body weight in macaroni and
cheese since her primary diet the past few days had consisted of nothing but pie—she could go back home and
resume feeling decidedly *not* fine. This was all part of
her grand plan to fake it till she made it. In the immortal
words of Taylor Swift, she could do it with a broken heart.

"Oh goodness. There you are." Cathy burst outside,
and the screen door slammed shut behind her, making
Peaches flinch. Apron strings flying, Cathy bustled toward Belle with her arms flung open wide. "Do you have
any idea how worried we've been about you?"

The tackle hug caught Belle off guard. Cathy had
been nothing but welcoming every time Belle visited,

but she'd never been quite this physically demonstrative. Before Belle had a chance to brace for impact, she found herself wrapped in a hug so stifling that she could barely breathe.

"Your father told me what happened. You must have been scared to death. I'm sorry, honey. I'm just so sorry." Cathy ran a hand in soothing circles over Belle's back, and Belle sank into the embrace.

This was different than being hugged by her father. Everything about Cathy was soft...maternal. And it felt so nice that she had to squeeze her eyes shut to keep from crying.

"I'm glad Dad has you," Belle murmured into Cathy's shoulder. "I don't think I've told you that yet, but it's true."

Cathy pulled back to cup her face. "I'm not just your Dad's, hon. I'm yours, too. I know no one can take the place of your mother, but that doesn't mean we can't be family."

If she'd uttered that sentiment to Belle a week ago, Belle would've bristled. She never talked about her mom, with *anyone*, much less someone whose existence had been kept a secret from her for six full months. Just hearing the phrase *your mother* was disorienting.

But a lot had changed since she'd first met Cathy. Right now, Belle was too raw inside to resist such a simple kindness.

"I agree," she said, and then she realized her face was wet with tears.

What was happening to her? Walking away from Cash had been the hardest thing she'd ever done, but it had been the *right* thing. She wasn't sure why she seemed to fall apart every time someone looked at her.

Maybe Taylor was wrong. Maybe she *couldn't* do it with a broken heart.

Don't be ridiculous. You knew the man for less than a month. You'll forget all about him, eventually.

What a whopper. Belle had every intention of moving forward and proving to herself, and everyone else, that she didn't need a man to take care of her. She didn't need Cash or his money and influence. What's more, she didn't want it. One thing was certain, though: she'd never forget him, or his little girl, for as long as she lived.

"Cathy, where's Dad?" Belle asked, eager to redirect her focus to the here and now. Come to think of it, her father's truck wasn't parked in the drive. Peaches had her nose pressed to the ground and was busy sniffing the perimeter of the trailer, searching for him like a little amateur bloodhound.

"He ran to the store real quick to get some charcoal for the grill. He wanted to make burgers to go with the mac and cheese. Maurice says that's your favorite meal." Cathy gave her arm a squeeze. "Oh, look. Here he comes now."

Peaches greeted him with a full-body wiggle as soon as he exited his vehicle, carrying a large brown paper grocery bag from Bluebonnet General. Belle couldn't help but laugh. Her safe, predictable world had been so topsy-turvy lately. It was good to know that some things were constant. If she could count on one thing to remain true, it was Peaches's affection for her father.

"Hi, honeybun." Dad shifted the grocery bag to his left arm and wrapped the other around Belle's shoulders. "How are you holding up? All good?"

"Great," Belle lied, and she could feel Cathy's curious gaze on her. She'd just gone all wobbly over a simple hug, and here she was, trying to tell her father there was nothing to worry about.

But this was how Belle and her dad had always operated. They glossed over things, and Belle was fine with that. It didn't mean they didn't love each other. Her dad had always put on a brave face when she was a little girl. He'd doted on her and done his best to give her a magical childhood, even in difficult circumstances. Perhaps that was why they still didn't delve too deeply into painful subjects, even now that she was an adult. It was no wonder it had taken him so long to talk to her about Cathy.

"I'm going to pop inside and check on the mac and cheese." Cathy wiped her hands on her apron and headed for the trailer with a wink. "Why don't you two stay out here and get the grill started?"

"Can do," Dad said, as he set the bag with the charcoal down next to the grill.

Belle sat in one of the patio chairs, and Peaches hopped into her lap.

Dad lifted the lid of the grill, opened the bag of charcoal and began arranging the briquettes, just like Belle had seen him do a thousand times before. "I made a few extra burgers in case you decided to bring Cash and Lucy with you today. You didn't mention they were coming, but I thought it best to be prepared."

Belle's hand stilled on Peaches's slender back. "Thanks, Dad. That was really nice, but Cash isn't coming tonight."

Or ever again.

"That's a shame. I like him. Lucy too. She reminds me of you when you were that age." Her dad looked up from the grill, tenderness etched in the lines on his face.

"Me too." Belle's throat constricted. She swallowed hard, pushing down the emotions that kept rising to the surface. "But things aren't like you think between Cash and me. I was working as Lucy's nanny over spring break, that's all. We're friends, that's it."

Dad kept his gaze glued to the task at hand as he lit the charcoal. "You sure about that? He asked about you when I ran into him at the store just now, and I have to say, he seems awfully fond of you."

Belle's heart nearly stopped. "You saw Cash? Just now, when you went out for charcoal?"

Dad nodded. "He was there with his dog, stocking up on pet supplies."

Again? What on earth could Sparkles possibly need?

"That Frenchie has him wrapped around her little paw," she said, hoping to move the topic of conversation away from her relationship with Cash and on to safer territory—dogs.

Her father shook his head. "Not Sparkles. He was there with his other dog."

"Cash doesn't have another dog. Just the one," she said.

Dad chuckled. "No, he got a second one—a shiny black Lab. And let me tell you, that poor man has his hands full with that animal. It was dragging him all over the pet supply aisle of the store."

It was a good thing Belle was sitting down, because she felt like she might pass out.

You're worried about the stalker's dog now? Cash's voice came back to her, filled with warm humor and just a dash of wonder. She heard it as real as if she'd been transported back to his kitchen...back before things had gone so terribly wrong. *That might be the most Belle thing I've ever heard. And it's also one of the many reasons I've fallen in love with you.*

Surely he hadn't gone to the police station to check on the whereabouts of Stetson's dog and ended up adopting Lasso, all because she'd been worried about the dog? That would be crazy. He wouldn't.

Would he?

"Cash adopted a black Lab?" She couldn't believe she was uttering that question out loud. "Are you absolutely sure?"

"I saw it with my own two eyes, honeybun."

"Was the dog's name Lasso?" she asked.

"No, it was named something else. Cookie, maybe? Snickerdoodle? Wait, that wasn't it." Dad punched the air with his spatula. "I've got it. Oreo."

"Oreo," Belle repeated, and the tears came hard and fast.

Cash had adopted Stetson's dog, and he'd done it for her. He'd actually found a way to woo her that would show her in no uncertain terms exactly how he felt about her. The fact that he'd renamed Lasso showed her he knew precisely why she'd been concerned about the poor dog. It was a fresh start. A whole new life, free from whatever had happened in the past. Oreo was part of a loving family now, and sure, there would be an adjustment period. Cash would make mistakes, and he'd *definitely* let that dog sleep in his bed. The road might be rocky at times, but they'd figure things out. That's what families did.

Could there possibly be a fresh start for her and Cash, too?

"Belle." Her dad dropped the spatula and came to squat in front of her. "What's wrong? What is it?"

Belle sniffed and tried to get hold of herself. But

maybe that needed to stop. If Lasso could get a new start, then maybe she and her dad could, too. Maybe it was time to finally have a conversation that was decades overdue.

"Dad, I'm in love with Cash," she blurted. "But he's not who you think he is. He's a McAllister."

Dad's forehead creased, then his mouth curved into a smile and he chuckled. Seriously? He was laughing... at a time like this.

"What's so funny?" she asked through her tears.

"The idea that you thought I didn't know exactly who he is. This is Bluebonnet, honeybun. I knew he was a McAllister the second he walked inside my trailer."

That made sense. Ugh, sometimes small-town living was the worst. She should've seen this coming, obviously. Belle had been so careful to avoid using Cash's last name, though. She'd been so intent on protecting her dad's feelings that she'd actually believed it was possible.

"Then you know he's rich." She pulled a face. "Really, really rich."

"I'm aware." He chuckled again.

Belle shook her head. "And that doesn't bother you? After everything that happened with mom, I mean?"

She was going there. And weirdly, it felt perfectly natural to ask the question, even though they'd been tiptoeing around the subject of her mother for years. A weight lifted off her chest, one that she hadn't even realized she'd been carrying.

"Honeybun, I know what it probably looked like from the outside. Your mom left me—she left *us*—for someone else. And yes, that man wasn't exactly poor. But we'd been having trouble for years. It wasn't the money that made her leave, and it wasn't you, either. We were really young when we got married, and I think she acted impulsively when she left, because she'd been struggling and never really considered how hard real life and marriage could be at times." He paused to take a deep breath, then he covered her hands with his. "And I also think she probably came to regret that decision."

"You think?" Belle wasn't buying it. But what did it matter? She had her dad, and that was enough. *He* was enough—he always had been—and she needed him to know that.

"I don't see how anyone couldn't regret leaving you, of all people. That's what I think," he said.

"I love you, Dad." She wrapped her arms around him and hugged him so hard that Peaches, sandwiched between them in her lap, let out a little yip.

Dad pulled back and gave the dog a reassuring pat between the ears. His gaze was serious when he lifted his eyes back to Belle's. "Now don't tell me you're going to let a little thing like money stop you from being with Cash. Because that would break my heart, honeybun."

"A 'little thing'?" Belle wiped her face. "Dad, it seems huge."

"Why?" His forehead creased. "Seriously, why? What's the real reason?"

Her dad knew her so well. He always had.

"Because I'm afraid it makes me like her," Belle said, confessing her deepest and darkest fear—the one that had raised its ugly head when Stetson cornered her in Cash's backyard. "And I don't want to be like Mom. If I'm going to be like either one of my parents, I want to be like you."

"Oh, honey. You already are. You're the apple of my eye. If I don't say it enough, then I'm sorry. But you're not me, and you're not your mother. You would never make the same choices she did. I know that with my whole heart and, someplace deep down, so do you. You're just scared, that's all. But take some advice from your old man. Don't let fear stop you from following your heart." He stood and looked down at her with his hands loosely placed on his hips. A dad pose, if she'd ever seen one. "The only way that Cash's money could truly come between you and Cash is if you let it."

Chapter Twenty

The school board meeting on Monday was a packed house. Belle nearly ran smack into a whole row of people as she pushed her way through the door of the Bluebonnet High School auditorium while juggling her pile of Book Buddies data in one arm and Peaches in the other.

She'd spent the entire morning finalizing everything in preparation for her presentation...well, *almost* the entire morning. First, she'd had another thing to take care of. After the heart-to-heart with her dad last night, she'd made some decisions about her future. As much as she couldn't wait to see Cash again, she hadn't wanted to face him until she'd gotten all her ducks in a row. If she was going to tell him she was ready for a brand-new life together, she wanted it to truly start fresh.

The rest of the day had passed in a blur while she'd made handouts and spreadsheets, all liberally sprinkled with adorable pictures of Peaches working with kids in the library. Last night, Belle had given the Cavalier a bath and a blowout, and she was looking especially lovely this evening, ready for her big moment in the spotlight.

If only Belle could get her way to the front of the au-

ditorium, where the Comfort Paws girls had promised
to save her a seat...

She jostled her way through the crowd, half wondering if she'd gotten the date wrong. School board meetings were never this well attended. Usually, the only
people who showed up were the board members, a few
teachers and a handful of parents. Maybe the school was
having a performance or something after the meeting.

"Oh, good. You're here." Adaline, situated smack in
the front row next to Maple and Jenna, gathered her
purse from the chair beside her and motioned for Belle to
take a seat. "Sit down quick. You have no idea how many
times I've had to stop people from stealing your spot."

"What's going on? All these people can't possibly
be here for the school board meeting?" Belle looked
around. She did a double take when she spotted her student Mason Hayes.

He waved wildly at her, and she waved back.

"Actually, I think they are. At least a dozen people
have come up to talk to us since we sat down. They recognized our Comfort Paws shirts." Adaline plucked the
fabric of her bright red logo hoodie.

"We thought you invited them," Maple said. "Nurse
Pam is here from County Hospital. She mentioned something about speaking during the portion of the meeting
when the board hears comments from members of the
community. She has a whole speech prepared about the
impact our program has had on patients in the children's
wing and how she believes our dogs can positively im-
prove student well-being in the school library."

Belle's jaw nearly dropped. "Are you serious right
now?"

"Completely serious." Maple tilted her head. "If you didn't tell her about this meeting, then who did?"

Belle had spent countless hours preparing her data, but she'd never considered asking people to come give live testimonials about their experiences with the Comfort Paws dogs. She'd thought Peaches's presence alone could seal the deal. Belle had never met a soul who could resist her sweet Cavalier's puppy-dog eyes.

But this...

She glanced around the crowded room, scanning the crowd for familiar faces. Her gaze landed on the educational psychologist the school always used for dyslexia testing and diagnosis of learning challenges, then her eyes darted three seats over to the chairperson for Bluebonnet Elementary School's committee on state standardized testing.

Belle swallowed hard. Whoever had thought to invite all these people here was a genius. What's more, she had a feeling that particular genius had eyes the color of her favorite wildflower, a recently acquired Labrador retriever and a penchant for thinking outside the box.

Heart pounding, she turned her head toward the stage, where the school board members sat around a long table. Belle had quite purposefully avoided looking in that direction until now. She'd have been nervous enough about this meeting without the added pressure of coming face-to-face with Cash for the first time since she'd told him she needed some space. But she needn't have worried. When her eyes met his across the crowded room, she saw nothing but pure love looking back at her from those bluebonnet eyes. His face cracked into a smile, and he winked.

"Ladies and gentlemen." The school board president pounded her gavel on the podium. "Thank you for being here this evening. I must say, we've never had a turnout like this before. It's encouraging to see so much enthusiasm for the great work our teachers, staff and administrators are doing here in Bluebonnet. I hereby call this meeting to order."

A nervous flutter passed through Belle. This was it—the moment she'd been working toward all school year. The Book Buddies presentation was slotted second on the agenda. All she had to sit through first was a summary of old business from the emergency school board meeting that had taken place the week before.

She held her breath and counted to ten in her head, more nervous than she'd ever been in her life at the thought of taking her place onstage just a few feet away from Cash. How was she going to get through this when all she wanted to do was walk straight up to him and kiss him silly?

"Psst, Belle." Adaline jammed her elbow into Belle's side. "Listen. They're talking about the Reading Rumble. Isn't that the game show type thing you do every year?"

Belle blinked and refocused her attention on the board secretary, who was reading the list of approved motions from the prior meeting.

"The board hereby approves the motion put forth by Cash McAllister to host the districtwide Reading Rumble at the McAllister Mansion on Main Street, in lieu of canceling the event due to budget constraints. Mr. McAllister will work with school principal Ed Garza and librarian Belle Darling to organize said event."

What?

This is what Ed had meant when he'd texted her and told her she owed Cash a thank-you for saving the Reading Rumble? He hadn't written a blank check to the school, after all. He'd actually volunteered to host the event himself…at his home. And he wanted to help organize the Reading Rumble alongside her and her colleagues.

Her throat went tight as her gaze homed in on Cash. He gave a small, nearly imperceptible shrug, invisible to anyone but her. Why hadn't he said anything when he'd come home from the meeting that night?

Because you just assumed. You never gave him a chance to say otherwise. Not then and not Friday morning before you walked out.

Regret burned hot in the pit of her stomach. Cash hadn't been the only one who'd made mistakes. Belle had made more than her fair share, as well.

There would be time to think about that later, though. Right now, she had to get herself together and speak on behalf of Book Buddies. The school president had already returned to the podium and called Belle's name. The room exploded into thunderous applause as she gathered her materials and walked Peaches up the stage steps.

"Hello, everyone. Thank you to the board for allowing me to speak tonight on behalf of Book Buddies, a program that I believe will help a wide variety of children learn to love books and reading, through the comfort and support of reading education assistance dogs." Belle licked her lips, and despite the vow she'd made to herself to avoid Cash's gaze while she was onstage, she glanced over at him and offered him a tentative smile—a smile that she hoped said all the things she'd fully planned on articulating after all of this was over.

I forgive you.

Please forgive me.

I never want to be apart again.

When he silently mouthed the words *I love you*, she knew he'd heard it all without her needing to utter a word.

Two hours later, after the board had praised Belle's presentation, been thoroughly charmed by Peaches and heard over a dozen testimonials from people who'd all worked directly with one or more of the Comfort Paws dogs, Book Buddies was officially approved as a vital element of Bluebonnet Elementary School's permanent curriculum. Belle tried her best to remain professional and not cry as one person after another took a turn at the microphone. Some of the comments caught her completely by surprise, including when Mason Hayes's teacher spoke of the profound impact his Book Buddies sessions had on his mental health. All this time, Belle couldn't understand why he'd been chosen for the program when he was such a good reader. His teacher's voice wobbled as she explained that he was a quiet, gifted student, and in a classroom full of kids with behavioral challenges, she rarely got a chance to interact with Mason one on one. He'd gone through class on autopilot until she'd chosen him for the Book Buddies program, and now that he'd had some individual attention from Belle and her dog, he'd blossomed. He was like a different kid, thriving both academically and socially. Even Belle hadn't realized the extent to which Peaches had helped the kids in her program.

But the real clincher came with last speaker—Lucy McAllister. There hadn't been a dry eye in the entire building when she'd told the audience how reading to Peaches had been the only time during the school day that she hadn't missed her mom. Now, thanks to Book Buddies, she had two dogs of her own at home. Plus, her Uncle Cash seemed way happier than he'd been before he met Miss Darling.

"Tell me the truth. Was that last part of Lucy's speech rehearsed, or did she come up with that all on her own?" Belle asked Cash after the meeting had adjourned and she'd practically skipped up the steps to meet him on-stage.

He held up his hands. "That was all her. I promise. In fact, I had nothing to do with any of the speeches. All I did was extend a few invitations. Everyone in this building spoke from the heart."

"Well, as long as we're speaking from the heart, I guess I will, too." She slipped her hand in his and tilted her chin upward as the stage curtains swished closed. The school auditorium buzzed with activity, but they were blessedly alone...save for Peaches, who was busy winding her leash around them, forcing them closer and closer together. "I am hopelessly in love with you, Cash McAllister."

"In spite of my last name?" He tapped the adhesive name tag tacked to the lapel of his suit jacket.

She was never going to live that down, and she didn't even care.

Laughter bubbled up Belle's throat. "What can I say? Your last name is growing on me."

"Good." They were just inches apart now, thanks to

Peaches, and Cash pressed his forehead to hers as his gaze dropped to her mouth. "Because I was hoping it might be yours too someday."

"If that's a marriage proposal, my answer is yes," Belle bit her lip. "So long as you're okay with your wife being Tumbleweed Print's newest children's book author."

Cash's smile widened until it seemed infinite, and in that moment, Belle could see an entire future in his eyes. *Their* future. "Really? Weren't they your very first choice?"

She nodded. "Really. I contacted them this morning and told them I'd gotten an offer from Southern Dallas University Press, and the editor immediately threw her hat in the ring. I hope you understand. I needed to make this happen for myself, Cash."

"There was never any doubt in my mind that you would." His thumb moved over her bottom lip, and if he didn't kiss her soon, there would be no book party at Bluebonnet Bookshop someday, because she might just die. "Are those your only terms on your conditional acceptance of my proposal?"

"I just have one more." She lifted her mouth to his and smiled against his lips. "If all those dogs are going to sleep with us, we're going to need a bigger bed."

"Done," he growled.

And then he kissed her until the rest of the world fell away, deep in the bold, beautiful heart of Texas.

* * * * *